Also by Mark Harris

NOVELS

City of Discontent

The Goy

Killing Everybody

Lying in Bed

*Something about a Soldier**

*Speed**

*The Tale Maker**

*Trumpet to the World**

Wake Up, Stupid

NOVELS IN THE MANNER OF HENRY WIGGEN, BASEBALL PLAYER

*Bang the Drum Slowly**

*It Looked Like For Ever**

*The Southpaw**

*A Ticket for a Seamstitch**

**Available in Bison Books editions*

The Self-Made Brain Surgeon and Other Stories

Mark Harris

WITH AN INTRODUCTION BY JON SURGAL

UNIVERSITY OF NEBRASKA PRESS
LINCOLN AND LONDON

Acknowledgments for the use of previously
published material appear on pages 207–8.

∞

Library of Congress Cataloging-in-Publication Data
Harris, Mark, 1922–
The self-made brain surgeon, and other stories / Mark Harris;
with an introduction by Jon Surgal.
p. cm.
ISBN 0-8032-7319-3 (pbk: alk. paper)
1. United States—Social life and customs—20th century—Fiction.
I. Title.
PS3515.A757S35 1999
813'.54—dc21 98-42925
CIP

This book is for my wife

Contents

Introduction

Jon Surgal

Open up a book by Mark Harris, and the feeling you get is like walking into a big-league ballpark before a game. You know you are about to see first-rate talent at work. You know that between the covers of a Mark Harris book the playing field will be dazzling in the sharpness of its detail, and you know that by the end of the book the field will have suffered rips and tears that commemorate the struggles of men, also sharply observed. You know that the chalklines laid out to circumscribe their endeavors will be blurred by these struggling men, that revelations will emerge from both their achievements and their failures.

The difference between baseball and Mark Harris is that Mr. Harris never disappoints his audience. He is, however, a chronicler of disappointment, one of the best. His characters sometimes succumb to their disappointments, more often overcome them, but almost always come to accept them, and the humor that so frequently attends this acceptance is a measure of the author's discriminating heart, his deep affection for people in spite of themselves. The game, for Mr. Harris, is seldom over when it's over. Disappointments, like successes, have their consequences.

I had occasion to consider these matters when, not so long ago, I paid my first visit to Fenway Park, baseball's preeminent temple of disappointment, site of the great wall in left field that is known as the Green Monster.

"Did you know," said my companion, a former college roommate, "that the Persian word for paradise translates as a green field surrounded by a wall?"

My former roommate is by profession both a doctor and a priest. For him, too, the game is not over when it's over. When science fails, there are always last rites.

"I am surprised," said I, "that there are not more Persian ballplayers in that case. I am acquainted with many Persians, although this is no longer what they prefer to be called, but I have never met a Persian ballplayer. I have met many Nicaraguan ballplayers, and Mexicans, and Ecuadorians, and Panamanians, and even Cubans. A few of them, I have to admit, will cross themselves when they come to the plate, although in my experience the Cubans never do so, at least not while they are living in Cuba."

"In the Christian tradition," said my former roommate, "the walled garden was called the *hortus conclusus*. It was a replication of Eden, which is to say it was an enclosed space where the grass seemed greener than green and the sky bluer than blue. It was where you went to contemplate your relationship with the divine presence. By the time of the troubadours, it becomes secularized, and the walled garden becomes the place where the lover contemplates his beloved, much the way the crowd is doing even as we speak."

"Their enthusiasm is impressive," said I, "considering that the last time the Red Sox won a World Series, the mourning period for Queen Victoria had not yet officially expired."

"My theory," said my former roommate, "is that baseball is not about winning. The best pitchers get scored on. The best batters get a hit fewer than four times out of ten. Every game ends with the expulsion from Eden. What baseball is about is learning to cope with failure. It is a dry run at learning to cope with mortality. This is my theory."

"It puts me in mind of the work of Mark Harris," said I.

"So I would imagine," said my former roommate. "What do you want with your hot dog?"

It is my privilege to welcome you here to the *hortus conclusus* of Mark Harris. Those of you who have already taken a tour of the park may encounter an old favorite or two among the short pieces collected in this volume. You may recognize here and there among the fictions a character from one of the Harris novels, for the fictional world of Mark Harris—like those of Anthony Trollope and John O'Hara—is a continuum in which characters from many novels share connections both business and social and reappear from time to time in each other's books. Those of you making your first visit are in for a treat. You are about to become a fan.

This book is itself walled round with contemplations of baseball. It begins with the 1946 essay "Jackie Robinson and My Sister," in which a young Mark Harris cheerfully deflates the last ditch argument so commonly advanced by baseball segregationists in the early days of the "Robinson Experiment." The cheerful tone is in this case deceptive, chosen for its rhetorical clout. Intolerance, as it happens, is the only human failing for which Mark Harris has no tolerance. The book concludes with "The Bonding," written by Mr. Harris in his seventh decade, in which the act of dropping a fly ball provides the occasion for him to articulate his thoughts on coping with failure.

"Everybody learns in her/his own way about losing," Mr. Harris tells us. "For me, baseball taught me losing and winning, taught me never to let anything get me too far down or too far up. You not only can't win 'em all—you can't win much more than half, hard as you try, long as you live." He is, he tells us, sustained by the truths he has learned from baseball. Baseball, he tells us, has been his path to self-knowledge. It has also been his path to fame. Mark Harris is best known for his baseball novels, and among them is the best-known of the genre, the classic *Bang the Drum Slowly*, in which the process of coping with loss is a matter of life and death.

But Mr. Harris is equally adroit in depicting loss on a smaller scale, as these pages demonstrate. In both "Carmelita's Education for Living" and "Flattery," the walled garden is Academe, and the loss in question is a minor matter of self-esteem. In "La Lumière," the title not only suggests that illumination which deprives the protagonist of an ancient illusion, it is also the name of the restaurant to which the greater part of the story is confined. In "Conversation on Southern Honshu," a simple loss of communication is at issue, and we are reminded that from time to time every man is, like Honshu itself, an island. In "The Self-Made Brain Surgeon," losses of one kind and another are assuaged within the walls of an ordinary grocery store stockroom.

In these and other stories, Mr. Harris reveals himself as that literary rarity, a writer of novels who can turn his hand with equal skill to the creation of a compelling miniature. He transforms everyday disappointments and the revelations which accompany them into flights of surprising, even quirky, narrative. Like knuckleballs, these stories dance from his skilled fingers in unpredictable, sometimes elliptical, arcs, which nevertheless manage to cut the heart of the strike zone.

Now and then, however, Mr. Harris employs the short form to address the large questions, the big losses. For these occasions he reserves his "purpose pitch," the high heat aimed to make you duck, a warning that some losses are permanent, irreversible, deadly.

Which doesn't necessarily mean they aren't funny. If you had the job of editing the First Book of Chronicles, fresh from the author's hand—and this is the task which faces the narrator in "From the Desk of the Troublesome Editor"—would you not be inclined to question the "crazy wrath" of King David, the "personal spite and violent vengeance" of Yahweh? This is very funny stuff as Mr. Harris presents it, but the fact remains that it is an indictment not only of our worst impulses as a species but also of our religious and ethical shibboleths, and the man who dares to indict them risks expulsion from the Eden he has charged with imperfection. And what are we to make of "The Iron Fist of Oligarchy," in which a young man, bowing reluctantly to authority, finds himself transformed into television's most famous dog and consequently, if understandably, actually loses his mind? "You will never again hear of anything so tragic," the narrator tells us, but this narrator, an interested party, is untrustworthy. The young man's fate is *worse* than tragic. Tragic elements we might expect to find in a Greek myth—metamorphosis and madness—are demoted by their context to the category of the ridiculous, a loss of status that is the *coup de grâce* of the young man's misfortune. In the world of Mark Harris, it is risky to defy authority, risky to accept it. Fate is not only cruel but capricious as well.

In "The Bonding," you will read of a series of letters written by Mr. Harris in his summer camp boyhood. In these letters he attempted to convince a childhood friend that he was playing baseball in a semi-professional "Inter-Camp League." Successful in persuading his friend of this fiction, Mr. Harris failed not long thereafter in persuading the same friend that the glory of patriotic martyrdom was also a fiction, and the other boy died in the invasion of Normandy. There is risk in both credulousness and skepticism. The capricious distinction between, as Mr. Harris has put it, "one boy early-doomed, the other surviving, continuing" has played itself out time and again in his novels.

As a grown man, accompanied by his eight-year-old son, Mr. Harris encountered the father of his childhood friend in Grand Central Station: "His face was seamed, wrinkled, he was generally well, and he told me that my mother telephoned him regularly—'every year, on Norman's birthday'—smiling as if to say how really unnecessary it was, how long ago the event was, and how grief had surely healed." While Mr. Harris struggled to imagine how such grief could ever heal, his son dashed recklessly about Grand Central, prompting Mr. Harris to imagine him lost amid the tunnels, crushed by a hurtling train. This incident provides the basis for the story "At Prayerbook Cross," perhaps the most sobering of the collection, in which a father experiences a brush with the worst of losses, expressing, as Mr. Harris noted in his journal, "my own outlaw wish for my child's death, as being at least a method of relieving me of all *further* anxiety about his death, the worst having happened."

Mark Harris is given, as he says, to "imaginations of disaster." Disasters befall us all, but the imagination of Mr. Harris is unique. Implicit in every contest is the possibility of loss, but the dread of loss has created in Mark Harris a distinctive voice unparalleled in American fiction, while the coping with it has spurred him to the creation of more than twenty published books of unsurpassed quality.

We can boast of no American writer more talented, more compassionate, more attuned to the subtleties of life's struggles. In the ballpark of his own devising, he hits, hits with power, runs, fields, throws, pitches left-handed and provides the perfect color commentary.

What more could you want with your hot dog?

The Self-Made Brain Surgeon and Other Stories

Jackie Robinson and My Sister

Some time ago the Brooklyn Dodgers signed Jackie Robinson to a baseball contract. That is, they signed him to a Montreal contract. Brooklyn owns Montreal. If Robinson turns out to be a good enough shortstop he will be promoted from the International League and sent to Ebbetts Field.

I was very interested in this because I am extremely interested in the Dodgers and in any shortstops to whom they might acquire title. I have always believed, not without prejudice, that Brooklyn shortstops were limitless in ability. It is my wish that Brooklyn obtains the best, most durable shortstops in the whole world.

This is hardly an ideology for a St. Louis newspaperman to possess because nobody in St. Louis has any special love for Brooklyn baseball players. If he does he is wise not to bandy the information about.

So, without committing myself, I scouted around to find out what St. Louis people thought about Brooklyn's new shortstop.

Some people did not have any opinions at all and some said they couldn't blame Brooklyn for wanting to corner the market on infielders.

Other people, however, asked a question instead of answering mine, the way some people do. They wanted to know how I would like it if my sister married Jackie Robinson. They even hinted that such a union was imminent.

Since this is such a popular question I feel it deserves an answer.

I understand, of course, that the matter is not up to me. Robinson says he plans to be married in January to a trained nurse. It would probably be difficult to induce him to change his mind at this point. It would also entail consulting the trained nurse, who is not likely to be any more sympathetic than any other woman in such a situation. Maybe less so, loss of sympathy being an occupational disease peculiar to trained nurses.

Furthermore, he is in South America at the moment, traipsing around with a bunch of norteamericanos, some white and some Negro like himself, playing baseball for their good neighbor aficionados to the South. I cannot see my way clear at this time to run around after him and get him married to my sister before January. And if I don't get them married I won't be able to say how I like it.

Martha, my sister, lives in Mount Vernon, New York, and is in the sixth grade at William Wilson Junior High School. It would not be unkind to say of her that at this time she is not a hot potato. Robinson, at twenty-six, has, by this time, lost all interest in young ladies of twelve.

She last wrote to me just before Halloween, for which she was preparing with traditional enthusiasm.

In her letter, written in reverse slant on blue-lined notebook paper, she hinted that she is now in love with Raymie Carucci. This is not surprising, the Caruccis having always been a lovable bunch. I can distinctly remember being in love with Theresa Carucci off and on during many a school year.

Martha was in love with Billy Pelkus when I was last home. During the winter, however, he smacked her in the eye with a snowball, putting at end what had been, at best, a one-sided affair.

I do not believe Martha has ever heard of Jackie Robinson. She has never been a student of the sports pages and I have never known her to follow with any degree of avidity the fortunes of the Kansas City Monarchs, for whom Robinson short-stopped last season.

And I am certain my mother will not permit her to marry before she has completed junior high school.

It does not seem probable that Robinson can be inveigled into marrying my sister before his intended trip to the altar in January.

And my sister's present attachment to Raymie Carucci appears to be a determined thing. If Raymie backs out there's always Billy Pelkus.

The whole thing is out of the question.

Carmelita's Education for Living

There came to Horatio recently—to his office—a young lady with blonde bangs and blue eyes and bare legs, and in her arms her Packet. Horatio was charmed. He was thirty years old, a college student counselor, and his fields of concentration were Middle English and modern women.

"Come in and sit down and tell me your name and all the most intimate things in the world about yourself," he said. And she went in and sat down and told him her name, "Scott, Carmelita B.," handing him her Packet. "I take it," said Horatio, "that you've completed all your Lower Division, Scott, Carmelita B."

"Yes," she said, "I'm a new English major."

Horatio unsealed her Packet and shook it, spilling onto his desk various documents of various sizes and various colors. They were certainly not very interesting, at least to Horatio, but he pretended to read them carefully: the longer he lingered over Carmelita's documents the longer she would remain in his office. She had been, in addition to being beautiful, President of the Sophomore Class, a cheerleader, and an honors student. She held the University record for Woman's Breast Stroke. Her father (the Packet said) was a farmer, her mother a farmer's wife, her hobbies were swimming, dancing, reading and "social participation of every kind," and she had come to the University (again, her own words, in faint blue ink) "to be educated for living."

"My, but you're beautiful," said Horatio, looking up from her Packet and into her face.

"That's what everybody says," she said.

"And your Minor is—" He often left sentences unfinished. It was a classroom device, but a habit which clung to him even in his office, like chalk stain.

"Psychology," she said.

"Why psychology?" said Horatio. "Any particular reason why psychology?"

"No, no particular reason," she said. "Only I've got to minor in something and it might as well be psychology."

"Well, now," he said, "in what way can I counsel you?"

"I think all I need is my Program signed," she said. She took from her notebook a blue card upon which, in a firm, controlled hand, but in an almost invisible blue ink, she had indicated her intention to carry three courses in English—Introduction to Chaucer, Introduction to Shakespeare, and Introduction to Grammar—and, in her minor field, one course, Evaluation of Personality: Theories of Individual Difference, taught by Gilbert Schaachtmann, an Assistant Professor of Psychology, unknown to Horatio.

"How's this man Grammar?" said Horatio.

"Sir?" she said, retrieving her Program. "Oh, no, that means grammar. *Grammar.* It's not a man, it's a thing."

"I see," said Horatio. He regained the Program, balanced it upright on his typewriter, folded his arms, and read it at a distance. "Do you think you're ready for Chaucer?" he said.

"I've got to take Chaucer sooner or later," she said, "and it might as well be now."

"I'm wondering, though, if Chaucer might be easier for you

if you take a course in Middle English first. You might take Introduction to Middle English."

"I've decided against it," she said.

"One terribly attractive thing about Introduction to Middle English," said Horatio, "is, I teach it."

"When?" she asked, consulting her Time Plan. "No, I couldn't. I dance."

"It's easily possible," he said, "to dance and take Introduction to Middle English at the same time."

"But not at the same hour. I dance in the lunch dances."

"Every day?" he said. "You know, I think I might come and dance with you sometime on a Tuesday or a Thursday."

"I never knew faculty danced," she said.

"I've danced at many a lunch," said Horatio, signing her Program and handing it to her, sliding the various documents back into her Packet, and rising and placing her Packet atop his filing cabinet. She also rose. "So you think I'm too old to dance," he said. "How old do you think I am? Tell me. Be frank. How old?"

"Thirty-five?"

"You're way high. Anyhow, give my regards to Mr. Grammar."

"I will," she said, "and I want to thank you for all your trouble," and down the corridor she went, her blue Program in her lovely white hand, and she disappeared.

Now, ordinarily Horatio never saw his Counselees except during Counseling Week. He might receive, from time to time, official notice that a Counselee had dropped or withdrawn; or he might be requested to send a Counselee's Packet to Guidance, in the event a Counselee seemed to need it, and this he did unless he forgot. The Packets (in a manner of speaking, the Counselees themselves) were ultimately removed from the top of the filing cabinet and filed—filed *in* it—by a graduate student named Ursula Poindexter, with whom, upon an afternoon of leisure, Horatio had once discussed, at a distinctly abstract level, the possibility of an affair. He had thought to pursue the discussion, but no further opportunity presented itself, and such passion as he may once have felt for Ursula cooled beyond recall.

So it was with Carmelita B. Scott. Flickeringly, Horatio contemplated dancing with her at noon on a Tuesday or a Thursday, but somehow her image was never in his mind at precisely those hours.

Indeed, so blurred did his memory of her become that, for a moment, when he found her note tacked to his door, he could not assign the name a face. "It is urgently important," the note read, "that I contact you at three (3): Miss Scott (Carmelita B.)." It was penned in blue on the reverse side of a blue receipt. Horatio saw that Carmelita had recently bought, at Kampus Kredit, a sweater, a bra and a book, and he said to himself, "Ah, contact," summoning to memory the blonde bangs and the blue eyes and the bare legs. When three o'clock came he was waiting, studiously casual and studiously young, his books hidden, his shirt sleeves rolled above his muscles, his tie loosened, his feet upon his desk and his eyeglasses in his pocket, and she knocked, and he called, "Come!" in his youngest voice, and she said, "I hope I'm not disturbing you, but it's my thematic apperception."

"Well, we all have trouble with our thematic apperception," he said, swinging his feet athletically to the floor. "What in hell is thematic apperception?"

"I finally thought about you at the last minute," she said. "You're supposed to evaluate somebody you don't know too well, but it seems like everybody I know I know very well." She opened her notebook. "You look at these little pictures, and you tell me what you see."

"What I apperceive?"

"Yes. I know you're busy, but it won't take long."

Horatio, peering at the first picture, so-called, saw nothing. It looked, to Horatio, like an ink blot. "I see your slender, inky fingers," he said.

"You're supposed to look more at the picture," she said.

"I see light-blue ink," he said. "It looks to me as if you spilled your light-blue ink."

"But does it have anything thematic about it?"

"If you wish," he said, "I'll see a theme even if I don't."

"Go on."

"The theme is, There's no sense crying over spilled ink. But actually," he said, looking up, "I'm afraid I'm just not thematically apperceptible."

"Everybody sees *something*," she said.

"Tell you what I'll do," he said. "I'll see my mother murdering my father. How's that?"

"Show me which is which," she said.

"Here's ma, here's pa."

Carmelita tore from her notebook a sheet of blank paper, and she wrote in blue ink, "Personality X." She drew a line beneath it. "You're Personality X," she said.

"X for Excellent," he said.

"No," she said, "just X for unknown quantity."

"This first figure," said Horatio, "is imploring this second figure to do something. To *see* something. He's pointing at something."

"Try to perceive what he's pointing at," she said, her pen at the ready.

"He's pointing at the air," said Horatio, "and he's saying, 'Can't you *see*?' "

"Can't see what?" she said excitedly.

"Can't see that the air is an illusion, that there isn't all that air between them, all that distance, it's only her stupid and innocent illusion, imploring, imploring—"

She said, very suddenly, "I've got you evaluated," and he laughed at her. "Me?" he said. "Me, who all these years I still haven't even begun to evaluate? You're a genius."

"It's due, though," she said, "and he grades you down for late papers. I'm not a genius, but I *am* rather good at thematic apperception. Everybody says so."

"I don't say so," said Horatio, "and I'm somebody. I think you're rather *poor* at thematic apperception, if there's any such thing to begin with. I think you're *stupid* at thematic apperception."

"Anyhow I've got to go," she said. "I want to thank you for your time and trouble. Everybody around this whole University is always so helpful."

"Do you still dance at noon?" said Horatio. "I've been meaning to come over and dance with you sometime."

"That's what you said last time," she said.

"I intend to," he said. "Sometime. I'll tell you the reason I haven't got around to it." He paused to rally reasons and the pause was ambiguous enough to allow her to mistake his words for a promise to be fulfilled not now but—as he said—sometime. Through this ambiguity she slipped and was gone, down the corridor, and away, with a wave of her lovely hand.

Horatio could not help chuckling at her innocence, and after he had chuckled for a moment in this superior way he found, in his filing cabinet, where Ursula Poindexter had filed it, Carmelita's Packet. In the Packet he found the blue Program he had signed during Counseling Week. It had, since he last saw it, traveled the bureaucracy—been stamped by the Registrar, initialed by clerks in the Departments of English and Psychology, and finally been, for vague but traditional reasons, returned to Horatio. Horatio saw that her instructor in Evaluation of Personality: Theories of Individual Difference was one Gilbert Schaachtmann, whom Horatio, to his positive knowledge, had never seen. Yet Horatio, subtle fellow that he was, addressed a note to "Dear Gil," asking to know, "if I might, unless it be contrary to your procedure, Carmelita B. Scott's evaluation of Personality X. Miss Scott," he added, "is one of my Counselees." He deposited the note in the campus mailbox, and he went about his business which so largely consisted of complaining to his colleagues of the impossible distance between professors and their students.

To Horatio's surprise—and it gave him pause—he received at week's end the following reply:

Dear Horatio:

In *re* evaluation by your Counselee Scott (Carmelita B.):

"I found difficulty in finding somebody I did not know too well. Finally found Personality X. But Personality X was also too emotionally involved with his Evaluator to supply valid apperceptive data. Personality X would like to have an intrigue with Evaluator but cannot descend from abstract."

You are right to be concerned about this Counselee. She needs help.

Yours,

Gil

cc: Guidance

Conversation on Southern Honshu

Once a week Lou Brown and Mr. Shibayashi engaged in a form of conversation. This conversation, or form thereof, proceeded in its mystifying way between October and the end of the year. Not until Bill Flynn's New Year's Eve party was the mystery relieved. Three days later, returning a book to the library, Lou saw Mr. Shibayashi for the last time.

Mr. Shibayashi would knock upon Lou's office door, and Lou would call "Dozo," one of forty words embraced by his vocabulary in the company of two dozen noun phrases and a complete sentence: *Wareware wa J. A. L. de kyonen no hichigatsu ni tochyakushimashita*—We arrived last July by Japan Air Lines. Mr. Shibayashi entered and bowed. It was a ninety-degree bow, entirely dignified but granting to Lou Brown all the entitlements of superior age and education. Lou bowed to the extent he was able, his worthiest international intentions still stiffly imprisoned by his past, and set water to boil upon the electric plate. After the water boiled they drank *ocha* and smoked cigarettes. Subsequently Mr. Shibayashi offered to rinse the cups, Lou rejected the offer, bows were again exchanged, and Mr. Shibayashi departed.

Invariably their conversation began with a brief discussion of the enormous problems confronting university libraries in Japan, and touched upon the problems confronting libraries in Seattle and Denver—the two cities visited by Mr. Shibayashi during a 27-day tour sponsored by the Librarians' Council of Southern Honshu—with a glance at libraries in Northern Mexico, Hawaii, and Manila, by which route Mr. Shibayashi had returned home. The problems of libraries in all those places, Mr. Shibayashi maintained, were staggering, a conclusion Lou found agreeable in principle, although his own investigations had been conducted on a more limited geographical basis, and rather as patron than as librarian.

Mr. Shibayashi usually brought this introductory phase of their conversation to an end by asserting, as a loyal Japanese citizen, that no libraries of the world exceeded in chaos the libraries of Japan. In response, Lou Brown offered his opinion that the libraries of Japan were equal in quality to libraries in those regions of America familiar to his experience. "It is kind of you to say so," said Mr. Shibayashi, "but in Japan, books are not to be found in their proper places."

"Often in the U. S.," said Lou Brown, "books are not to be found in their proper places."

"In Japan," said Mr. Shibayashi, "books are often lost, stolen, catalogued in carelessness, and in poor repair. Especially is it embarrassing to observe that we possess only one copy of even the most famous volumes."

"In America," said Lou Brown, "likewise."

Mr. Shibayashi once again emphasized the kindness of Professor Brown and of (introducing at this point the second principal subject of their conversation) Americans in general, here submitting as the living example of American kindness Bill Flynn, local director of the American Cultural Center.

Bill was a lanky, blond man of visible energy and effective

good will. Lou found him immensely congenial, although he would hardly have applied to Bill Flynn the word *kind.* Bill was somewhat too analytical ever to be purely kind. Bill was *lucid.* Bill was *keen, sharp,* the operations of his mind conducted along the firm lines of reason. A silent fellow, long on meditation, when he spoke he spoke to the point with brevity and clarity—*shrewdness,* Lou thought—and he was remarkably perceptive in his appraisal of people and events.

"We have felt ourselves fortunate," Mr. Shibayashi said, "in the possession of the kind presence of Mr. Flynn."

"He's very astute," said Lou, pouring the boiling water from kettle to teapot, replacing the lid of the teapot, disconnecting the electric cord, wiping out the cups, and awaiting Mr. Shibayashi's documentation of the everlasting kindness of Bill Flynn.

"During my travels in America I encountered only kindness. Especially in State of Washington and State of Colorado is America extremely kind to foreigners."

"Toki-doki," Lou said. "We also have a history of not being so kind, not all of the time."

Mr. Shibayashi discounted this as the right-minded impulse of any man to diminish the fame of his own country. "Mr. Flynn," said Mr. Shibayashi, "is typical of American kindness."

Soon, when Lou filled the cups, Mr. Shibayashi would ask, "Are you fond of Japanese green tea?" Lou had lately endeavored to pour at the moment when Mr. Shibayashi was most deeply engaged in his relation of the biographical highlights of the life of one Miss Kumashiro (her name, Mr. Shibayashi would eventually say, means, in English, White Bear). Lou no longer wished to be asked whether he was fond of green tea, since he had reassured Mr. Shibayashi on this score not once but six times. "Mr. Flynn has been most kind to Miss Kumashiro," Mr. Shibayashi said.

"Miss Kumashiro," Lou said without interest. He had not met her. And the story of her triumphant young life, which had so profoundly moved him when he first heard it from Mr. Shibayashi—which had at that time appeared to him a tale he would want to carry home as an illustration of the courage of the Japanese student—was now powerless to capture his emotion. It merely numbed him, like the sixty-fifth close description of tragic and anonymous want in the annual Christmas exposition of the One Hundred Neediest Cases.

"When Miss Kumashiro was at the pinnacle of her discouragement," Mr. Shibayashi said, "Mr. Flynn was her rescuer. Under him she is enabled to continue in her course of study, although all difficulties are not yet past."

Flynn's rescue had consisted of his employment of Miss Kumashiro at the Cultural Center, at a wage not low by Japanese standards nor high by American, in the capacity of translator and interpreter. Her English was superb and her grasp quick in any given situation, a dual skill of unmistakable service to Flynn, to the Center, and of course to herself insofar as she was now relieved of the financial stress which had at one point threatened an end to her academic career. "As to her program of scholarship," Mr. Shibayashi said, "Miss Kumashiro was at one time amused by the literary category of William Shakespeare, but she has now become permanently amused by the literary category of James Boswell. Had you heard," Mr. Shibayashi asked, "concerning *Life of Johnson* by James Boswell?"

Lou Brown had heard of that book. Even now he was reading it, as Mr. Shibayashi well knew who had located it for him on the library shelves. Therefore he did not reply to the question but poured *ocha* from teapot to cups. "Are you fond of Japanese green tea?" Mr. Shibayashi asked, waiting for Lou to drink, then raising the cup to his own lips, setting it down, and reporting in a brisk style that Miss Kumashiro's native place was a village in the northern sector of Yamaguchi Prefecture, a region famous for cedar; that she had attended the public schools of that county, distinguishing herself morally, academically and athletically; that she had farmed the family paddy in every weather; that she had saved her little money for books in English purchased by mail from Tokyo; and that she had at length, after intensive and isolated study, completed her preparation for entrance examinations to the University, passed them with eminence but been prevented from immediate admission because of tuberculosis. Tuberculosis, Mr. Shibayashi explained, was widespread in Japan but unknown to America, a conception he had formed in conversation with an Indonesian medical student at the Denver Y.M.C.A.

Nor would it be fair to imagine, said Mr. Shibayashi, offering Lou Brown a Peace cigarette, that Miss Kumashiro's convalescence was hastened by news of the death of her father in a lumber accident upon a hillside of her native place.

There followed an enumeration of the difficulties and disappointments encountered by Miss Kumashiro during her years of interrupted but determined attendance at the University, a recital now so devoid of surprise that Lou seized the opportunity, in these moments, to organize in his mind odds and ends of the day's business. Meanwhile he sustained a posture of attention. This he achieved by holding his head erect and slightly tilted, thrusting out his chin and blinking his eyes at intervals to avoid the appearance of fixity. Thus he was largely able to insulate himself, although in spite of his best efforts at concentration—more accurately, non-concentration—he could never remain wholly indifferent to that chapter of Miss Kumashiro's life, as related by Mr. Shibayashi, devoted to degrading labor.

Apparently, upon the advice of an employment agent who told her, in effect, that penniless fatherless girls can scarcely command choice positions, she accepted appointment as a maid-of-all-work in a dormitory occupied by railroad workers. This category of men, said Mr. Shibayashi, is drunken and vulgar, unlike American railroad workers, whom he had observed from train windows near Seattle. Returning briefly to her native place in Yamaguchi Prefecture, a region famous for cedar, Miss Kumashiro secured her *futon*, traveled south again, her *futon* on her back, and devoted herself to her new position.

She was to have received three thousand yen a month, a dry room, and good food. Within a short period she should have been able to save enough money to provide for her family and guarantee her own return to college, but she had omitted from her calculations the employment agent's fee, and she had failed at the same time to anticipate the invisible moral cost. "As a Christian," said Mr. Shibayashi, "you are first concerned to know of her moral condition."

Lou Brown never knew which end of this statement to confront. "I am not *precisely* a Christian," he sometimes said, or, on other days, "The first concerns of a Christian are not *always* moral."

"Morally speaking," Mr. Shibayashi said, "among the drunken and vulgar railroad workers she reached the pinnacle of her discouragement." From daylight to dark she labored, and then, when the day's last task—the firing of the baths—was done, and she hoped for an hour of solitary reading upon her *futon,* she was yet subject to the drunken and vulgar advances of the railroad workers. For Miss Kumashiro (whose name in English, Mr. Shibayashi said, means White Bear) it was an existence neither her health nor her spirit could long have borne. How fortunate it was that at this moment of her life the position became available under Mr. Flynn.

Mr. Shibayashi's offer to rinse the teacups now signaled the concluding stage of their exchange. Lou Brown rejected Mr. Shibayashi's offer. Mr. Shibayashi rose. Lou Brown rose. Mr. Shibayashi apologized for his necessity to depart. Lou Brown forgave him. At the door Mr. Shibayashi bowed once more from the waist. Lou Brown bowed from the shoulders. Mr. Shibayashi said, "You have been very kind."

"Sayonara," Lou Brown said.

"Of course Shibayashi is nothing," Bill Flynn said at his New Year's Eve party, "if not indirect."

Fumiko-san, the Flynns' maid, weeping as she worked, restored the *kotatsu* with new charcoal, and then they all lowered themselves again into the warm well. She had been weeping all evening because the whiskey was warm. Ordinarily, said Emily Flynn, she did not cry until the middle of the month when, at some convenient hour, usually in the morning after Bill left for work, she wept away an accumulation of travail. Clyde Pettit told in his soft Texas accent an excellent joke newly imported from the United States, and everyone laughed except the mining engineer from Oil City, Pennsylvania. "Then why don't she chill it?" he asked. "Because the iceman's three-wheel truck broke down," said Emily Flynn, a morose failure which plunged the gentleman from Oil City into a developing gloom. The Japanese kimono, said Hester Brown, who had been admiring Fumiko-san's new kimono, had been wisely adopted in Japan, where it flattered the figure, but Clyde Pettit disputed this point upon the grounds that Japanese women are not really *much* thinner than Westerners. "Don't ask me to reveal my source of information," he said, at which everyone laughed except the gentleman from Oil City, who contended that all Japanese women are ugly. Fumiko-san served sandwiches, and Lou Brown searched her face in vain for ugliness. The man from Oil City, finishing his sandwiches and declaring that the Japanese are insane, struggled to his feet from the *tatami*, told the Flynns to tell Fumiko-san to phone for a taxicab, and afterward returned from the cab to tell the Flynns to tell Fumiko san to instruct the driver.

"And of course you can figure out Shibayashi's indirection," Bill Flynn said, "if you're patient."

Emily Flynn plugged in the tape-recorder, and Fumiko-san sang *The Light of the Firefly* which—she was astounded to hear—enjoyed a certain currency in the Western world under the quaint title *Auld Lang Syne.* At midnight the Browns and the Flynns and Clyde Pettit and Fumiko-san were toasting the new year with Very Rare Old Special Suntory Liquor Whiskey when the iceman arrived. And it was then, in the act of plunging the pick into the block, that Bill Flynn cried "Haaa," and again, "Haaa," and swung upon Lou Brown with a vehemence that might have been thought wrath except that his face was wide with smile. "Lou," he said, "for Christ sake, Lou, take back that goddam Boswell to the *library.*"

The Iron Fist of Oligarchy

You will never again hear of anything so tragic as the career of Sy Appleman. However, let me begin with Mrs. Governour. One must begin somewhere.

Mrs. Governour was a tall, thin, insane widow of fifty-five living in Richie, Illinois, with a Toy Manchester Terrier bitch named Champion Princess Gloriosa, whose bloodlines were beyond reproach. She was fourteen years old (the human equivalent of ninety-eight), and so it was natural that one morning she died, dragging her little rug into the living-room, curling herself up, and expiring. "Gloriosa!" screamed Mrs. Governour. "What are you doing here, you naughty child? Bad, bad girl, get back where you belong," beating the dog with a supple maple twig.

Of course the dog refused to stir. The veterinarian was summoned, one Logan McLean, a brother, as it happened, of Walter McLean, owner of Radio Station KRIC in Richie, for whom Sy Appleman worked for two years. "There's not too much sense beating her," said the veterinarian, "the animal's dead. I'll tell you what I'll do, I'll just dispose of the remains."

Mrs. Governour had other plans, however, for the repose of

her dog. "You can't possibly think," she said, "that I'm just going to throw Gloriosa down a hole in the ground." Therefore, with the veterinarian's assistance, she groomed the dead dog, dressed it in a plaid vest, tied blue ribbons to its collar, and drove with this burden a hundred miles to St. Louis. When Logan McLean presented her with a bill for five dollars she refused to pay it, accusing him of having murdered her dog. Eleven months later he brought suit against her in Richie Municipal Court, introducing witnesses to prove that he could have had no possible motive for murder, and after a trial of a day and a half he was awarded his fee and legal costs. It was a struggle.

In St. Louis she witnessed the interment of her dog in a vault sold to her by Laughter In The Glen, Inc., which promised her that fresh lilies of the valley would be placed regularly before the dog's resting-place, and assured her that the vault was immune to flood, fire, or other natural disaster. Service was read by an officer of Laughter In The Glen, choosing as his text *Genesis* VIII, 17, "Bring forth with thee every living thing that is with thee, of all flesh, both of fowl, and of cattle. . . ." Then he presented her with a bill for $600, which she immediately paid.

Now, Sy Appleman, whose true name was not Seymour, as you might suspect, but Samuel, or Sam, was at that time the all-round man, or boy, at Radio Station KRIC in Richie. He had been born in New York City, where he had received a degree in Dramatic Art, son of Harry Appleman, a Radio producer of note in the heyday of Radio, later transferring his talents to Television, where he is highly thought of throughout the industry as a man of dynamic magnetism. The job in Richie was Sy's first. He had accepted it more or less to please his father, who had gone to some effort to make the connection.

Radio, in Harry Appleman's opinion, was then on the threshold of becoming an Art form, forced into an agonizing reappraisal of itself in view of the threat of Televison, and therefore really only in its infancy, screaming for young men of talent and ingenuity to revolutionize the industry, exactly the medium for Sy's fine voice, his expressiveness, his clean-cut nature, and his co-operative spirit. In short, a challenge.

Of course Richie was terribly hot, and Sy never took the heat well, gasping and suffocating at seventy-five degrees or over, but he loved every minute of the job up to a point. Everything that a voice could do in small Radio was his to do, his finger was on the pulse of the town. He was always courteous, always anxious to promote good public relations, meanwhile forming a sound sense of community life, and learning Radio from every conceivable point of view. What enthusiasm he had!

And what a small salary! He was paid $32.50 a week, raised to $35 in his second year, which he budgeted very carefully in order not to depend upon his father. If his father sent him a check he sent it back. He rented a small room in the home of people named Klein, owners of a jewelry store in Richie. They had a daughter, Teddy, an intelligent girl who wore no make-up and read magazines containing articles entitled "The Iron Fist of Oligarchy." At first, Sy's tastes at this young stage of life directed him toward girls less intelligent but more glamorous than Teddy, with the result that he formed friendships with several, although never concurrently, skating on the lake in the winter, or walking arm in arm about the town late at night, Sy, as they walked, pointing out the important houses of the town and describing their residents' political or commercial affiliations. He was on speaking terms with every important person of the place since, in addition to reading local news on KRIC, he gathered it. He also read national and international news torn from the teletype, enunciating well, and allocating to each item proper feeling and respect, never reading with cynicism what ought to have been read with gravity, and clearly differentiating in tone between commercial announcements, on the one hand, and items of importance to mankind. He was a true humanitarian, God bless him, we need more of his type. He made every effort to pronounce the names of foreign persons and places in a manner even a native would have approved, and to distinguish between fact and hearsay, charge and conviction, or wish and actuality.

In the summer, his preferred destination was the slaughterhouse, which was refrigerated, although I cannot doubt, as he has told me, that most of the girls of Richie disliked it, since it smelled bad and was splattered with blood. He often went there with Teddy Klein, who did not object, and who even found in a slaughterhouse rich material for serious conversation. In the slaughterhouse they talked about man's relationship to animals, of the ethics of killing them, and of the wonders and dangers of man's technological control of his environment, thoughts which you and I had when we were younger.

Well, why should I keep you in suspense? Just before he eventually left Richie they were married, and in time had four children, the first a boy, named Richie, simply Richie, not Richard, as you might suspect. Perhaps he has a middle name, poor little darling, but if so I was never informed of it. Thus you can see that he retained a favorable memory of Richie, Illinois, where his pulse had been on everything, and where his work had been full of variety, as it cannot help but be for an all-round man in small Radio. She was not beautiful, but they were devoted. Afterward, when his pockets spilled over with nothing but money, and he could have picked and chosen among varieties, or his father at the drop of a hint could have boosted a girl to national prominence in a single night, he took no liberties. His agent in Hollywood, Peggy Flanagan, not only thought the world of him but was eleven or twelve times as beautiful as the former Teddy Klein, but Sy never so much as pecked her forehead. The three other children were born on the Coast, where Sy and his growing family lived in a splendid home between Hollywood and Topanga, thoroughly air-conditioned, and blessed with a swimming pool shaped like a star, for the house had been built by the late Star Weber, hero of more than two hundred Westerns, a tragic story, but not this one. Suffice it to say he returned home one night, announced to his widow that he had been first on the draw at the pass two hundred times too often, drained the pool, leaped onto the divingboard, and jack-knifed headfirst in.

Additionally, in Richie, Illinois, Sy was soon conducting his own morning show, which unquestionably revolutionized Radio, at least in Richie. It was a work of Art, carefully planned, although not without its moments of sheer inspiration, as I shall relate. It was a *balanced* show. In music, for example, he reduced the quantity of pop and increased the quantity of classical, most of the latter from his own store of records. One portion of his program he called Human Take All, absolutely unrehearsed, unrecorded, untaped, and unnetworked, during which he interviewed a scholar or artist if by chance such a person appeared in the vicinity of Richie. If no scholar or artist were available, he invited to the studio someone entirely undistinguished, as, for example, a slaughterhouse worker, an electrical repairman, a policeman, a barber, a grocery clerk, a schoolteacher, inquiring into the details of their jobs, what hours they kept, what their principal problems were, what their secret ambitions were, whether they were bored, and so forth. I have heard recordings of these shows, and you may believe me they were every inch original. Moreover, there were no complaints.

One day, after delivering a commercial announcement on behalf of the Ralston Purina Company of St. Louis, advocating the use of Purina Dog Chow For Eager Eaters, and Purina Kibbled Meal For High Energy Requirements, Sy thought, in a moment of sheer inspiration, to embellish his statements with a few barks such as a happy and appreciative dog might make after a meal of such variety. Mr. Walter McLean, owner of KRIC, looked up from his desk and smiled at Sy, for he was always proud of the young man's resourcefulness, and a few moments later the telephone rang.

Sy allowed it to ring several times. Little did he know that this was the ring of Fate. Had he known he would have snapped up the telephone in a twinkling, for he was much like all of us, anxious to know his Fate, good or bad, sitting and waiting for *the* telephone call. One receives many, until sometimes life is nothing but a ringing, and one considers unlisting his number. On the other hand, one keeps his number listed, never daring to disconnect himself from Fate. It was Mrs. Governour, demanding to know whose Toy Manchester Terrier she had just heard.

"It wasn't actually a Toy Manchester Terrier," Sy said politely.

"You're being impertinent, young man," she said, "because I guess I ought to know her when I hear her."

"It wasn't a her," Sy said, "it was a him."

"You're not being truthful," she said.

"Just a minute," said Sy, "I'll look." He laughed. (Laughing at Fate, what an irony!) He whispered to Mr. McLean the substance of Mrs. Governour's remarks. "By golly," said Sy back into the phone, "you're right, ma'am, and many thanks for calling."

"I want to see her," said Mrs. Governour.

"But you really can't," said Sy. "Frankly, ma'am, it was only a sound, to be truthful."

"Has she been altered?" Mrs. Governour inquired.

"Hang up and tell her to go to hell," said Mr. McLean, but this was not a thing Sy Appleman could do. If anything, he was a humanitarian, and therefore, in response to Mrs. Governour's request, he called the dog to the telephone, saying, "Here, doggie, speak to the nice lady," which the dog did, barking several times into the phone until Mrs. Governour at last permitted Sy to leave the line. When he met Teddy Klein for lunch that day she said "Woof." (First laughing at Fate, and now saying "Woof" to Fate, irony piled on irony!)

Had Mrs. Governour been satisfied with one single telephone conversation, things might have been different, but she saw no inconvenience to anyone in calling every day to speak to the dog, so that what first was humorous soon became an annoyance, almost in the nature of a pain in the ass, even to a humanitarian like Sy Appleman. Once she came to the studio in the hope of seeing the dog. Sy told her it had died in the night, but this was a possibility she was unable to grasp. Therefore he said the dog had gone away on a two-week vacation. She described to him the murder of the dog by Mr. Logan McLean, and the funeral in St. Louis, presented him with a copy of the script of the sermon, and she went home again, but in two weeks her calls were resumed, and Sy was able to tell her, with perfect truth, that *he* was leaving, not for two weeks but forever.

"And tell her you're taking your dog with you," said Mr. McLean.

"And taking my dog with me," said Sy. "But, ma'am, I have a plan if you have a phonograph. Mr. McLean says if you'll pay for the materials I can make you a little recording of the dog barking, and you can play it on your phonograph night and day."

"Will it be expensive?" asked Mrs. Governour.

"About a dollar," said Sy.

It was agreed. Sy made the record, beginning with a few moments of yipping and howling in his own voice, followed by a statement, "Here, doggie, here's your food," and the dog barked "Thank you," and later "Good morning" and "Good night" and "Where's my leash?" and what-not until Sy had cut a record of decent size, which he labeled MANCHESTER TOY TERRIER (*with Sy Appleman*).

That record will someday be a collector's item. More than that. It is not alone the record of a man imitating a dog, but a tragic poem illustrating the stage of civilization in the calendar year 1950. No doubt things have changed in the decade since, but in 1950, in Richie, Illinois, a young man of some talent received from his unseen audience only one request—to speak not in his own voice but in the voice of a dog. This is demeaning to a man. Sy Appleman had many intelligent things to say in his own voice, ideas he had formed on life from alert living, ideas on Dramatic Art from his studies at college, ideas on love from loving Teddy Klein, ideas on international news, ideas on budgeting for the simple life, ideas on heat, ideas on enunciation and pronunciation, even ideas on dogs. Soon after he reached New York the record was sent on to him by Mr. Walter McLean, since Mrs. Governour refused to pay the dollar charge.

It goes without saying, the experiences of Sy and Teddy Appleman in New York were nothing short of perfect bliss. Here were a healthy and energetic young man and his beautiful, or intelligent bride, free of all the restraints of childhood, and not yet apprehensive of the encroachments of age, surrounded by amiable friends old and new, and by cultural benefits of every sort, living on love, as the saying goes. From a financial point of view they could not be envied, but New York is a Paradise of open-air amusements, and the boulevards and parks are free.

Their apartment was not spacious. To be perfectly straightforward with you, it consisted of only a single room in a house owned by the University, although the rent was less reasonable than you might expect from a non-profit institution. When I first visited them they had no furniture except a crib for Richie, soon to be born, although they had also received, from a friend in the rug business, a rug. Sy's father, seeing their condition, sent them a bed and chairs, and they slept on the bed, I suppose, but piled the chairs in the corner until one night, after a furious argument with his father, Sy agreed to unpile them and distribute them about the room, although I never saw him actually sit on one. There is no questioning the fact that Harry Appleman in argument is a forbidding man. When angered, or even overcome by mere friendly enthusiasm, he pounds the fist of one hand into the other with such violence that it is reminiscent of whipcrack or gunfire. He is not a tall man, but he stands exceptionally erect on all occasions, and his hair is fully gray, and extremely striking. The room also contained a guitar, records, and a phonograph which we heard on the first night I made their acquaintance.

But rather than tell you all the details of their life in New York, let me give you a glimpse of Sy and Teddy such as I had one warm night as I walked down their street. They were sitting at the open window of their dark room, facing the street, he bare-chested and she bare-shouldered, he with his arm about her, sitting so peacefully, so completely fulfilled, so utterly content to be alone with themselves, so pleased with this moment and with the world and with all that was in it, that they would not have noticed me as I passed if I had fired a cannon into their faces. Chairs and rugs they did not need.

I was at this time writing a little family show which Harry Appleman was producing, but which was bound to fail. We perked it up for awhile with a kindly Uncle, suggested by Harry Appleman and subsequently played with such success for many years by Melvin Aloy. Following introductions, Harry encouraged Sy to play us the records of his days in Radio in Richie. Reluctantly he did so, sitting on a stack of books and closing his eyes and groaning, and saying after each record, "Well, that's plenty," but his father said, "No, go on, go on," and Sy put on another record. A father is a father. His father thought the records all very well, smiling and nodding or occasionally offering criticisms of a minor nature, such as "You were talking too much there, not allowing your guest to explore himself."

And finally! History! Because when Sy played the record of the Toy Manchester Terrier talking to Mrs. Governour his father became inspired, pounding his fist several times—a regular bombardment—leaping to his feet and losing all control, dancing a jig on the floor, laughing and holding his ribs, absolutely convulsed, and he said to me, "The dog is the missing ingredient over and above the kindly Uncle, minimize the family and accentuate the dog. Sy will read the dog. Do you realize that this is a country that can't get enough of dogs? Hail and farewell, my moment of truth is heralded by the voice of a Toy Manchester Terrier."

"It wasn't a Toy Manchester Terrier," Sy said. "It was just a dog barking, no particular dog."

"Sy, give me your answer and think it over later," said his

father. "Let me tell you something, Television is in its infancy, on the threshold of becoming an Art, dying and bleeding while waiting for young men of talent and ingenuity to revolutionize the industry."

"No," said Sy.

"For you," said his father, "Television will be easier than falling off a log."

"I don't want to do something easy," Sy said. "I want to do something hard."

"A tremendous challenge," his father said.

"To bark like a dog?" Sy asked. "Thousands of actors can satisfactorily bark like a dog. Why not get an actual dog?"

I will not bore you with the reasons why actual dogs have never been heard on "Kanine Kapers." For a short period of time in 1956, when Sy was sulking in his tent, or mansion, we attempted to work with dogs, but the chief problems are three: dogs are dirty and smelly; dogs do not always bark on cue, however well-trained, since they cannot read scripts; and the employment of a dog also requires the employment of a trainer, who is frequently more of a nuisance than the animal itself.

"As a favor to your father," cried Harry Appleman, grasping Sy by the shoulders and kissing him on both cheeks. "Now you are about to become a father yourself, change your little darling's diapers night and day, feed him his mush, bathe him, wash him, tie his shoes, wipe his nose and what-not else, shower him with gifts and protect him from the bruises of life until he can stand upright and manly on his own two sturdy feet, direct his intellectual development, nurture his genius and talent and ingenuity, pray that he will be wealthy—and rush at night a thousand times to the side of his cradle for fear he has stopped his breathing." Here Harry rushed to the cradle, laid his forehead on the crossbar, his arms dangling at his sides, and wept.

"Don't be so goddamn emotional," Sy said, standing by his father with an arm around his shoulder, but he was moved and so were we all.

Of course, you would never expect Sy Appleman to offer anything less than his absolute best. Bark like a dog?—just any old dog? Not Sy. If he were to bark at all he would bark accurately, because for him the point of life was not to fall off a log but to do whatever he was called upon to do with energy and enthusiasm, confronting not only the simpler demands of a given task but its most rigid complexities, believe me. The research he accomplished! He went to dozens of kennels in New York, Westchester, Jersey, and I believe southern Connecticut, soon learning to bark the bark of breeds most people will never hear of. Have you ever heard, let us say, of an Affenpinscher? A Bouvier des Flandres? A Keeshond? Welsh Corgis? Lhasa Apsos? Now you are speaking of rarities in the kingdom of dogs, and Sy Appleman knew them by their bark.

We shot three pilot films of the "Kanine Kapers" series in four days in a studio in Manhattan, everybody working for carfare from what looked at best like a risky script. Melvin Aloy played Uncle, Caldwell Burris played Father, and Rhoda Sibilia Mother, all remaining with us throughout the years. Unfortunately, from season to season we must recast the children as they outgrow their roles, although we always attempt to retain them as long as we humanly can. And then when we break the new child in, you may be sure we sweat hammer and nails while effecting the transition. You see, it is a business ridden with superstition, the reason being that nobody has anything definite to go on, so that we must depend exclusively upon omens and portents. When something works, nobody knows why. Succeed or fail, there's no accounting for it. For these three pilot films Sy was paid $110, retroactive contingent on selling a sponsor.

After the pilot series he retired, as he thought, from his career in Television. Never mind this getting on in life. This was an attitude he maintained even after the show was sold. He stood firm, literally unmoved. "It's sold, it's sold," his father shouted, but Sy replied calmly, "Things are sold every day, so don't be so emotional. Beef is sold every day in Richie, Illinois, rice in

China, coffee in Brazil, candy in Woolworth's, Coca-Cola in bottles. In short, leave me alone, I have only a certain limited capacity for rejoicing."

"Only thirteen weeks," his father said. "I plead with you, in memory of your mother. I'll pay you $220 a week. Consider your babe in arms. To sophisticated minds like yours and Teddy's the natural beauties and cultural benefits of the City of New York may be nourishment enough, but these things cannot pacify a baby. On top of everything," he added, "your father's problems have now increased beyond all possible control."

This was true. With a sponsor, our budget was relatively tremendous, the agency hovered over our every move, we were forced to infinite care with every detail, and all the members of the company were continually prostrated with nervous anxiety. Add to this the fact that we were shooting the new series at the same time we were trying to transfer the operation to Hollywood, and you will understand that Sy allowed himself finally to be persuaded to assist, carrying out his own end of things to perfection in spite of a severe collapse brought on by the heat. He bought a Frigikoola air-conditioner for his apartment, or room, although it burst through the limits of his budget, costing $299.99—let's say $300—plus installation charges. He quickly reimbursed himself with an appearance on the Ed Sullivan show, then in its infancy, where he imitated a True Boxer Type reading "From Here to Eternity" to a Dandie Dinmont, and a Rhodesian Ridgeback explaining Canasta to a somewhat backward Alaskan Malamute. This was so successful that he received numerous invitations to appear on Radio and Television, and another to appear before a convention of veterinarians in Dallas. The letter from the veterinarians he neatly tore in half and threw away, but later retrieved and carried with him for weeks. Whenever he took the letter from his pocket he became blue, downcast by the thought of going all the way to Dallas to bark like a dog, and yet he could not surrender it, although I encouraged him either to answer it or throw it way. But how could he throw it away?

The fee was $1,000 plus expenses, a sum he could not honestly deprive his family of, especially with another baby on the way.

He also kept his money in his pocket, I think in the hope he would lose it. Possibly the continual barking was getting him down. Think how often you have been praised for something you have done so many times that now you are beginning to lose interest in it—some anecdote, for example, which you are asked to repeat over and over again until you wish you had never told it the first time. Think how often we say of our job, "Yes, I know it sounds thrilling, but after awhile it becomes a bore, and I feel the need for a change." Let me even mention love and marriage, pointing out to you how often we change our husbands and wives, buy a new car, grow a mustache and shave it off, cook a new dish, drive home by a different route, anything for a change. "Variety is the spice of life." Good God, even a dog needs a change off from Purina Dog Chow to Purina Kibbled Meal as the days go by. The man was made for better things.

The public saw their first "Kanine Kapers" in September. Within thirteen weeks it was a national institution. In private conversation the industry expected it to decline shortly like everything else, but officially the agencies were taking no chances, so that we were soon underwritten eighteen months into the future. Harry Appleman himself had no idea how he had achieved what he had achieved. Nor did he care to know. He wished only to continue, and the way to do so is to repeat the performance over and over again, respecting the omens and portents, employing the same names and the same faces and the same voices and the same plot and the same music without variation or improvement or experiment or innovation, even down to the same cameras on the same lot at the same hour of morning on the same days of the week, throwing parties to reduce the boredom, raising wages to introduce the idea of progress, and promising that someday it will end, halfway hoping it will but halfway hoping it won't until someday, at long last, to everyone's relief and despair, it finally does.

The moment we saw we were in for a good thing we rushed back East, finding Sy studying for his courses on the floor, and rocking the cradle with his foot. We pleaded with him to return with us to the Coast, he had never seen the Golden West, but he complained that he had seen the show on Television, and it was infantile and foolish and a certain sign that the moment was coming which would witness the decline and fall of America, and so forth, further complaining that the show lacked *teamwork*, he never met the actors, the actors never met the writer, the writer had no control over the music, and he wished he were back in Richie, Illinois.

However, this is standard procedure throughout the industry, except in the rare event of a producer who feels it may be beneficial to all concerned to have a general idea of the total show, in which case a round-table is held beforehand, sometimes for an hour. To make a long story short, tears were followed by compromise, his father agreeing to inject a team spirit into the production by holding regular round-tables, in return for which Sy would come out for thirty-nine weeks at $440 a week, and I flew back with Harry. As I recall, Sy and Teddy and Richie stopped off in Richie, Illinois, where the Kleins were greeted with the first sight of their new grandson, and Sy staged a huge emotional scene, kissing the earth at the Town Square, then down to Dallas for the veterinarians, then a week's engagement in Reno, and then to the Coast, where they arrived in good health and spirits, and took up their new life.

It goes without saying, their experiences on the Coast were nothing short of perfect bliss up to a point. Their house was more unique than any I have ever seen, but at the same time by no means inexpensive. The truth is, in that environment there are only mansions or shacks, the middle class having withered away. There is no such thing as medium, although the house was somewhat cheaper than another of the same quality because of its history. In a community ridden by superstition nobody wants to live in the shadow of suicide, which is looked upon as a form of failure. For years nobody would buy the house from the widow, no matter how she disguised its past. In addition to pool and air-conditioning throughout, it was entirely mechanized, built along the lines of the Indian cliff-houses at Acoma, New Mexico, where Star Weber had shot many of his Westerns. In structure it consisted of one immense principal room with ladders leading upward into numerous small bedrooms, bath, kitchen, and what-not.

All things prospered, there were four children and they grew, sunburned from toe to crown, and Teddy increased in beauty, although she was widely criticized for refusing to wear make-up, and Sy's income doubled from time to time until it had grown beyond all reason. He forgot whose face was on the dollar bill, his voice was insured by his father for $1,000,000, he seemed serene.

Of course, especially when the weather was hot, he was a man of temperament, frequently threatening to leave us and return to Richie, Illinois, where he could always obtain a job for $35 a week in Radio, and supplement his income by helping out Teddy's father in the jewelry business. Often he bought tickets to Richie, carried them in his pocket awhile, then tore them up. He complained that his bark was now perfected beyond the wildest dream of man and dog, that there was nowhere left to go but down, and at such times he spoke of suicide, inquiring among his intimates if any had heard of a new and original way, never before tried, such as jumping out of a dirigible, burying himself in sand, or hanging himself from a Television aerial.

In 1956, as I have related, he left us for a short period of time, remaining in his home *incommunicado*, where he undertook to write a friendly letter to every person he had ever met in his life, under whatever circumstance and regardless of how briefly, as a means of returning to that point in his existence where he had taken the wrong turn, but little was accomplished. The fact was that he had passed the point of return. He could not return to Richie or to Radio or to school, not now. Too many people depended upon him, from his father to his smallest child, poor little darling.

Two years ago he broke off all direct relations with his father, refusing to speak with him, so that communication between them was conducted by his agent, Peggy Flanagan. When his moods were at their worst they sat for long hours in his pool, each on the tip of a star, Sy, Peggy, Harry, conferring until the mood had passed and his spirits were recovered, so that he appeared for work on the following day full of good cheer again, with a smile and a quip and a bark for everyone. Originally he engaged her to find other work for him in Television, which she promised to do, and perhaps tried, although why she should have tried I cannot imagine, since he was now earning $1,760 a week. Bark, yes, this she could have found for him all over town, besieged he was, make no mistake, because he was an omen and a portent of success. After all, the industry is the industry, you do what you do. A man turns a screw, as he does in Detroit. "I can play the piano or guitar," he said, "I can sing a little, even whistle, or hum, read from the classics, interpret philosophy, saw wood, wire electricity, I am a man of numerous parts, I have a face, I can speak," but the industry is vast, versatility is not required. Send out a call for two men who can hum, and a thousand will knock at your door. "Television is only in its infancy," he said, "soon it will be an Art, it is bleeding and dying for young men of talent and ingenuity to revolutionize the industry," but this is not so. He did not see things clearly in his mind.

One morning, about three o'clock, Teddy discovered him draining the pool, and I went when she called, throwing my clothes on over my pajamas, and thinking, "Fortunately such a beautiful pool takes a long time to drain." It was early June. Let me guarantee you I drove at breakneck speed, resolved that if I were not too late I would make every effort in the future to know him better, and understand him, and comfort him in his melancholy moods. He needed a vacation. We all needed a vacation. I had written eight thousand pages of "Kanine Kapers."

A mile away I could see the lights of his house, and the revolving red light of an ambulance, or police car. As I approached I perceived that there were several such vehicles, as well as emergency fire equipment, dozens of automobiles from all the neighborhood and scores of people gathered on the lawn beneath the floodlights, so that I almost had the feeling, with my pajamas beneath my clothes, that I was attending one of those come-as-you-were-when-invited parties, of which we have such a number these days. Then I heard the singing.

Everyone was singing "I'll Never Smile Again," Sy leading them with his hands, in his bathing suit, on the divingboard, and all the light pouring down. For an actor, it was Paradise. Among those present was Dr. Joe Jack, a physician and friend of the family, who, when he saw me approach, said "Sing, sing, for all you're worth," and I joined in song. There was a foot of water in the pool below him, or perhaps eighteen inches, as one of the firemen later estimated. With wrenches the firemen had turned the water on again, but the inflow was only, so to speak, a drop in the bucket. They had also endeavored to run a safety net beneath the board, but the width of the pool prevented their doing so. Floating in the pool was a rope with which a neighbor, Oliver Wells, a Western player, had attempted to lasso him, but this too, had somehow failed. When he saw me he barked in my honor, saying, "Here is the man who has written my speeches," howling and baying and setting up a howling and a baying in reply from all the dogs of the neighborhood, magnificent power and range of the sort I never knew he had, since we had never required it.

The firemen now struck upon the plan of nudging him with a long pole, in the hope that he would fall into the pool and suffer only scrapes and bruises. Joe Jack opposed this. The best course, he said, was to stall for the light of day, which might cast a different aspect upon things, and meanwhile sing according to Sy's directions for all we were worth. He also suggested that the children be brought, which they were, blinking and rubbing their eyes under the lights, falling asleep and waking, falling asleep again, but at last waking and standing together beside the pool and singing a song with their father which they had sung together on many evenings. It was from a Pooh book, Sy singing the words, the children singing the "tiddely pom," while Dr. Jack instructed the oldest, Richie, to call to his father, "Daddy, we love you, we will miss you, remember that you always told us to make sure the water is in the pool."

SY. The more it snows
CHILDREN. Tiddely Pom
SY. The more it goes
CHILDREN. Tiddely pom
SY. The more it goes
CHILDREN. Tiddely pom
SY. On snowing.

The boy's words had no effect upon his father. "Thank you for your sentiments," Sy said, "and I wish you a merry Christmas. Remember how versatile your father was, I can sing, lead the choir, bark, and dive." He prepared to dive, but Dr. Jack called, "No, just one more song, your versatile voice is entrancing us all," ordering the firemen to try the use of the long pole, as they had planned, which they in turn decided against, bringing instead a long hose which they intended to play upon him and cause him to fall instead of dive. He consented to lead us one final time, issuing instructions, and we sang it in the following way:

SY. And nobody knows
CHORUS OF VOICES. Tiddely pom
SY. How cold my toes
CHORUS OF VOICES. Tiddely pom
SY. How cold my toes
CHORUS OF VOICES. Tiddely pom
SY. Are growing.

"Let me bring you a coat," I shouted.

This he paused to consider, when his father arrived, and the cold spell passed, and he began to grow warm, wiping the sweat from his face, gasping, suffocating, strangulating, and calling out, "Turn on the air-conditioner," which Dr. Jack and I promised to do, bending with wrenches at the base of the board where it was attached to the ladder, informing him that we were turning on the air-conditioner, in the hope that we could loosen the board and tip him into the pool, where he might suffer only scrapes and bruises.

"Sy," his father shouted, pounding his fist into his palm, "come down off there before you make a fool of yourself," and Sy replied, "Don't be emotional," but even so, hearing the voice of his father he came, and the crew from the ambulance seized him. Tell me if it is not as tragic as I promised. His mind is gone. Sorely we miss him. For the time being we are finding it possible to transcribe his barking from the old films, and beginning in September we will gain time with thirteen weeks of Critic's Choices (re-runs), meanwhile training a new voice. We are not without confidence, but you may believe me that we are sweating hammer and nails while effecting the transition.

The Self-Made Brain Surgeon

I

I ordered the illumination extinguished in the power pole, but on the following day the cruising Streetlight Bench replaced it. It was the Electrical Overhead who referred me to the Streetlight Bench, again I ordered the illumination extinguished, but the Fire Department took issue, one Inspector Mahaffey there, complaining that he required the light, it illuminated the alarm box on the corner. Not enough co-operation, too much efficiency, men are double-barreled. I arranged with the Streetlight Bench for an independent circuit, they installed it in the ground at the base of the pole. A buried brook ran underneath the sidewalk. It emptied in the reservoir. I could kick on the power pole with my foot when I went home, or off, however I desired. Several nights I went home very late, I was constantly afraid, the neighborhood was unfamiliar to me.

Complaints were initiated in the neighborhood when the light was observed extinguished, and I observed in the dark beside the pole. But where else could I have stood? From any other point I could not have obtained a full view.

It was not Mr. Kayzee who initiated complaint, for he is not a man frightened by much. He possessed no gun, while his door he long ago took down off the hinges, so at night when he quits he drops and lashes a tarp, that's all. The hinges are there, but no door hanging, yet he has never been broken or entered.

His own illumination is all interior, except his beer sign, which throws a little blue light on the sidewalk. Late at night, when the fog blew in, it shone blue on the particles of the fog, and when the wind was right I could hear the foghorns. It was cold. Sometimes, when all was very quiet, I could hear his beer sign buzz, and yet I don't see how I could have heard it as far away as the power pole, but I thought I could. I became accustomed to the noises.

What you don't hear. Imagine if you could see as well as hear. I could hear the water running in the buried brook underneath my feet, babies crying and people arguing, dogs or cats barking or wailing, cars starting, doors slamming, brakes or honking, people whistling or singing, pianos or trumpets playing or blowing, bells ringing, radio or television, hammering or repairing. It is a great neighborhood for repairing, do it yourself. A man was repairing dents in bodies, one Lionel Hefley, age 44, residence 615 Twelfth, he was a moonlighter, he didn't really need the money but he needed the hammering. Nobody complained. Somebody shouted out a window one night: "Hefley, for Christ's sake, go to bed," then I heard the window slam, but it wasn't a peeve or beef, it wasn't anger, it is an understanding neighborhood, he needed the hammering. He was a patient of Mr. Kayzee's. Then little by little all around you the lights go out.

Sometimes he forgot to turn his beer sign off. He lives over his shop, when he switched his lights on upstairs he remembered his beer sign and came back down again. The mind is not such a mystery. If he had a patient he went in the back room. One night I went around the corner and down the alley, but I could not see in, nor was there entry or access there, although the Fire Department claimed that escapement was not impeded, one Inspector Farmholder there. What was he thinking? It was a small window, and I scraped it, but it was painted brown and blue on the inside, triangles all crisscross, and I could not see in, nor hear in.

One Mrs. Marinda Marveaux was a patient at that time, a housewife, age 24, residence 55 San Pedro, I stood aside when she left, the rear of the Marveaux house faces the rear of Mr. Kayzee's premises. Complaint was initiated by one Armand Marveaux, her husband. Another patient was his alleged bookkeeper, one Miss Denise Willerts, age 18, residence 689 Twelfth, a student at the Washby Office Machines School & Sales. Another patient was one Lionel Hefley aforementioned.

Never was a job more lonely or depressing, it was too little to do for the hours, standing and observing nothing happening. It is a quiet neighborhood, night after night, go out and buy a loaf of bread, a half a dozen slices of meat for the pail tomorrow, two cans of beer for bedtime. Where is such a life leading? I was so depressed, talking out loud under the pole was next in store for me, babies cry, people die, one night there was a wake for one Mrs. Theresa McQuinn, age 78, deceased, residence 714 Twelfth. Mr. Kayzee closed early and attended the wake, babies cry, people die, get up, and go to work, everybody waiting for some piece of luck to carry them out of the neighborhood. In front of Mr. Kayzee's store they were always talking, the word I could hear was "Money." Yet when will such a piece of luck float by, and for who? You can try to promote your luck, you can bet the horses, fly to Reno for the weekend, hunt for your Lucky Dollar in the newspaper numbers, you can drink or take a pill, but half the ways of promoting your luck are illegal or harmful to your health, and the harder you promote it the thinner your lines become, you lose patience, your habits become irregular, you become irked and irritated. Finally you lose your job. Most of them figured it was luck enough to be working. You can borrow, you can gamble, but you can't really win, or even if you win you won't be satisfied, for winning once is only half of winning twice, in the end the regular life is best, come home, eat your dinner, put the kids to bed, read the papers, look at the television, go out and buy two cans of beer, come home and drink it, argue with the wife, turn out the lights, and go to sleep. It is that kind of a neighborhood, just the noises, not much.

He was born over the store. He was named Hopkins in honor of one Hopkins, deceased, who held the first mortgage on the store for his father. His father's name was full of *k's* and *z*'s, such as Kzotszki, a foreign name, and when he was a young man he took out the *k*'s and *z*'s and called himself Kayzee. It was clever. I inquired of one M. J. Cavendish, age 84, retired, of 802 Twelfth (back): "What kind of a boy was Mr. Kayzee?"

He replied: "He was a studious boy, read books and ate fruit in the front of the store."

"Was he given to cutting up frogs and such?" I inquired. Information to this effect was divulged by Mr. Marveaux, complainant.

"Yes," replied Mr. Cavendish, "he was given to cutting up frogs and such. The boys all caught frogs in the buried brook. It ran diagonal to what is now called Twelfth. The boys caught frogs and the Kzotszki boy cut them up with a knife. He ate fruit and read books and cut up frogs and such."

In the old war he served in a medical detachment, 1917–1918, carrying, bandaging, and nursing. Following his military career he continued his career in his father's store to date, The Rite-By Market, 696 Twelfth.

Once every night I crossed the street and entered, purchasing a cigar. Cigarettes I kept lighting up and illuminating myself, maybe it was how I was observed, whereas a cigar could remain dead in my mouth for long periods of time and avoid illuminating myself. At that time I smoked three packages of cigarettes daily, I was on the verge of a nervous collapse. Once I cashed a small check, five dollars.

He always wore a white coat, and it was always clean, the sleeves turned back neatly one turn at the wrists. He wore a badge of blue and gold three inches in diameter, like an election button, it was a joke.

U. S. OFFICIAL
TAXPAYER

Every night he threw the coat in the hamper, the final action before turning out the lights, pinned the badge on the new coat, except on Thursday night he also set the hamper on the sidewalk prior to dropping and lashing the tarp. The liner of the hamper was removed on Friday morning by one Owen Segret, age 27, driver for the Pacific Linen Supply Company. The coats bore no stains or questionable matter other than ordinary, the pockets contained nothing informative, sometimes a coin or a register receipt. Segret returned the coins, if any, each following Friday when he replaced the new liner.

His books were kept by his alleged bookkeeper, one Miss Denise Willerts aforementioned. In addition to Miss Willerts he was assisted by his wife, one Dorothy, age 59, residence same. She was formerly a nurse at Letterman Army Hospital, 1951–1956, and elsewhere. Also by a delivery boy, one Warren Ponce, age 15, residence 685 Twelfth, the boy and the girl are relations. I can't describe how. Her mother and Ponce's father were formerly husband and wife, their marriage terminated, the wives exchanged husbands, the husbands exchanged residences. It was the second exchange, since prior to the termination of their marriages Mr. and Mrs. Willerts were married to each other, and Mr. and Mrs. Ponce also. The Willerts girl and the Ponce boy now reside again with their natural parents. Eight other children are also issue, residing at 685 and 689, three born to Mrs. Ponce and living with same (two by Mr. Ponce, one by Mr. Willerts), while five were born to Mrs. Willerts (three by Mr. Willerts, two by Mr. Ponce), all eight now resident with their natural parents except August Willerts, age 14, resident in the Ponce residence, 685. Mr. Willerts was arraigned but never tried for alleged attempt to defraud, June 1946, in connection with a litigation involving multiple disability claims for alleged internal injuries suffered in a collision of two machines at the intersection of Junipero Serra and St. Francis Circle *de facto* unoccupied when alleged collision occurred. He was represented by one Carlos Minna, age 57, an attorney, residence 113 San Pedro, also attorney for Mr. Kayzee.

In addition he employs one Alvin (Monk) Kuhnle, Jr., age 38, a painter seasonally employed, residence 134 San Pedro, who paints items and prices and occasional interior surfaces, who painted the blue door leading to Mr. Kayzee's alleged storage room, who painted the window in blue and brown triangles within, and who paints the numerous signs or decorations such as

MY MIND IS MADE UP.
DON'T CONFUSE ME WITH FACTS

or

DON'T CRITICIZE YOUR WIFE.
LOOK WHO SHE MARRIED

or

LOVE YOUR ENEMY.
IT'LL DRIVE HIM CRAZY.

These are the simple wisdom of ages. Kuhnle receives groceries and sundries in lieu of rates or wages. He was arrested in January 1953, for petty pilfer of the poorbox of the Church of Our Lady of Mercy, San Pedro at Thirteenth, charges were not preferred, he was represented by one Mr. Minna aforementioned and released in Mr. Kayzee's recognizance.

Except in the case of Kuhnle he pays standard rates or wages to Miss Willerts and Warren Ponce, withholding withholding taxes and Social Security deductions according to law, and $599 to his wife *per annum*, whereby he claims her as an itemized business expenditure while also retaining her as a dependent exemption, it is legal.

Nothing was illegal. He possesses authorization to sell beer, wine, liquor, or one or all and has no record of violation, possesses a Fire-Sanitation permit to burn trash during daylight hours in an approved receptacle, permit to encumber pedestrian right-of-way with cardboard or light wood cartons or crates or other pending removal by scavenger service, and permit to maintain storage space at the rear of his establishment not to impede escapement. I ordered a Fire examination of the alleged storage space, one Inspector Farmholder there, but he failed to observe contents as I directed, reporting only "adequate escapement." Co-operation is difficult. Persons in high stations are often negligent or indifferent.

I made numerous inquiries of nonperishable salesmen or truckmen dealing in such goods as bottled or canned beverages, packaged cereals or desserts or cake mixings, inquiring: "Does your business with Mr. Kayzee differ in any way from your business with other grocers operating establishments similar in size or kind?" I gained helpful information from all, especially one Jack Schindler, age 48, a salesman-truckman employed by the Twin Peaks Bottling & Distributing Company.

"I am forced to call daily on Mr. Kayzee," he replied, "whereas I don't call daily on anybody else."

"How do you account for this?" I inquired.

"Because he'll stock shelves or refrigerator facilities," replied Mr. Schindler, "but he won't stock storage."

"Why won't he stock storage ?" I inquired.

"Because he's not a progressive businessman," replied Mr. Schindler.

"Doesn't he do a good business?" I inquired. Then I stated: "He lives."

"You're asking a tricky-type question," replied Mr. Schindler. "He does a marginal business, he owns the building, he eats off his shelves, sure. Sure, he *lives*."

"But he has a storage room," I stated, and then inquired: "Why doesn't he use his storage room?"

"Because he performs brain surgery back there," replied Mr. Schindler. He laughed. Over the freezer was a sign painted by Kuhnle aforementioned in the old English style:

BRAIN SURGERY PERFORMED ON PREMISES.
ALL WORK GUARANTEED.

Everybody knew so. It was a joke in the neighborhood. Who cares? Anything goes, everything and anything is taken for granted, it was no surprise I became depressed. Consider the neighborhood. It is a neighborhood of churches, including the Church of Our Lady of Mercy, San Pedro at Thirteenth, the largest Church in the Diocese, and yet you will hear a great deal of criticism of the Priests. All persons follow politics but do not trust the politicians. It is heavy with the residences of municipal workers, Police or Fire or other, and yet the Department is not respected. It is a Union district, and yet the leaders of labor are not respected. The taverns are full, illegal betting is freely solicited, graft and corruption are everywhere, violations exist, scores of residents draw unemployment but will not work though bodily able, it is a neighborhood joke. Scores of residents draw disability but are not sick, respectable physicians sign statements, and everybody knows but nobody tells. The outstanding industry of the area is minding your own business. Information is difficult to develop. I saw children smoking on the street, the adults turned their backs. I heard vile language from women and children. Do my own children do this, does the wife swear outside the house?

Whereas when I was a boy the future was arranged, my father allowed me my way, but never too much, I swore on the street but nobody heard me, I smoked under the stairway, we respected our elders, or if anybody heard me or saw me it was definitely by chance, I ran around a little, I fought a little, I pinched a stick of candy here or there, an article of fruit, I cut school, I window-peeped, I sneaked into ball parks and films, we all did. I wrote my name in the municipal cement. But we never doubted the future was arranged, and when the time came we settled down.

The more I stood there the more depressed I became. I wore dark clothes. I surveyed his premises from across the street beneath the power pole. For three nights I stood there late, while after the first few nights I became almost too depressed to remain, sometimes I kicked the power pole on and went home early, though I put in far short of the hours.

His knives depressed me, he was always slicing fruit, the blades reflected from his interior lighting. He sliced a little, he laid the knives down carefully for a customer, he wiped his hands on his coat, rang up the money, and picked up the knives again. Over the bread and pastries was a sign:

ANYONE WHO REMAINS CALM
IN THE MIDST OF ALL THIS CONFUSION
SIMPLY DOESN'T UNDERSTAND THE SITUATION,

but he was calm, there was no confusion, his hands were steady. He sharpened his knives on a whetstone, and when he spoke he spoke slow, and he was calm, a deep thinker.

MAKE SURE BRAIN IS ENGAGED
BEFORE PUTTING MOUTH IN GEAR

On the east wall is a large sign:

GOOD RULES FOR BUSINESS MEN

1. Don't worry; don't overbuy; don't go security.
2. Keep your vitality up; keep insured; keep sober; keep cool; keep your dignity.
3. Stick to chosen pursuits, but not to chosen methods.
4. Be content with small beginnings and develop them.
5. Be wary of dealing with unsuccessful men.
6. Be cautious, but when a bargain is made stick to it.

7. Keep down expenses, but don't be stingy.
8. Make friends, but not favorites.
9. Don't take new risks to retrieve old losses.
10. Stop a bad account at once.
11. Make plans ahead, but don't make them in cast iron.
12. Don't tell what you are going to do until you have done it.
13. Speak up, for dignity is more than dollars.

Mr. Kayzee discovered these rules in the front of his Daily Reminder, a black book I examined, showing Domestic and Foreign Postage Rates, Table of Days Between Two Dates, Actual Rate of Income, Distances and Mail Time Between Cities in the United States, Distances and Mail Time to Foreign Cities from San Francisco, Common Stains and How to Remove Them, Rates of Interest in All States, Actual Time in Use in the Largest Cities of the World when it is Noon in San Francisco, Rules for Computing Interest, Points of Constitutional Law, Weights and Measures, Explanation of Weather Bureau Flag Signals, Help in Case of Accident, Approximate Weight of Substances, Presidents of the United States, Nicknames and Flowers of the States, Supervisors of the City of San Francisco, Assemblymen of the State of California, Population of Principal Cities, Legal Holidays in Various States, and other necessary information.

II

Complaint was initiated by one Armand Marveaux aforementioned, age 33, a plasterer, residence 55 San Pedro. San Pedro is only three blocks long, running parallel to Twelfth between Twelfth and Thirteenth, blocked at the east end by the reservoir, and at the west by the Nun Convent adjacent to the Church. The rear of the Marveaux house faces the rear of Mr. Kayzee's premises as aforementioned, she crossed her garden, jumped over a rock wall there, it was not high, afterward returning the same way and entering her own house by her own rear door. She was in love with Mr. Kayzee, afterward she loved her husband again, all was proper, it was only transference. San Pedro was known in former times as Vivian Lane, honoring a noted prostitute, one Vivian. Certain older residents of the neighborhood still refer to it as Vivian Lane, such as Mr. Cavendish aforementioned. They are incorrect. Complainant complained that his grocer, one Hopkins Kayzee, was engaged in alleged illegal or illicit relationships with his wife, one Marinda, in the storage room of the latter's premises and was performing alleged illegal or illicit brain surgery upon the head of same.

I was at that time assigned to Convention Protection. "We are the Nation's foremost Convention City, boasting splendid luxury hotels, unexcelled fine restaurants, a wide variety of sophisticated nocturnal amusements and daylight summit vistas, an average Summer temperature of 65 degrees (Fahrenheit), the world's largest International Airport, and a Cosmopolitan Atmosphere blended with a Frontier Tradition whose spirit encourages mature restraint as the better alternative to an unrealistic strict enforcement." It was the height of my depression.

I worked hotels and demonstration or display rooms with an old friend of mine, Archie Wilson. He also depressed me. Some months prior, coming home one night, he was attacked by hoodlums, his gun was stolen, he was beaten, his assailants were never apprehended. Requesting a change, I drew for a partner a young man of little experience, one Robert (Bob) McFee. Our work was limited to report. We were permitted to detain or arrest pickpockets or confederates only, McFee took it in stride, everything and anything he took for granted, and yet a college man. Is this the respect my children will be taught in college? We reported or observed, but we could not take action, we could only survey. Whereas with an arrest here or an arrest there it could have been cleaned up entirely, Convention Protection done away with forever, but it wasn't done, the idea being allow it to be professional but prevent it from being organized, let girls work, let card players work, only keep it in singles or pairs and off the telephones, keep pimps or heavy operations out. What were we doing? Do you wish your city to be no more than a protected operation? You will attract to it the dregs of civilization from Reno, Vegas, Denver, or other points.

When I awoke I inquired: "How can I face another day?"

The wife replied: "Let it pass, it's the summer season," while McFee took the same position, stating: "Let it pass, you're already an ulcer type, let it pass, let it pass."

"How can I see and not speak?" I inquired.

"Who would you speak to?" the wife inquired, then stating: "Limiting and containing is all you can do, accept it, it's the summer season," until I bottled it up inside me but could not release it, for who could be spoken to. She was right. "Speak up, for dignity is more than dollars." Men cannot always speak up. Men shoot themselves in the head in the locker room, it is a common occurrence.

Lt. Kline said a little rest would do me wonders, he gave me a week away, we left the children with my mother, the wife and I flew to Reno. We allotted one hundred dollars to the slots, we attended the nude shows, we slept in a hotel, we approached the end of our allotted money on several occasions, we hit, we were rich again, we laughed, but I wouldn't live there. When I returned Lt. Kline stated it was better for me to work slowly, relax a little, avoid tension, keep to myself. "What's this?" the Lt. inquired. He laughed. "Whose wife? The grocer's wife or complainant's wife? Investigate the back room, work slow, relax a little, avoid tension, is it a storage room, or what is it?"

Complainant is the father of three children, Marilyn, Lucinda, and Marilinda. I rang the bell, the children and the dog came running, laughing or barking, and Marveaux himself behind them, I stated my business. "Finally you came," stated Mr. Marveaux, walking out on the porch and chasing the children back inside. Then he himself went inside, coming out again wearing an orange leather jacket, and he zippered it up. In those days I never forgot anything, if a man wore a jacket and zippered it up it remained in my mind, my mind was a storage room of useless small facts, whereas I was out of touch with the big pattern of things. After he zippered up his jacket we walked down San Pedro and around the corner. "What right has any man got," inquired Mr. Marveaux, "to be tampering with another man's wife's ways?"

"No right," I replied.

"When your wife goes to the grocery store," inquired Mr. Marveaux, "do you expect the grocer to be asking her all kinds of questions or making her all kinds of suggestions regarding her sexual activities with her husband?"

"Certainly not," I replied.

"A grocer is a grocer," stated Mr. Marveaux, "a grocery store is a grocery store." We crossed Twelfth and stood under the light of the power pole, his hair was cut in sideburns, he smoked Oasis cigarettes, and his jacket was illuminated, shining orange. It was called The Rite-By Market. "Don't you think a grocery store is a grocery store?" inquired Mr. Marveaux. "Is he permitted to call himself a brain surgeon?"

"We must know the facts," I stated, and then inquired: "Does he actually call himself a brain surgeon?"

"He performs brain surgery," replied Mr. Marveaux.

I inquired: "He actually cuts people's heads open with a knife?"

"He tampered with my wife's sexual attitudes," replied Mr. Marveaux.

"He cut open your wife's head with a *knife*?" I inquired.

"It was brain surgery," he stated. "He shifted around her brain, causing her to alter her image of herself by brain surgery."

"With a knife?" I inquired, then stated: "If it was a knife she would have come home bleeding. Answer me," then inquiring again: "A *knife*?"

"Go read the sign," he replied. "See the knives."

I crossed the street, he remained where he was. I entered the store, I bought a package of cigarettes. Over the freezer was the sign aforementioned:

BRAIN SURGERY PERFORMED ON PREMISES.
ALL WORK GUARANTEED,

in his hands a knife, he was slicing an apple. He put down the knife, he placed his apple on the scale, he gave me my cigarettes, rang my money, gave me change. Then he picked up the knife and the apple again. I went back across the street and leaned against the power pole again. "It's just a joke," I stated.

"It's no joke," he stated. "He made a regular sexual fiend out of her. She was just an ordinary girl, after six years you don't suddenly develop along the lines of a sexual fiend unless somebody's been tampering with your attitudes. It was surgery."

"With a *knife*?" I inquired.

"Formerly it was now and then, take it or leave it, *comme ci, comme ça*, my background is French. She's also of French background."

"Answer me. Did she come home *bleeding*?"

"She came home a fiend. 'Where are you going?' It's seven o'clock. 'I'm going down to The Rite-By for a loaf of bread.' It's eight o'clock. It's nine o'clock. I'm all alone. Where is she? 'Where have you been?' 'I went down to The Rite-By for a loaf of bread.' 'Since when does it take two hours to buy a loaf of bread?' 'He was slicing it. It was unsliced bread.' "

"Slicing it with what?" I inquired.

"A knife."

"*Was she bleeding when she came home*?"

"It was brain surgery."

"You can't leave the house," I stated, "at seven o'clock and have brain surgery and walk in at nine and not be bleeding."

"She never walked in, she ran in, she leaped in my arms after six years, she loved me, I was tired, I'm a plasterer all day. She had a new image of herself. Formerly she was who she was, now she is Marinda Marveaux, French lady of the night. 'Where have you been?' 'I've been in the back of the store with Mr. Kayzee.' 'Doing what?' 'Receiving brain surgery.' Everybody in the neighborhood is having brain surgery in the back of Mr. Kayzee. Ask around. Read the sign."

"Mr. Marveaux," I stated, "brain surgery is a job done by medicine men of long experience and training in many colleges, and you bleed. You lie around unconscious for many hours afterward, and they send you a big bill." Then I inquired: "Does Mr. Kayzee send you a bill?"

"Only for groceries," he replied. He leaned against the power pole, thinking of Mr. Kayzee. "He's a very fair dealer. I like him. He has done wonders for the wife."

"Then why did you issue complaint?" I inquired.

"I didn't issue complaint," he replied.

"You called the police," I stated.

"Well, it's all right now," he stated. Again he leaned, thinking, and soon he stated further: "I withdraw complaint. I'm not complaining any more."

It was Wednesday. Thursday I ordered the illumination extinguished in the power pole, but Friday the cruising Streetlight Bench replaced it. Monday they installed the independent circuit, I could kick it off or on with my foot, however I desired. The cigars depressed me. The noises depressed me. The water in the buried brook depressed me, flowing, flowing, flowing, flowing, babies crying, people dying, I could feel it in the vibrations of my feet. It never ended. I began going crazy from depression. It became foggy at night, and the people were a blur, sometimes it was difficult to view the movement or motion within his store. What was I accomplishing?

Miss Willerts, Mrs. Marveaux, and Mr. Hefley were patients on the first three nights of the week, Monday, Tuesday, and Wednesday. Thursday I went home early. I was cold. Friday night I cashed a small check, five dollars. He took the check and placed it in his pocket still wet. "Will that be all?" he inquired. I bought a cigar, that was all. "That will be all," I replied, and he stated: "I thank you very kindly." I turned around and started out, he further stating: "Oh, by the way Mr. Cop, last night you forgot to kick the power pole back on."

"What power pole?" I inquired. Then I stated: "You're crazy, Mr.," and I continued walking. Yet why deny it? I had made many inquiries, I was illuminated by cigarettes, one way or another it was bound to get back to him, it was how the neighborhood is, he is appreciated, he extends credit and courtesies of every sort, he has lived all his life in the neighborhood, raised his children there, maintains his property, respects the peace, such a man is respected in that neighborhood or any other. I stated: "You've got no license to dispense."

He stated: "Maybe you're crazy, too."

"O.K." I bent my head, I removed my hat, it was a joke. "Here's my brain. Cut." He laughed, I laughed a little also, he dropped and lashed his tarp and turned out the lights. "Don't forget your beer sign," I stated. He went back and turned out his beer sign, in his hand was his knife. In the storage room he took off his white coat, unpinning his badge, then pinning it on a fresh coat. The room was dark, his coat was white, he turned his lamp toward the window, and it shone against the triangles brown and blue. Behind him was a shelf of books made of crates standing side by side.

"What's the tapecorder for?" I inquired.

"To talk in," he replied. "I record their lives."

"Play me a life. Play me Mrs. Marinda Marveaux."

"I erased her," he stated. "Tapes are expensive. She is a woman who expected perfection, but men are not perfect, men are double-barreled, smoke if you wish." He turned the tapecorder on, a small red light shone, the spools went around and around, reflecting on the ceiling. In former times I was hypnotized by the spools going around and around, but later I did not mind them.

"Turn it off," I ordered. He turned it off.

He gave me a sheet of paper, *Good Rules for Business Men*. "This is all I dispense," he stated. "This is all I dispensed her, these are the simple wisdom of the ages. I recommend especially Number 13, speak up, for people must tell their troubles to one another, they discover their own mind with help, the mind is not such a mystery. They cannot pay much. Poor people cannot go downtown to the high-priced men. Accept the world, it's a low-income neighborhood."

I inquired, "This is all you dispensed her?"

"That's all," he replied. "We discussed the imperfections of her husband, which are numerous, but also his qualities, which are also numerous, he is steadily employed, he does not drink, he does not gamble, and he beat her only once in six years."

"You've got no license or authority to dispense," I stated.

"Why not eat your apple?" he inquired. He ran a small electric heater, the room grew gradually warmer, the heater switched off, the hour still was early, I agreed to eat my apple.

I inquired: "Where can I wash my apple?" He took me to a lavatory adjoining, it was clean but cool, I washed my apple, it was good to return to the warm room again. "Since when," I inquired, "does it take two hours to dispense a sheet of paper? Tuesday night she entered your store at 7:09, you turned out your lights, you entered this room, she departed at 9:11."

"We also talked," he replied.

"Where was she?" I inquired.

"Sitting where you are," he replied. I was in a leather chair.

"Did she sit or did she lie back flat?" I inquired, for the chair leaned back for comfort.

"*Comme ci, comme ça*," he replied. "However she desired."

"Where were you?" I inquired.

"I was right here," he replied.

It was a comfortable chair, my head rested on a barber-pillow, I leaned back, I sliced my apple, while outside the wind blew fog down the alley. "Go ahead and eat it," he ordered. "Enjoy something. An apple is an apple, don't be so cautious, the health of the apple overpowers the germs. Why are you so cautious? You screw the cap on your pen too tight, your pen clips too tight in your pocket, your writing is extremely small and cautious, your hat is a half a size too small, it leaves a red mark on your forehead. Do you think the world is lying in wait to steal your fountain pen?" He informed me that in former times he also was an extremely cautious man. He spoke in a soft, steady voice, I loosened my shoes, I loosened my tie, I smoked cigarettes. In those days I smoked three packages daily. We discussed smoking. When I was a boy I smoked cigarettes under the stairway, I thought nobody saw me, but Mr. Kayzee suggested that the smoke drifted up, I was observed by my father and others, I agreed it was a possible theory.

"Take off your coat," he advised. "Take off your gun, too." He possessed no gun, and he inquired whether I had ever shot a man or not. I replied that I did not know, for I shot into the shadows twice after Archie Wilson was attacked by hoodlums unknown. He inquired whether he might hear the story of Archie Wilson in the tapecorder, I agreed, the red light shone and the spools went around and around on the ceiling. Upon later occasions I heard my own voice on the tape. My voice grew stronger in later weeks, I became less depressed.

The hour grew later and later, and the wind died, but I did not leave, although it soon was midnight, and I became afraid, stating: "I cannot go, you must at least walk me to my machine, the hour is late and the neighborhood is unfamiliar to me."

"There is no reason to be afraid," he stated.

"Even in a machine a man is not safe," I stated. "You dare not even stop at the light at certain intersections, they are on you in a minute. Our own municipal streets are no longer even safe."

"The front page of the papers," he stated, "is not the story. Don't be afraid."

"I'm not afraid," I stated.

"Good," he replied, "because there is little to be afraid of."

"Then walk with me," I stated, but he refused. I could not go, I could not stay. What could I do? "You do not know the number of crimes committed every night, we are under-staffed, we are not respected, we are without power, young thugs are running wild, attorneys defend them, the judiciary is far too lenient, social workers bleed their hearts out, the boy had a bad beginning, excuse and forgive, meanwhile they leave court in a stolen machine full of billiard balls in high stockings, the streets are not safe, I cannot go," yet he refused to go with me. He unlashed his tarp and lifted it, and we stood on the sidewalk in front of the shop.

"Cross," he stated, "and kick on your power pole, walk to your machine, do not run, and drive home," but still I could not do as he directed. The wind was down, I lit a cigarette. "Consider," he stated, "that you were observed smoking under the stairway, not only by your father but by all the neighborhood. You were loved and protected by your neighborhood, although you thought it was filled with enemies. But the truth is, let a thief enter, let a man be lewd or molest a child, let a man assault, and the neighborhood will rise and crush him, then or now or anywhere or any time, the neighborhood defends itself. The police are few, the residents are many, the neighborhood is its own Department, it cures or mends, it regulates itself. There is some danger tonight, but there was always some danger every night, not more and not less, so cross."

I did as he advised, and I continued afterward for some time until my depression faded away. We said goodnight, I crossed the street, I kicked the power pole back on, I walked to my machine, I drove home, I advised Lt. Kline on the following day complainant withdrew complaint, I ordered the independent circuit discontinued, I resumed Convention Protection at that time.

At Prayerbook Cross

In the winter of my twelfth year I was stricken by the death of my classmate Esmond Bright, whom I had hardly known but whom I now pretended to have known better than I had because of this distinction which had come to him.

He died beneath the ice of a pond in a meadow within sight of his house. I had been to that pond only once with him, for an hour or less, helping him to dam the outlet, our trousers rolled to our knees. It was his plan, by damming the pond, to deprive the town of water, although he must have secretly known that the pond no more watered the town than fireflies lit it. When the dam was done, and he was satisfied of his power, he demolished it with a flourish, permitting water once again to flow to the parched people.

His death had occurred in the act of crossing the pond, but whether by the cracking of the ice beneath him or by a fall from a floe was never certain. At the request of his father no inquiry was pursued beyond the certainty that the boy had died in a voluntary act of daring. In my mother's scrapbook the newspaper clipping telling of the event asserts that no witnesses had been present, although I heard at the time the boasts of other boys—all, too, seeking distinction—who, never quite close enough to have *seen* the catastrophe, produced versions and reports remarkable for their detail.

Esmond Bright lived in that neighborhood of our town whose streets were named for trees common to the region—Maple, Oak, Sycamore—in a large, distinguished house with many chimneys. It had belonged to his family for generations. Before it, a flight of white steps provided the illusion, at a distance, of a solid wall. I was never within.

His parents, too, by the standards we all understood, were distinguished. His father was an attorney, afterward town judge, whose name appeared frequently in the newspaper, usually briefly, as, "Judge Bright presided," or, "Judge Bright postponed sentence until May 24." The Judge was always reelected to his office, endorsed by all men and all parties, universally trusted and admired. It occurs to me now that he must have been a man rare for his wisdom and restraint, his virtue so apparent as to exempt him from even the routine gestures of opposition. Although he must have had enemies the only enemy known to me was my mother, whose contempt for the Judge, after Esmond's death, formed, developed, hardened, and became permanent.

Her cause was simple. After the death of the boy she had sent his parents a message of mourning. It was a printed card chosen at random from her wide collection of greetings for all occasions. She was a celebrant of all landmarks, of births, weddings, deaths, christenings, communions, *bar mizvah*, installations, graduations, honors, awards, and honorable mention, and for every landmark she owned a selection of cards to which sometimes—not always—she trusted herself to add a line in her own hand—"We are *so* happy for you . . . May this be only the *first* of many." Sentiment was her occupation. As her health slowly failed, and she was less about, she was more and more represented everywhere by printed messages. She calculated the mails: She knew to send me to the mailbox Tuesday night with a message ideally suited for delivery Thursday morning. She never failed instantly to acknowledge replies to her messages, and in some cases lifelong correspondence ensued between her and people whom she had never, to begin with, quite known. No correspondence ever lapsed by *her* omission: She had always the last word. And she was prompt besides.

In reply to her message to Judge and Mrs. Bright my mother received a letter seeming strange both to her and to me, for if we were sentimental we were also unlearned, together lacking in every subtlety. It was a poem in the hand of the Judge, legible but unintelligible, nor bearing in any way, as far as we could tell, upon either the death of his son or the message of my mother. That it was a poem we could tell by the arrangement of the lines, with the name of the author entered below. I suspect that the author was one of the world's poets, but he was unknown to us, and I should like to know now who he was and what the lines. A search, however, of my mother's scrapbook fails to uncover the Judge's letter. In fury or chagrin she must have allowed it to become one of the few documents of her possession which never entered her archives, destroying it because of its coldness, its inappropriateness, its unintelligibility. Unfeeling, it dishonored the boy who was dead.

The wife of the Judge was familiar to my sight. I cannot say that she ever spoke more than a few words to me, but I cannot say that when we met she failed to see me, for she offered the sense that children were entitled to notice. She was a frequent observer at school functions, and since she was sometimes seated upon the stage during important assemblies I assume that she was a volunteer officer of the school. Once, between the schoolhouse and the waiting yellow bus, she held an umbrella over my head. I see her as having been an awkward girl, her sunniness intended to divert attention from her great height, and yet it must have been natural, too, not cultivated, for her face in whatever repose issued kindness. After the death of her son I saw her but once.

During the winter days following the death of Esmond Bright my brooding took the form of assembling all the scattered moments of our acquaintance, enlarging them until their brevity and their faintness became prolonged and firm. Nobody of my acquaintance had ever died, and as far as I knew nobody would again. Therefore my memory worked hard to accommodate this contrast between life and death.

I engaged in his resurrection. I walked beside the pond where he had died, where we had dammed the outlet, expanding our single continuous hour together until it was a summer. I gazed upon the house where he had lived. The enlargement of my memory enlarged my emotions, too, and I wept for the friend he now became.

My mother consoled me, insisting upon the great idea she herself could never believe—that death was of life—and who, herself, in the presence of my own awe, increasingly resented the heartlessness and the obliqueness of Judge Bright's response to her card of condolence, increasingly spoke of the strangeness of his behavior, and finally took her angry stand against that injustice whereby I who was but a friend more deeply mourned Esmond Bright than his very own father. From that anger she would never recover.

But early surrender was alien to her. She would try once more. Therefore, once again, as if she had not done so the first time, she sent a printed message of condolence to Judge and Mrs. Bright, adding, in her own hand, "My son was a close friend of your son and is shooken by your sad tragedy."

No reply was received. In a sense she awaits it yet, holding it forth as a possibility, as if her unanswered message still lies, thirty years afterward, among odds and ends of matters slightly delayed, upon the table of Judge and Mrs. Bright.

During the first weeks of waiting her mind engaged in a speculation sufficiently flexible to permit her to bear upon herself a portion of the blame for this failure of exchange. Perhaps, my mother argued, the fault was not the Brights' but ours; perhaps it would have been proper if I, deeply affected friend of the dead boy, as a supplement and enforcement to her second note (which became, in her mind, the first), personally, face to face, called upon Judge and Mrs. Bright at their house. There I could express whatever it was my mother's message had failed to carry. Undoubtedly, my mother argued, *that* was what the Brights expected, that was what they were *waiting* for, the man was a Judge and he knew the proper way.

I declined. Chilling enough that the boy was dead, to call at his house impossible. She insisted. Why not? What was I afraid of? Had I not built bridges and tunnels and dams summer after summer with Esmond Bright? She outlined true duty to me, emphasizing the grief of parents, but the picture she drew for me of the violence and depths of that singular variety of grief became so vivid that her objective became actually less and less attainable: If it were true, as my mother said, that grieving drove mothers and fathers mad, what might those madmen do to me when I called at their door? If parents in grief became deranged, the Brights in their derangement would seize me, possess me, keep me prisoner in their house, make me their captive son to replace their own.

Oh, no. Several times I declined. Once, in the hope of ending the matter, I told my mother I had called upon the Brights, but she knew a lie when she heard one.

As I declined to visit them, I trusted further that I should never see them under any circumstances. Declining to place myself in their presence, I guarded against the chance of their placing themselves in mine. I kept a careful lookout, especially at night, entering no enclosed places without first assuring myself that they were not there. I glanced about corners before venturing down streets. I imagined that they lurked waiting for me in dark movie-houses, behind parked cars. They hired G-men to track me down. They crouched behind the seats at the back of the town bus. I thought, once, that I spied Mrs. Bright in the corridor of the schoolhouse, and I fled.

In my dreams they pursued me, and I ran as well as I could in dreams, knowing in dreams the inevitability of their finally overtaking me in waking life. When at last they did I was luckily in the company of my mother. "Isn't that the Brights?" she asked. It was the Brights.

My mother and I were walking on an afternoon in early spring in my twelfth year still, along the garden path encircling an abandoned mansion. The mansion, its grounds and gardens, then in decline, has since become a public park. I thought to flee, but the presence of Sunday strollers comforted me.

If I was too old to cling to my mother I was nevertheless young enough to place myself slightly behind her. Judge and Mrs. Bright came swiftly toward us, not in recognition but because we stood in their route. The energy of their stride baffled me, astonished me. Where was this forlorn insanity in grief my mother guaranteed? Far from being downcast, the Brights were gay, briskly walking, spryly, arm in arm. The Judge's head was high, he was drinking the day, its freshness, its greenness, and the newness of the season. Their mood was joy. We waited. They approached and stopped. We stood a minute there, not more. My mother spoke to them, and they to her. My mother said, of course, something about their loss, for no other subject lay in common between them.

The Judge replied at too much length and with too deep a complexity to reach me, so that I remember only one short sentence, and that with doubt, for I have never been entirely clear whether I heard it from him or heard only my mother's repetition—then, or immediately afterward, or over the years. She repeated it often, to me, to my father, and to everyone her indignation encountered, as the ultimate evidence of the brutal and unnatural character of Judge Bright. "Oh," said the Judge, "the worst has happened."

Like their bearing, their joy, their energy, their buoyance, and their delight in the day, that sentence of the Judge remained to perplex me for thirty years. His words were the summation, I assume, of his struggle against the terrible thing that *had* happened, his recovery, his means to his equilibrium, his message of ease for his wife, their means of going on. *The worst has happened.* Life must proceed. He could not have imagined that his sentence would inflame my mother so long as she lived, and perplex me for thirty years. Judge and Mrs. Bright walked forward upon their way, and my mother and I upon ours.

Thirty years passed, my son was in his twelfth year, and our dispute was constant, for he believed himself immune to danger, and I knew better. I told him once of Esmond Bright, and he jeered at me, since everybody knew, he said, that ice never forms in San Francisco. He swam with sharks. He bicycled down Market Street no-handed.

Enraged, I once sentenced him to a week's confinement in his room, relented on the following day, and for a new outrage beat him the next with absolute fists. He crumpled in defiance and laughter. I have moved from the town of my boyhood. My mother, enfeebled, remains bound to her house, and Mrs. Bright, I hear, to hers. Judge Bright has retired to his garden. His house stands, but the meadow is gone and the pond sunken. New streets in that neighborhood have lately become so numerous that the most recent—Palm, Spruce, Cypress—confess the exhaustion of native names.

One day not long ago in San Francisco my son and I went to Prayerbook Cross, a monument atop a wooded hill in the heart of Golden Gate Park. Beside the Cross, charging from the earth, the waters of Rainbow Falls spill upon the rocks. Two miles west, framed by evergreen, the Pacific Ocean is visible. The day was Sunday, the winter rains just ended, the bare earth soft, and the grass slick. I questioned the necessity of climbing this particular hill on this particular day. I suggested alternatives.

But my son was determined to climb, here, now. We would

be the first white men, he said, to discover the source of the falls. We must imagine, he said, that nobody was ever here before, his voice slightly assuming the velvet tones of the eyewitness reporter. There were already, I knew, hovering helicopters with telescopic cameras. In his jacket pocket his transistor radio played one hundred top tunes.

We climbed the hill, he before me, the music of his pocket soon drowned by the crashing of the water upon the rocks of the ravine. The sound was intense, heightening excitement and a sense of dread. My ankles turned in the soft ground, and where I doubted my possibilities for forward progress I climbed crabwise. He had soon climbed beyond me, out of sight, to the pinnacle. At length I overtook him.

There, a steel fence inhibited his fantasy, blocking our way to the source of the falls. Clearly the Park Commission had preceded us, and our own poor human eyes were only second.

Alas, we were worse than that. Twenty feet away, arriving by a safer route, a group of Japanese men in business suits approached the Cross. Their cameras were slung, and they were already shooting. They were accompanied by a young lady—Japanese in features, American in bearing—who gave them time to read the inscriptions, front and back, offering them nothing by way of explanation, nor did they ask.

Late indeed! The inscriptions carried back the history of this summit to 1579. "Before you were born," I said to my son, who was not amused. "Before even I was born," I said. *Soli deo sic semper gloria*—and then, in American fashion, the Cross claimed for its location all the primacy it could, "first Christian service in the English tongue on our Coast . . . first use of Book of Common Prayer in our Country . . . one of the first recorded missionary prayers on our Continent."

Their picture-taking done, the Japanese men wandered from the base of the Cross to the fence defending pilgrims or tourists from the naked ravine. To fall was death. I wished that I were on their side.

My boy declared that he would leap the channel. Four hundred years late, thwarted by a man-made fence, possibilities for daring yet remained. "I like to live dangerously," he said.

"And die down there," I said.

"It's nothing," he said.

"Don't you dare," I said, but with insufficient authority.

And then, as if admitting at least a minimal danger, he removed his transistor radio from his pocket and handed it, still playing, to me. I turned it off. My act of accepting it permitted him to interpret consent. Quickly he gauged his distance and rallied his body.

All danger now lay in any outcry I might make, for his balance was cast, his weight in motion, his resolution beyond the point of return, and I saw with the worst moment's anguish of my life that his aim was false, that his leading foot, instead of striking the foothold my eye had chosen for it, would strike somewhere lower, and he be gone below forever.

In the moment of my boy's flying through the air I saw two images. I saw, first, the eyes of the Japanese men at the fence, peculiarly lacking in alarm. Was it Oriental? Or could they see, at an angle hidden from me, a safe foothold my son had chosen?

And I also saw in that moment, as if they were among the Japanese men at the fence, Judge and Mrs. Bright approaching, as I had seen them on the garden path of the abandoned mansion in the fullness of their joy, where, standing slightly behind my mother, I heard the mystifying sentence of the Judge, *the worst has happened*. Not the present moment, not my boy's danger, but my sudden break with thirty years' perplexity overwhelmed me. The worst has happened. The worst is therefore past. Now Judge Bright was free, now I was free, for the death of my son was the worst I could imagine, and its having happened would release me now and henceforth and forever from fear, from rage, and from all morbidity: The worst having happened now rendered the worst impossible, releasing me into immunity and perfect safety. Nothing henceforth lay ahead but joy.

His leading foot landed securely upon the target he had chosen, and the momentum which had carried him across the channel lifted him easily upward from his foothold to the flat, sound earth above. Then, turning, again gauging, stepping down to his foothold and springing, he lightly returned to my side of the channel. The eyes of the cameras poked through the woven wire fence, but my son in contempt of mere tourists disdained to turn to view either the span of his daring or its witnesses. He held his hand for the transistor radio, turned its volume loud, and slid it back into his jacket pocket. Then he began his descent down the path we had climbed, and I followed.

Touching Idamae Low

Auerman was a lame duck. His office at Kemperer was no longer the office it had been. Some matters formerly referred to him now bypassed him for consideration elsewhere. He said to his wife, Elizabeth, one night, "Do you realize that I'm no longer an authorized signature?"

Nobody knew where he'd be going, or when, and few people suspected that he himself did not know. Between the Fourth of July and Christmas he'd gone off six times to six corporations, no secret about it, two days here, three days there, for which he had claimed from Kemperer travel expenses three times but paid his way the other three, according to his determination whether he had gone more truly on company business or his own.

To sound out the job he had in mind for himself, Auerman had traveled to Tipex in Seattle, Park Products in Portland (Oregon), Whitman Tool in Los Angeles, Dennis O'Toole Tool in Denver, Tourtour in Minneapolis, and Toba Steel in Pittsburgh. With his own company, Kemperer, where he was now an unauthorized signature, these were seven of the "big eight" of a not very big industry. Winckton was the eighth. For no particular reason it hadn't entered his head to try Winckton up to this time.

Some people said Auerman was playing his cards close to his chest, but he had never been a card player. His game was golf and his customary opponent was his wife, from whom he had never won a match in his life. Her handicap was twelve, and she knew they'd go nowhere that didn't have a good golf course and a good veterinarian. Their children had dispersed in the friendliest ways to distant parts, leaving dogs and cats behind.

Kemperer's success was partly due to Auerman, who was director of personnel. People knew that he knew what he was doing. He had said yes or no finally to questions of the fate of five thousand persons entering or departing Kemperer's work force over the years, and the older he grew, the shrewder. He never pretended to know things he did not know. If he was doubtful he said, I am doubtful. Whatever he said, it was trustworthy.

He was a little eccentric, but not much. He was consumed by the moral necessity to do the right thing rather than the wrong thing. He had done the morally wrong thing on three or four occasions in the past, and his conscience had troubled him.

On those occasions he had been especially helpful in the way of employment at Kemperer to women to whom he had been attracted on sight. He had affectionately touched them when perhaps he should not have . . . oh, well, he had had a love affair or two or three. Thereafter he had felt obligated to those women. He gave them more positive endorsements than he would have given young men or plain women with equal qualifications.

It was the danger of touching. All religions knew the danger of touching and kept the bride and groom apart beforehand. The three or four women whom Auerman befriended were slender, tall, handsome, long-legged women who carried themselves well. They were upper-middle-management, and therefore sophisticated if not formally educated, and he continued to be helpful to them in their careers at Kemperer long after he had lost his strong desire to touch them: His moral obligation outlived his passion.

When Winckton invited him down, Auerman never questioned how it had come about. Word went around the industry, people bumped into people at conferences, airports, golf courses. The person who telephoned to invite Auerman formally was Mr. Kinnealy, a vice-president.

"I doubt if you'd want to come down here," Mr. Kinnealy said, "but I thought I'd give it a try. Maybe you'd come for a little get-acquainted visit." Mr. Kinnealy spoke in a low voice, always subject to interruption. He seemed to be a listener, and Auerman admired listeners. On the other hand, Auerman at first mistrusted Mr. Kinnealy's low voice—people with low voices were often making promises they knew they couldn't keep.

"I suppose," said Auerman, thinking of Elizabeth, "you've got year-round golf down there."

"Nine months, we say," Mr. Kinnealy said. "Wait until March if you want the golf. Let's have our secretaries put their heads together over the calendar and set a date." They spoke for five minutes, arranging to arrange. Mr. Kinnealy would set up meetings at which all the people of Winckton at various ranks and levels would be able to meet Auerman and decide what they thought of him. "The employees really make the decisions," Mr. Kinnealy said.

"I like it that way," Auerman said. "I wouldn't have it any other."

But Auerman did not wholly believe that the employees made the decisions at Winckton or anywhere else. It was his experience that when it came to a particular case at a particular place a decision was made not by groups but by one single, determined person, and for his own practical purposes Auerman would want to know who.

Several days after his conversation with Mr. Kinnealy, Auerman received a letter from Winckton; handwritten, on plain stationery, signed only "Idamae," its author referring to herself as "Assistant to the Director of Planning." In her letter, Idamae greeted Auerman in the name of all Winckton and enclosed a copy of the tentative schedule he had already received from Mr. Kinnealy's secretary. The schedule was comfortably flexible, indicating that on the day of his arrival he would meet with small groups of people at stated hours and places all subject to change at his will; and on the following day he would "tour and talk" with five Winckton executives. On Idamae's copy the entry "lunch at new clubhouse on our new golf course" was emphatically underlined.

Idamae's copy also included two words of additional information, referring, apparently, to day two: the words "Low, breakfast," were penciled into the margin and were almost invisible. Perhaps the problem was, Auerman thought, that the waxlike paper was not meant for pencil. And yet "lunch at new clubhouse on our new golf course" took pencil well enough. Therefore, thought Auerman, who was, after all, paid a high wage to read intentions, second thoughts, lies, and evasions into the scratchings-out and erasures of applicants at every level, "Low, breakfast" was a message Idamae really had no right to deliver and therefore delivered cryptically, fearfully, invisibly, on a Xerox page accompanying her unofficial letter on plain stationery.

A few weeks later, Auerman flew from winter to spring, Kemperer to Winckton, one thousand miles south. Beside Mr. Kinnealy at the airport stood a little woman of thirty-five or so, carrying at her breast manila folders and computer printouts folded in squares—in her arms, it would seem, all the business of the corporation, to be transacted on the spot; and looped over her shoulder her vast leather purse, once shining brown, now faded, worn with use, and packed with all the business of at least a second corporation.

From her hat two frayed feathers with tassels soared above her head, antennae to catch everything everybody said, although she did not at first impress Auerman as a listener. Constantly she interrupted Mr. Kinnealy, and when she did he did not seem to mind. He stopped, as if he had nothing so special to say that he cared to fight for it.

She was a small, female person. She was compact. In the first moment of Auerman's view of her, the thing that fascinated him was her powerful concentration upon him. She could not have been more transfixed by him had he been her imported groom. At length, shaking off her trance, she shook his hand, told him her name, and added: "I'm the one you had the letter from."

"Did you bring your clubs?" Mr. Kinnealy asked.

"Clubs?"

"Golf clubs," Idamae said. "We have a brand-new golf course. Everybody plays golf here."

"I'm afraid I must have exaggerated my interest in golf," said Auerman. "I never take clubs on a trip."

"Avis rents clubs," said Mr. Kinnealy.

"Now, my wife is passionate about golf," said Auerman.

"I don't play golf at all," said Idamae.

"I never play more than once a day," said Mr. Kinnealy.

Idamae had not yet smiled. Perhaps she was too tense to smile. For some reason not clear to Auerman, this was a critical occasion for her, it made her nervous; among the manila folders and computer printouts at her breast her hands trembled conspicuously. Why had she carried all those papers from the car to the airplane gate? He must ask her that. Perhaps her paper work was protection, defense, concealment. And yet, if she did not care to be seen, why wear antennae with tassels from her hat and a blouse striped in all the colors of a circus wagon? Hiding not her body but her lies, perhaps, one moment saying we all play golf here, the next moment saying she didn't. Waiting at the baggage carousel he asked her why she'd said *everybody* plays golf.

"I don't *care* for golf," said Idamae, "so I don't play it. Everybody *else* plays golf. All we're really talking about there is one little word. Isn't that right?"

Auerman thought, when she smiled, that her face was fine. Her smile had power, commanding him to cease his silly probing. She smiled at the liveried driver of the Winckton limousine, who appeared to seek his instructions from her.

"We're leaving the airport," Idamae announced. Between the airport and the hotel she delivered a summary or travelogue—not for the first time, Auerman supposed—of the countryside and the city, their history and their statistics, speaking very deliberately, honoring all her syllables. She was a model of clarity in her description, although her narrative was tinged with ironic phrases: she offered names and dates with the warnings "if anyone cares" or "I can't imagine why I remember such things," playing it safe, respecting the data without insulting any larger mind that might find the data trivial.

Her recitation could be interrupted easily. Auerman soon saw that he had only to begin to speak to make her stop. She was as acquiescent as she was aggressive, as silent as she was voluble, as reticent as she was forward, seeking the right relationship between herself and this man she did not know. By the time they arrived at the hotel her data and description of Winckton and environs had turned rather satiric as she began to size up Auerman's nature. Apparently she wished to be whatever he wanted her to be.

"We are arriving at the hotel," Idamae announced. "It's the only hotel with no name." The Winckton hotel was a tidy brick structure with twenty suites used for exactly the present purpose—to house, as Mr. Kinnealy put it, "visiting firemen." No money changed hands between the guest and hotel. Their driver, who was also bellman, carried Auerman's suitcase and All-In-One garment bag from the car to his suite, drew the drapes for sunshine, flung open the windows, and asked at the door for instructions.

Auerman replied that he would instruct if he knew what the plans were—better ask Mr. Kinnealy; but behind the driver, in the doorway, so small she was hidden, Idamae spoke. "We can rest for a while if you wish," she said, "or we can begin now." She came a step forward. *We* can rest? Did she intend to remain with him while he rested? He supposed she would if he asked her to. Little scandal if she did. He was in no danger of touching her. She was not one of the slender, long-legged women of Kemperer whom he had affectionately touched and to whom, thereafter, his morality inconveniently obligated him. Idamae was different. "No, begin now," said Auerman, hanging his All-In-One, which swiveled on the hook, stepping over his suitcase, and returning with Idamae and the driver to the limousine. "I came to see it all," he said. "I didn't come to rest."

Indeed he did not come to rest for twelve hours, returning to his suite at half an hour past midnight, his suitcase lying on its side where he had left it, All-In-One swiveling again in the breeze he created. For twelve hours he had had almost no rest, no silence, no privacy. He had shaken hands and talked for twelve hours with a wide variety of people at all levels and extremities of life at Winckton.

He had dined more or less formally twice, lunch at a vegetarian restaurant with employees of middle rank and dinner of two-inch steak at the home of a vice-president. Auerman participated in many dialogues at coffee breaks in various corners of the plant, and twice in the cafeteria known as the Breakfast Room.

It occurred to him now, in the privacy of his suite, that the last time he emptied his bladder he was in the men's room off the Breakfast Room with the deposed director of personnel. The deposed director was "very happy" to be leaving, he didn't know where he'd be going, the farther the better because Winckton, he said, was a nightmare, a mystery, he hadn't pierced the reasoning in a single major decision for two years. "I can't fathom the T.O.," he said.

Winckton thought it lived by its table of organization. Auerman did not believe Winckton lived that way, but it did not matter—each corporation had its mythology, and Winckton's was as good as another: an extensive table of organization roughly the shape of an airplane, flying from the walls of a dozen executive offices and scattered public rooms. Winckton could blame its woes on the inflexibility of the T.O. or the too casual flexibility of the T.O., as if the people of Winckton were the T.O.'s creation, not the other way around.

In the men's room the deposed director had said, "Here at least you're free of Idamae Low." True, Idamae had gone everywhere with Auerman, dogged him for twelve hours, punctuated every silence, kept him on schedule, and somewhat upset the vice-president's wife, who had not expected her for dinner.

"I take it," said Auerman, "Idamae has a reputation for ubiquitousness."

"For what?"

"For being everywhere? For being ubiquitous?"

"She *is* everywhere," the other man said.

"What does she do?" Auerman asked.

The deposed director of personnel frowned. He was puzzled. "The question never occurred to me," he said. "I know where she is on the table of organization. She's a little bird on the extreme wing tip of a very big airplane."

"Then she's nothing?" Auerman asked.

"She's just everywhere," said the deposed director of personnel. "When you come to think of it I don't really know *what* Idamae does. I wish you lots of luck," he amiably said.

And so Auerman was horizontal now on the sofa of his suite where the telephone was, smelling of dry sweat; dry of throat and high upon adulation. He had seen that everyone liked him, that the job was quite his if he cared to accept it, barring someone's veto from a source still invisible to him. It was only natural, only right, that he should step so easily from Kemperer to Winckton—he could go anywhere he cared to go in the big eight (except remain at Kemperer). It was his payoff for a lifetime of hard work that now, at his age, at the crest of his career, he could live at a level of easy mobility. "This is really the place," he said to Elizabeth on the telephone.

But Elizabeth was always skeptical, less given to hope. "That's what they said when they discovered Utah," she said. "How was the flight?"

The flight. She didn't understand. It was not as if he had just arrived. This morning's flight was ages ago. "I'm already here," he said. "I'm writing letters in my head to lots of people at Kemperer."

"Have you seen the golf course?" she asked.

"Tomorrow," he said.

"How many people did you see?" Elizabeth said.

"Millions," he said.

"And you mean there's not an enemy in the crowd?"

Idamae Low crossed his mind's eye, hidden behind the driver at the door to his suite, but he did not mention her name to his wife.

"Do you like Mr. Kinnealy?" she asked.

"Jesus," he said, "I forgot all about Mr. Kinnealy. I haven't seen him since before dinner. He didn't come to dinner with us. He disappeared." Somewhere along the way everyone had disappeared. People joined him, accompanied him from meeting to meeting awhile, drank a cup of coffee, and dropped from his caravan. He had gone the whole way from noon to midnight. No wonder he was tired. Only Idamae had gone the whole long way with him and seen him at last to the door of this little hotel. He began to think she was in love with him, but this he did not mention to his wife.

Auerman wound and set his alarm clock for eight-thirty. He turned pages of the Bible and the *TV Guide*, gifts of this nameless hotel where no money changed hands. On the TV at this late hour one band of men on horseback pursued a second band of men on horseback. This was not a new experience for Auerman, and he was about to turn off the television, feeling himself ready for sleep, when he saw that one of the bands of horsemen was led by a woman. At this point, however, a commercial interruption occurred lasting so long it extinguished his curiosity regarding the lady on horseback.

He darkened the room and tried for sleep, but he must have been higher than he realized, for it was two o'clock before he slept, and seven o'clock when his telephone rang. Not enough. Not enough sleep.

"Good morning," said Idamae Low, "I hope you had a *fine* night."

"Not enough of it," he said. He did not instantly know her voice. He thought she was the hotel operator. "Why so early?" he asked. "Did I leave a call? I didn't leave a call."

"I'm awfully sorry," said Idamae, but she did not urge him to go back to sleep, as someone might who was truly awfully sorry. "I thought you wanted breakfast," she said.

True in its way, Auerman thought. "Everyone wants breakfast," he said. "It's seven o'clock. I could have slept till eight-thirty." He was angry. But she was doing her job, he supposed. She had obviously been assigned to convey him from place to place, and he thanked her, therefore, for ringing his phone, and he said he would be down shortly.

Let her wait. He shaved and showered and dressed. How he would love to sleep another hour! Deprived of sleep he was less secure about his position than he had been at one o'clock this morning. But he was now too agitated to sleep, and he certainly never slept when someone was waiting for him, even if someone was only a bird on the wing tip.

Therefore he decided to consider his wake-up pill. It was a prescription drug whose effect was not only to awaken him but to improve his day in every way by reducing irritation. He had carried these pills with him for years, using them less and less as his own sense of command increased. He shook one pill from the bottle, broke it into two, returned half to the bottle, and wrapped the other half in a square of toilet tissue, which he dropped into the change pocket of the coat he had selected.

Auerman ate breakfast in the Breakfast Room. Idamae Low ate no breakfast. She sat with her folders and printouts at her breast, carrying them as she had carried them first to last yesterday. Her leather bag was slung from her shoulder. Her antennae flew. Today she wore a checkered blouse no less colorful than the stripes of yesterday—a blouse like the official's flag at the Indianapolis 500, or a cereal box.

Auerman said, "Can't you stash all those papers somewhere? I didn't see you look into them once yesterday."

"I might need to know something any minute," she said.

"You know things nobody else knows," said Auerman.

His insight seemed to dismay her, and she glanced about the Breakfast Room as if to see whether anyone had observed her exposure. He knew that she had chosen the Breakfast Room so that she might be widely seen, identified from the beginning with the new director of personnel, herself strengthened by reflected power. In the Breakfast Room Idamae knew everyone, and everyone knew Idamae, blue collar, white collar, waitresses, busboys.

"You know everybody," Auerman said.

"I know everybody who was hired longer than a month ago," said Idamae. "I make it a point. I like *people,* Mr. Auerman, even if some people don't."

How old was she, Auerman asked.

She was twenty-nine, she said.

"Twenty-nine going on what?" he asked. Years and years in personnel had made him good at judging ages.

Thirty-three, she confessed. She was thirty-five. He was glad he had not taken the pill. The pill made him uncritical, passive, too nice. With the pill in him he'd not have challenged her age. He began with a luscious grapefruit.

"This breakfast was not on my schedule," Auerman said.

"It *was,*" she said. She braced.

"No," he said, "it was penciled in by you. On a Xerox copy. And very lightly, I must say."

"I wanted to have a chance to fill you in," she said. "I want to be all the help I can."

He considered this. To whom? To herself? "To whom?" he asked.

"To you," she said, but this seemed to strike even Idamae as unlikely, and she partially revised it without restoring the whole truth. "To you and Winckton," she said. "You'd be good for Winckton. Of course I can't speak for everybody, but speaking for the people I did manage to talk to yesterday and today . . ."

He interrupted. "Today?" he asked. When *today* could she have spoken to anyone? She had sat alone in the empty lobby of the hotel from seven o'clock until he had joined her.

"Mostly yesterday," she conceded. "We aren't going to get hung up on *time*, are we? My impression is that everybody likes you a great deal although they maintain an attitude of wait-and-see. Their main concern is their own department."

When Idamae said "everybody" she'd mean, on the whole, herself. Of that Auerman could be sure. Experience had taught him so. "Everybody's main concern is probably even narrower than that," he said.

"Of course they don't know you all that well yet," she said.

"I see," he said.

The waitress brought him his eggs and his toast. He had been looking forward to the last of the juice in the rind of his grapefruit, but the waitress removed his grapefruit, and his irritation rose within him. His sleeplessness imposed itself on him once more, and his fingers felt for his half-pill in its square of toilet tissue in his pocket. But he did not take it, resisting it, struggling for tranquility without chemistry.

Every motion Auerman made in Idamae's direction evoked her response. If he bent his head toward her she bent her head in reply. It was no illusion, Auerman knew, that she yearned for his touch, or that she yearned to touch him. Her envelopes at her breast were her restraint. They occupied her hands. Perhaps she had known trouble produced by her hands. Somewhere in her past, he guessed, he'd find among her records a job gone bad in the quicksands of a commitment someone had made to her too soon, too deep, from which he had tried to withdraw.

"Start your egg," she bluntly said. "It's nearly nine o'clock."

Obediently he cracked an egg, and he sensed without seeing that the Breakfast Room was emptying—a movement toward the doors, a lowering of the level of conversation. "At nine o'clock I'm supposed to be somewhere," he said.

"I'll get you there," she said. She observed closely his method of eating his eggs.

"Idamae," said Auerman, scraping his eggshell clean, "just what do you do?"

"Do I do," she said.

"At Winckton."

"I love Winckton," she said.

"Yes," he said, "but specifically what do you do?"

"I'm the assistant to the director of planning," she speedily said.

"Yes," he said, "that's your title or what you give me as your title, but what I asked was what do you *do*."

"Mr. Auerman," she said, "you're cross-examining me. I'm not accustomed to that. I'm a respected, valuable employee of this company. I work very hard."

"At what?" he asked, in spite of the hatred in her eyes.

"I'm the assistant to the director of planning," she said

"You are *an* assistant to the director of planning," Auerman said.

"What did I say?"

"You said you were *the* . . ."

"We're not going to get hung up over a *syllable*, are we?" she asked.

"You know," said Auerman, "I don't think you do anything."

"I don't know what you're saying," she said. "I'm in Mr. Patterson's office. You'll meet him this morning, he'll tell you I'm a respected, valuable employee of this company. Ask Mr. Kinnealy. You spent a lot of time with him yesterday. You had a lot of opportunity to ask him anything you wanted to."

"Whenever I asked him something," Auerman pleasantly said, "you answered."

"Everybody knows he's a quiet man," said Idamae. "Finish your coffee."

"You're in Patterson's office?" Auerman asked. "I thought you were in Mr. Kinnealy's office."

"I'm in both," she said.

He walked with Idamae down a long corridor from the Breakfast Room to the distant end of the building. Her heels drummed at so rapid a rate on the hard tile floor one would have imagined she was walking swiftly, but that was an illusion. The illusion amused Auerman. She was small and he was tall, short legs and long. He had never loved a tiny woman, although he had no scruples against it, love was love. But it was a fact that the women he loved, like Elizabeth, tended to be long-legged and slender. He was a man of imagination, he was afloat with fantasies, but he couldn't imagine himself Idamae's lover.

But Idamae was no longer in love with him anyway. Her love had died at breakfast. Swept away with the grapefruit. In and out of love in twenty-four hours. Well, she would be gone in a few moments, he was at the end of her. They came into the sunlight to the limousine they had ridden in yesterday, and yesterday's driver, and four men and a woman waiting for Auerman. One man was Fred Patterson, Idamae's "superior" (a word abolished by Winckton on the table of organization); another was Bob Peterson, sufficiently confusing, the more so since a third man was named Bob, too . . . these names Auerman would seize as the day progressed, although he tried to take them in now, and at the same time to shake Idamae's hand, to thank her for all the time she had so generously given him, to thank her for piloting him about, good-bye for now, hoping to see her soon, surely, only to discover that she was already seated in the limousine.

Auerman was mildly astonished, as the vice-president's wife had been last night to discover Idamae was her guest. In the limousine Idamae was telling one of the gentlemen that she and he (she and "our visitor, Mr. Auerman") had been "conferring at breakfast." Auerman would not have called it that, but he supposed that that was what they had done—conferred. The gentleman to whom she was talking was the second "Bob," but his last name was even more distinguished: he was a Winckton and therefore invested with whatever power or influence the family retained in the corporation. So they were Fred Patterson and Bob Peterson and Bob Winckton and Mr. Kinnealy and a slender, distinguished woman who was director of testing, and Idamae and the driver and Auerman.

Auerman adored the director of testing on the spot for her openness, her wisdom, her nice discernment, and her long legs.

"We're driving through the golf course first," Idamae announced. She had instructed the driver. But who had instructed Idamae? This was unclear to Auerman, who began to perceive that in the absence of clear command Idamae had assumed it.

"Do you play golf?" Auerman asked the director of testing.

"Not especially well," she said, "but I hear that you do."

"I play," said Auerman, "but my *wife* plays especially well."

"How good is well?" asked the director of testing.

"She has a twelve handicap," Auerman said, "but I think my interest in golf has been somewhat exaggerated."

"Then what are you interested in?"

"Well, golf for one thing," Auerman said. "This *is* a beautiful course. What am I interested in? Golf, dogs, cats, children, comfort, justice, the right job for the right person."

"We're leaving the golf course at this point," Idamae announced. "We'll be back." The limousine sailed softly down the highway to the animal hospital—"the best little veterinary clinic you could ask for," Bob Winckton said, "your dog will thank you." Auerman was introduced to the physician on duty, who assured him that a physician was *always* on duty. Apparently the veterinarian had been briefed on Auerman's coming, for he said, "I suppose you've seen the golf course, too."

"We're driving back to the clubhouse right now," Idamae announced, leading the party back to the limousine.

It was likely, Auerman thought, once again pondering Idamae's presence in the limousine, that his fellow passengers imagined she was along at his request. But of whom would he have requested her? Who was in charge? Nobody was in charge. Everybody thought someone else was in charge. Into the breach little Idamae stepped.

The clubhouse smelled as new as it was, of wood sawed fresh, of new leather, new cork. It had not yet been polluted by the smoke of men and women oddly here for their health in the first place. The new cork floor was still unpunctured by spikes. A service crew waited for them with white wine. The party was alone in the clubhouse. The view of the rolling hills from the grand window pleased Auerman, but the glare troubled his eyes, which were growing heavy with fatigue. The director of testing, observing his discomfort, lowered the transparent green screen, softening the glare, and he thanked her.

Nevertheless, to his own surprise, suddenly with a sip of cool white wine Auerman popped his wake-up pill. He had unveiled it in his pocket. Presto! Magic! Out of a square of toilet tissue came a powerful pill. In a few minutes he would feel refreshed, cheerier, his amiability up, his critical nature down, love up, irritability down, and that was what he wanted, for he knew that of all the places of the "big eight" from Seattle to Pittsburgh the place he liked best was Winckton and everyone in it but officious, presumptuous, deceitful, dishonest, self-appointed, hidden, weaseling Idamae Low.

"Can you talk about the employment of women?" asked the director of testing.

"I'm an absolute equalitarian," Auerman said.

That was not enough for her. "Can you elaborate a little?" she asked.

"Well, starting negatively," Auerman said, "backing in, I know what I don't *want* it to mean. It mustn't mean hiring people in categories for whom no jobs exist. We have to have a program designed before we hire people for it. It's one thing to build a corporation in the image of the civilization we'd like to be, but it's another thing to be sentimental and wasteful. I've never seen it go right unless we planned it. At Kemperer we have a cross section of the world—black, brown, red, white, yellow, citizen, alien, veteran, handicapped, heterosexual, homosexual, and a lot of variations of those . . ."

"Unmarried women," Idamae blurted. Apparently she could not help herself. She had not meant to speak, and Auerman, in kindness, would have pretended not to have heard her, but everyone had heard and waited for him to reply.

"What about unmarried women?" he asked. "Yes, we were talking about that at breakfast, weren't we? We want to know what a person actually *does*, don't we; not the title of the job but the work of the job. Everybody who's employed has got to *do* something."

Auerman saw Idamae whiten with hatred and with fear. She had set aside her folders and her computer printouts, but now she went further: She slipped the leather strap of her purse from her shoulder. She drank her wine swiftly, restoring her color to her face, but her fear and her hatred dwelled in her eyes.

One of the men of the service crew refilled her glass. He had been hovering about her as if she, not Auerman, were the honored guest. And at this moment a distressing idea came to Auerman's mind, a suspicion, a revelation, and then almost a certainty; that his future at Winckton lay not in the judgment of Bob Winckton or Mr. Kinnealy or Fred Patterson or Bob Peterson or the director of testing or the masses at coffee breaks or at lunch or at dinner, but with Idamae Low leveling her glance at him above her freshly-filled wine glass.

Yes, it was true. He could not doubt it. He knew her too well for her comfort. She had no job, no task, no duty, no skill, no art, no craft, no family, and probably no lover. Her work was only the continuation of herself by the endless cultivation of her own power, and *that* work she would do at all cost. She would block his way. She would ruin him. He would fly home to Kemperer on the wings of goodwill only to hear in a week, two weeks, a month, by phone, from Mr. Kinnealy in his low, listening, interruptible voice, that somehow the support for Auerman at Winckton had eroded, something had happened, he couldn't say what.

Auerman would know what had happened, and Idamae would almost know. From the hour of his departure she would malign him. She was the reigning authority on Auerman. Had she not been seen everywhere with him? Like old friends, they had been inseparable since the moment of his arrival, they had conferred together at breakfast, and something about him *worried* her, she'd say—she was troubled for Winckton, she couldn't name it, perhaps it was her intuition—wasn't she being ridiculous? And everyone would assist her with reassurance, no, she wasn't being ridiculous at all, she should trust her feelings, speak right up.

Well (speaking right up), he'd been wonderful the first day when he went around meeting everybody, but the second day he began to wilt, in the limousine, at the club with top executives, Bob Winckton and the others, it was only her impression . . .

Auerman, at the clubhouse table, felt his wake-up pill beginning to work within him, and the cool white wine. He condemned her for ruining him. And yet, how could his balanced mind condemn her for fighting for her life? If she did not fight for herself, who would? She was a small, female person fighting for her place in this animal scheme. He would now require of himself a pragmatic descent from moral purity, a touch of legitimate hypocrisy. A touch indeed, even here at this open table in everyone's sight, for this was the moment. If he permitted this moment to pass he was doomed, Winckton was lost to him, he would never return to this burgeoning place with its long season of sun, nine months of golf for Elizabeth, and the slender, long-legged director of testing.

He smiled at Idamae. The anger softened in her eyes. And when he leaned toward her his motion evoked her response, as it had at the breakfast table; and when, with one finger, he touched her cheek the anger in her eyes, already softening, altogether dissolved. She received his touch as a commitment, a promise. Auerman would preserve her secret. No one would know that busy, bustling, hustling, scurrying, hastening Idamae, laden with folders and printouts, was titled but idle, a lady without work but forever employed, everywhere, ubiquitous. Her fear vanished from her face, she hoisted the strap of her purse again to her shoulder, and he knew she would fight for his appointment with every weapon.

La Lumière

When Boppo was a much younger man he fell in love with a woman he thought of as fabulously beautiful, as she might have been. Hard to judge early judgments. Memory was deceptive. Photographs were lost—the photographs they had taken on beaches and innocent excursions had been somewhere lost during that spacious interregnum between then and now when nothing much had happened to him except two wars in Asia, two fortunes acquired and one lost, two wives and four children scattered now to five States of the Union, connected to Boppo only by occasional lines dropped into the mail and by telephone lines cleverly strung from coast to coast by the Bell company. Boppo owned sixty thousand shares of the company, and other gems, some of which he now and then distributed to two of his children—the second child of his first wife and the first child of his second wife—who were habitually improvident and needful. He loved them all, money-takers or not.

Everybody called him "Boppo," which was not his name. The name was affixed to him accidentally by the fabulously beautiful woman, Ella, as they were celebrating with friends at a tavern at the corner of Liberty and Postal Streets thirty years ago. Ella, who was either slightly drunk or pretending to be, challenged him to a boxing match. She swung a roundhouse punch at him and cried "Boppo," as if she had connected. It was very funny at the time. All that evening he was called "Boppo" by their laughing friends, and the next day, too, when they met again to sober up from their bout of more or less pretended or exaggerated drunkenness, and all that week, and into the future. He carried the name, although all the friends of that night, but one, dropped away, through Asia, through his hard-scrambling moneygetting days, and through his two marriages and his two busted families.

The name seemed not to fit him any longer, but he didn't much mind. Didn't mind and didn't not mind. All that mattered was that he was well and life was filled with pleasures of the heart, the head, the belly and the loins, and as free as possible of too many oppressive regrets. "The hard part about getting older," his father had once told him, "is the burden of memory." That was the price of advancing age. If he remembered too much he understood too much.

He thought of that long-gone Ella as Ella One now because of Ella Two. They were the only Ellas he had known. Ella One had married the magician Konstantinople, famous in his craft for escape, mentalism, and tricks of fire. Boppo had not seen Ella in thirty years and he did not suppose he cared to. What could it possibly lead to?

Thus he received with mingled emotion this evening at dinner at *La Lumière* with Ella Two, Ella's mother Vivienne, and Ella's young friend Lance, the news that after dinner they were to attend a performance of Konstantinople the magician. Oddly, Boppo assumed that since Ella One had married Konstantinople she was still married to him. She would do that, stay married forever. Boppo's assumption was based upon nothing much. He had not known her as well as he thought he had, although at the time he believed he knew her very well, for they went "everywhere" together, to parties and skating rinks, free concerts, summer beaches, winter carnivals; they were pals, they were chums. Indeed they were. He had never been, as the expression goes, *intimate* with her, and so perhaps had never known her as well as he had thought he had. He had not known there was more to know. Even as such a young man he had been enormously sophisticated in certain ways, but enormously innocent in others.

"Of course you needn't go if you don't want to," said Ella's mother Vivienne. She and Boppo were lifetime friends, and they were frank with one another.

"Why wouldn't I want to go?" Boppo asked.

"You turned off when I mentioned the magician. Last year we had those gymnasts. I didn't have the feeling you liked them either."

"They weren't bad," said Lance, the young man who was Ella's friend. It was the height of his evening's enthusiasm. He appeared to Boppo tonight to exist in a state of irritation, frustration, the reason for which was clear enough. The young man cared little for the idea of the magician, or for anything else connected with this night (in spite of which he ate a vast dinner eagerly). He cared for Ella, or thought at least that he did, although he was coming these days to the end of his hope. Tonight's occasion was the anniversary of their meeting, the annual fund-raiser for the League Opposing Violence Everywhere—LOVE—and their relationship had never progressed in depth or affection, really, beyond the first weeks so tentative, so promising, and so soon cool or impeded.

"I think I once knew the magician's wife," Boppo said, "if she's still his wife. That was years and years ago and he was from Yonkers, not from Constantinople at all, and a good thing, too. If you can't spell it you shouldn't be from it."

"When was this?" Ella asked, who kept in her head a developing biography of Boppo. She wished to know everything about him she could possibly know. She adored him.

"Oh, I was only a boy," he said. "Your mother knew her, too.

We were all a sort of aimless, pointless gang, just beginning to learn to drink, and playing practical jokes which make us laugh a lot, and building up a mythology of ourselves."

"You were only a boy?" Ella asked.

"I was a boy and she was a woman, I suppose. We were the same age."

"Women are so much maturer than men so much sooner," Ella's mother, Vivienne, announced. She suspected that her daughter was Boppo's mistress, and she craved a philosophy to justify the event. "You were the same age but not the same maturity."

"You make me sound like a corporate bond," Boppo replied.

"You say I knew her," said Vivienne.

"Her name was Ella," said Boppo. "Like your Ella. They're the only Ellas I've ever known. She was often with us at that beery old place at Liberty and Postal. She's the one that christened me 'Boppo'."

"A slender girl was she?" asked Vivienne. "Long blonde hair that kept falling down over her face all the time . . ."

"Yes," said Boppo eagerly, "what a mind you have!"

"She had a bad complexion," said the mother of Ella Two.

"I don't remember that," said Boppo, "although I suppose it's true if you say so. I remember her as having a *fine* complexion and I'm hot for complexions, it's the first thing that strikes me in a lady, her complexion."

"No," said Vivienne firmly, "her complexion was bad."

"Then she hid it from me," said Boppo.

"I wouldn't be surprised," said Vivienne. "She hid it behind her hair."

"I see," said Boppo, who was always seeing something new.

This conversation between Boppo and her mother amused Ella, for she had heard something from Boppo of this other Ella, Ella One, who had baffled him in those ancient days by her mysterious disappearances. Over the bridge and gone, that was Ella One. After a few days she returned with tales of where she had been, which Boppo, silly boy, absolutely believed. Young men, of course, were easy to deceive. They were raw, gross, lacking in subtlety. Now that Ella knew Boppo, young men were more than ever unacceptable to her, foolish hot-blooded things, perfect of body, imperfect of mind.

"I was easily fooled, I'm sure," said Boppo. He spoke somewhat carefully, aware that he was to some extent describing Lance as well as himself. "I was inexperienced. She called me a soda-pop boy because I kept drinking soda pop. She introduced me to wine and water. Water had never occurred to me before, but I gave up soda pop on the spot." Ella would be a bit angry at him for putting it this way. It resembled so much things passing between her and Lance. But then, she was often a bit angry about something or other. It was fun to be angry with Boppo, he could take it, nothing could shake him, and her own anger warmed her and sent her blood coursing into all her farthest parts, her fingertips, her toes. Boppo never objected to her anger at all, but parried it deftly like some superb swordsman or boxer, and her anger turned to passion.

Lance made no sign that he recognized himself in Boppo's account. His mind was absent. It was familiar, he thought. The same sort of thing had happened to him. But he had learned to enjoy wine, and it magnified his passion for Ella, if such a thing were possible. It was not possible. His passion was already total, maximum. He loved her deeply and would love her forever except that lately he was often impatient with her, somewhat angry with her, somewhat mistrustful, disappointed and enraged and—yes—sometimes almost physically sick about her, for she held him at a distance although he was dying for her. He imagined their bodies in the long embrace of bliss, even as he began to understand that such a moment might never occur, that his most persistent dreams might never come true. When? That's what he wanted to know—when? "When we're ready," she replied, "supposing that we'll ever be ready, but I don't know. We can't hurry." "I'm ready," Lance said, "we should announce our engagement. I feel engaged. I know you don't. Now I understand why they invented engagements—so at least you know where you're at, and everyone else knows. You know the score. You know that if you don't go to bed now you'll go to bed later because you're engaged. You don't go to bed with anyone else." His little speech prompted a thought in his head, suggested to him some days ago by a detective. Lance was ashamed now of having visited the detective, and yet the man had posed some good questions. "Do you go to bed with someone else? Lately I feel I'm beginning to mistrust you, and I don't see how we can go on mistrusting each other. Can we? It's not a feeling I like, believe me. I hate it." "You have no reason to mistrust me," Ella said.

But of course he had. Suspicion without known cause remained suspicion nonetheless. Ella was going to bed with someone else—it was exactly the language of his question—with Boppo, for she loved Boppo, or assumed she loved Boppo, who was such an experienced, skillful lover, absorbing her romantic passion as adroitly as he absorbed her anger. He could do anything. And she was so comfortable with Boppo, too, he was so much at leisure, he knew all the perfect places to go and all the perfect things to do. He was rather rich as well, and that helped; not so *very* rich, her mother guessed, but decently rich, his income was fixed but abundant, even discounting for inflation.

Ella cared nothing for the figures. She tried to think that the money did not really matter, and he said so himself, lavishing things upon her she really could not have afforded herself. She loved Boppo for his kindness and the comfort he gave her, for his wisdom and his cleverness, which his money merely made possible. He opened all the world to her.

Mistrustful of Ella, and not very pleased with himself, either, Lance had gone a month ago to the office of a detective named Spritz, whom he had met at tennis one day. Lance might even have engaged Spritz, but the detective's rates were terribly high—Lance had never imagined that level of money, and he had none of his own, poor fellow; he got by from week to week as well as he could; the night before payday he was broke. When the detective Spritz saw that Lance had no money he lapsed into mere wisdom, saying to Lance, "Maybe you don't want to know anyhow."

"I want to know all right," said Lance. "I can take it."

"Maybe you'll be sorry if you found out," the detective said. On the wall behind his head a small sign read *No Guns*.

"I'll take my chances," Lance said. "I know how to face things."

"Sooner or later you'll find out," the detective said. "You find out everything in time."

"I want to know *now*," Lance said.

"But you haven't got the *money* to know now," the detective said. "Where do you *think* she goes? What do you *think* she does?"

"I haven't thought it all the way through, I suppose. She doesn't say where she goes, or she says she's going somewhere and then it turns out she wasn't. There's no telling."

"Why don't you follow her?" asked Mr. Spritz, and when he observed the expression of shock on Lance's face he asked, "What's the matter? Do you think following her is indecent?"

"I guess I do."

"So you'll hire me to do your indecent thing," the detective said, "or at least you would if you had any money, which you haven't. My experience tells me that's the problem. I suspect she's got a rich old man."

"He split the scene years ago," Lance said.

"No," said the detective, not smiling. "Not father. I mean old man, as in sugar daddy. Tell me, does she live beyond her means? Does she have a job? Ask yourself how much money does she earn and how much rent does she pay, and multiply it out."

"She's a student," Lance said. "She gets straight A in everything."

"A grade-A girl," the detective said.

"Woman," Lance said. "I suppose it's *possible.* Some other man. But I really can't believe it. No, I don't believe it. It's something else." The rivals of his life had always been boys, not men. Another boy he could believe, but not some old man, some sugar daddy. The idea was alien.

"Then if I have no reason to mistrust you," Lance fiercely whispered now, at table in *La Lumière,* "tell me where you were this afternoon."

Boppo, appearing to be attentive to Vivienne, listened at a tangent for Ella's reply. Vivienne, too, was listening.

"I was in the library," Ella replied. "I was in the library from about the middle of the afternoon until it closed."

"What door did you leave by?" Lance inquired.

"I can't believe you're putting me through this," she said.

"I can't believe a lot of things," he said. "I looked everywhere and I telephoned everywhere." He resumed his normal voice, to avoid the appearance of a crisis between them. And he approached his pastry with some pleasure.

"We must have missed each other," she foolishly said. She hated this lying. Truly she did. If not for Lance she'd never need to lie. She lied to her mother, of course, but that was old stuff, she'd been lying to her mother all her life. Besides, her mother knew the truth anyhow, or guessed, if not precisely then approximately, that Ella had not been at the library but somewhere else in somebody else's company, somebody else's arms, perhaps in Boppo's. On the whole, her mother approved of Boppo, he was an old friend, reliable, and his taste was good. Her mother's view of Lance, on the other hand, had never been wholly positive, though there was no telling, she said, how the years might ripen him.

Ella placed her hand upon Lance's on the table. It was a bit of a patronizing gesture, he felt, as if he were a little boy and not quite bright. Maybe he was. His psychological counselor said just the other day that all men had little boys in them still, and maybe that was true, Lance thought, even of himself. Lately he was hearing many new things. His troubles were making him alert. He was filled with doubts that were new to him. Oh what a damnable liar Ella was! He withdrew his hand from hers, but gently, to be sure, not as if his action implied a meaning. Could such a beauty lie? It seemed to him a contradiction in terms, for truth was beauty, beauty was truth, and yet she lied. He was absolutely certain she had not been at the library this afternoon, for he had searched the library room by room from top to bottom, and afterward he had sat himself on the long bench in the pale sun with his weary feet up, watching everyone who came or went for an hour and a half until closing. Not in a thousand years could she have eluded his sharp eyes.

If only he didn't love her so much he *could kill her*, he thought. No, of course, not that, it was only an outlaw thought. He was a gentle boy whose anger had never taken the form of violence. When he was most angry he was most solitary. He sat on public benches until the mood dissolved, and he played tennis, at which he excelled. He had been playing tennis almost from infancy, and he could smash the ball with the speed of a bullet. Since his involvement with Ella had drifted into conflict he had neglected his tennis awfully, and felt much the worse for it, sluggish in his veins. His long muscles ached for action. He should really get back to it. Ella herself recommended that he resume. "Put your mind to it," she said, "you'll feel a million times better and you won't be thinking so negatively." It would improve his color, too, she thought, for lately the fine brown of his skin had whitened.

But he *had* put his mind to it. Tennis had always taken his mind off everything but tennis itself, until he had been driven nearly bughouse by this frustration with Ella, so that he had lately begun to play tennis not for itself but to take his mind off Ella. And what was the result? The harder he played tennis the more comprehensively she monopolized his mind. While he was playing tennis *where was she*? She ruined his concentration.

She was seldom where she really said she was. She'd say she was at work. She wasn't. She'd say she had been to see a certain film. She hadn't. She'd say she was at the library. She wasn't. He quizzed her on the film she said she'd seen. She could answer none of his questions. And he found out quite by accident that she had not been on her job for several weeks and was not expected back. If he asked her where she'd been she said, "Nowhere, and you mustn't make me tell you anything when I clearly don't want to. It's not you, Lance, don't you see? It's only that I want to be by myself more and more these days. We have plenty of time together, don't we?"

Now Lance saw other signs, too, of a change in himself, a new viewpoint. He had begun to notice in spite of himself (he had begun to notice himself noticing, one might say) many young women here and there about town who appeared to be quite alone. Often they gazed at him appealingly, as if to say, "Why don't you come and talk to me?" They seemed to be sending him a message. Well, why shouldn't they, he was a healthy good-looking fellow. But then it would all so soon fall to pieces. As soon as young women heard about Ella they lost interest in Lance. "Oh, one of those," one young woman said, "I can't live with your broken heart."

"Told them *what* about Ella?" Lance's psychological counselor asked.

"When they hear that she's my—"

"What?"

Yes, that was a problem area all right. All the young women he encountered assumed that he was taken, spoken for, that he was "going steady." But going where? On this point his psychological counselor pressed him diligently. "What does everybody mean when they say you're going steady?" the counselor rhetorically asked, replying to himself, "They assume that two people of your age and your economic class and your educational level and your religious informality and your heterosexual preferences are going to bed. So when you say she's your—your something or other—I've got to ask you, your what?"

"I don't want to lie to you," Lance said.

"Going where then?" the counselor asked. "Going steadily where?"

"Well, not to bed," Lance said. There was no point wasting his time and the counselor's as well if he wasn't going to level with the counselor. Tell the poor man the truth of things, Lance thought. No, he said, he'd not been to bed with Ella, nor ever really been in any way "intimate" with her in the way people meant. They danced, they skated, they swam, they did all sorts of healthy physical things together, but these things were always public, never private. They did everything sporting except play tennis together (there weren't six people in the city Lance would play tennis with), but on the sexual side she held him off.

These facts delivered so truthfully and so straight seemed to disappoint the counselor, and for this Lance was sincerely sorry. He was as apologetic as he could be. "It isn't as if I haven't tried," he assured his counselor, but if the truth be known he was no longer even trying. He had quite given up. For three months he'd hardly even mentioned the subject. And their innocent physical life together had waned, too. He had become, if anything, a shopping companion, a chauffeur, a department store freak, wandering up and down the escalators while Ella and Vivienne surveyed the sales, and he was reduced to an occasional social event like this, tonight, dinner at *La Lumière*, and a magician afterward, the annual fund-raiser for Vivienne's League whatever it was—LOVE.

Lance was moving toward a decision. Think of all the other beautiful young women in the world! Think of all the other beautiful women right here in *La Lumière*. Looking about him, Lance saw several tables of women unaccompanied by men. At several other tables women outnumbered men. The world was waiting for him to circulate. At moments he was struck by the absurdity of his concentrating his energy so totally upon Ella, and lately the tension between them had uncomfortably increased.

He would quit her. He would leave her. That must be, he felt, the decision toward which he felt himself moving, and it frightened him to think of life alone and Ella-less. He could not at first imagine it, but as soon as he began to live with it, it became both real and possible, and he prepared his remarks. "Ella, I can't go on, and I think you know why, that's all there is to it, it's really the end, but enough is enough, the tension is getting me down." It was ruining his tennis, too, but he would not mention that for fear of his seeming trivial. He could not believe he was thinking such harsh, decisive, aggressive thoughts here in the elegance of *La Lumière*.

But immediately he began to think them again, plunging forward with his planning. He would give back to her some object she had given to him, something symbolizing continued affection and yet the end of things, not in a spirit of anger or remorse but in the mood of disappointment. She had given him the Regular Patron Ticket to the Sports Arena, where he went now and again for various events on nights when she was busy somewhere, requiring solitude. He might return that to her. Better still, the *Young Unmarrieds Cookbook* they had bought together and shared, passing back and forth. The recipes seemed to assume that the "unmarrieds" shared the same kitchen, too. He would give her the book, insisting it was hers now forever, and with it the Bridge Pass, too, which they had shared as they had shared the cookbook. It was she, not he, who was always going off over the bridge these days. These little gifts had seemed to say, "We're here forever, this is our town together," and his returning them to her would seem to say, therefore, that they had arrived together now at the end of things.

When Boppo was a much younger man he had seen in Asia a great deal of the world's violence without its having destroyed his peaceful principles or pressed him into a posture of cynicism.

He had met Ella (that is to say, Ella One) at a political meeting in the garden of some people in Muskrat Hill he would then have thought of as wealthy. They might have been. "I was just getting out of uniform," Boppo recalled—

"In the garden?" Ella asked. "Good show."

Anyhow, it was about that time, he recalled, and he had either just begun or was just about to begin his first real job, and the world was splendid. All the big wars had ceased.

"What kind of meeting was it?" Ella asked in *La Lumière.* Boppo sat to her right. Her mother sat facing her, and Lance to her left. At a small perfectly square table she nevertheless held the center. Well, she *was* the center. She was Boppo's lover and Lance's friend and her mother's daughter. She was also, as part of her own education, Boppo's biographer, historian of the generation past seen through Boppo, told by Boppo. He was her connection to the vanished past, even as he was her connection to those places and luxuries and pleasures of the present which without him would have been as remote to her as Boppo's youth.

"Oh, I can't remember," Boppo said, "it was some sort of League like your mother's League condemning violence. I'm sure it was Save Something or Protect Something or Friendship with Somebody—friends with Russia, friends with China, friends with the Negro people. That was the term we used in those days, the Negro people."

"As I recall," said Vivienne, "she was a rather political person. She was always wearing buttons on her—if I may say so—her rather modest breast."

"I've thought since," said Boppo, "that she went to a lot of political meetings partly as a social thing. Saving things and protecting things and also looking for somebody."

"Looking for a man," said Ella's mother. "Everybody was looking for a man. Pity me, I found one."

"She'd never go to a meeting alone," Boppo said. "To be alone would have reduced her in her own eyes. Something in the way she was brought up had taught her to think people would look down on her if she went anywhere alone."

"People would think she couldn't *get* a man," Vivienne said.

"Sometimes," said Boppo, "she kept her telephone off the hook so people would think she received a million calls a night." When Boppo first met her, in the garden in Muskrat Hill, she was surrounded by so many young men, and he thought he stood very little chance of winning his way through the crowd to her. And yet in no time he seemed to be hers. Hard to believe. Impossible to believe. He, Boppo, sole escort to Ella! It stunned him, and gave him a new view of himself in the same swift magical way, in a silly moment in a tavern one New Year's Eve, she gave him a new name for himself. "She was my young manhood. For me, this whole city is a kind of monument to her. I can't go very far without coming on some place she and I once went together, little theaters we went to that are skyscrapers now, little houses where we went to parties that are freeways now. A lot of our past is torn down. I don't mind their tearing things down, but it seems to me they should put up some sort of plaque, 'Boppo and Ella walked here.' "

"Did you sleep with her?" Lance inquired.

"Never," Boppo promptly said.

"That's shocking," said Vivienne, but whether she meant Lance's question or Boppo's reply was unclear. The question had been in her mind as well.

"What will you say if you see her tonight?" asked Ella.

"Will she be there?"

"I think she might," said Vivienne.

"She might not even remember you after all this time," Lance said.

"She'll remember him," said Ella's mother. "I'd remember him and there really was never anything between us."

"I'm not sure there was anything between her and me, either," Boppo said. "It was always the greatest mystery to me.

It was the most shocking thing that ever happened to me. I wouldn't want to go through it again. Not ever."

"How long did all this take to develop?" Lance inquired.

"I thought it was years," Boppo replied. "I suppose it was only months. I thought she was mine, I thought everything was more or less understood, I assumed I was her main man. I assumed I was her *only* man. Then all of a sudden one day she said, 'Boppo, I've got something to tell you.' We were walking down Tin Street near the Boulevard. All right, tell me. She said, 'I'm going to marry this Konstantinople, this magician.' I was really quite suicidal."

"This very same magician we're going to see?" Lance asked.

"I assume so."

"Did you ever meet him?"

"I don't know about that," Boppo said. "I've often thought about that, and it seems to me I might have because there was one man who might have been he. He was old enough to be her father."

"This is interesting," Lance said. "How did you manage to recover?"

"From what?" Boppo asked.

"*From losing her,*" Lance said in a voice heightened with impatience. "*What we've been talking about,*" he added, fierce again, as he had been fierce with Ella on the question of her movements this afternoon.

"I'm sorry," Boppo said, as indeed he was. Tragic hero of his little tale, he had in fact lost all feeling for the event, as an actor might who plays a role too long. For Lance, however, it was living, breathing drama. He identified. It was indeed "interesting," as he had said. "Honestly I can't really remember," Boppo said.

"You said suicidal," Lance said.

"That passed. Quickly. I remember being very down, but I can't say if it was days or weeks. It wasn't months, I know that, and I suppose that what happened was that there were other young ladies to console me."

"We had expressions for such things," said Vivienne. "There's a lot of fish in the ocean."

"Were there a lot of fish in the ocean?" Ella asked Boppo, rebuking her mother, and he replied as tactfully as he could. "There are lots of fish in the ocean," he said, "but when you're in love there's only one. Never mind fish. I thought I'd lost the most beautiful girl in the world."

"She was plain," said Vivienne, "nothing out of the ordinary."

"But he thought so," Lance said sympathetically.

"Yes, I thought the whole world was laughing at me. I'd been in heaven for a long time, and then suddenly it was over."

"It probably wasn't all that sudden," said Ella's mother. "She might have warned you in a number of ways, but you weren't listening. You were wet behind the ears."

"Boppo wet behind the ears," laughed Ella. "I can't believe it."

"I can't believe I'm going to a magician," Lance said to Ella.

The waiter brought the check, and the boy read the bottom line with his quick athletic eyes. He was astonished, and for a moment he was assailed by the sudden fear of some sort of misunderstanding, that he was expected to share the expense of the meal, which he was not in the least prepared to do. He soon saw, however, that this man Boppo, whoever he was, whatever he was, handled the matter. Boppo did this every year, took Ella and her mother and other guests to dinner before the League Opposing Violence Everywhere fund-raiser, it was all in a good cause. "I really must thank you very much," Lance said. "I don't eat like this every night."

"Or drink," said Ella, for the boy was warm with wine.

"The last time I saw a magician I was a kid," the boy said. "I always thought magicians were for kids."

"This is an adult magician," Vivienne said.

"How so?"

"I don't know," she said. "He says political things as he goes along. I guess that's why we hired him, impossible escapes and mental tricks, all really amazing. He can guess the number of a dollar bill in your purse, add the year of your birth and the dates of all the coins in your purse and give you the sum in a twinkling. He's as fast as a calculator. The escaping tricks are marvelous, just perfectly amazing. He stands in a locker. He's locked in there. You can walk all around it, examine it from every angle, you march back to your seat in the audience, and the next thing you know he comes walking back on the stage from the wings smoking a Turkish cigarette. The locker is still locked."

"Oh, mother, you're so gullible," Ella said affectionately.

"You'll see for yourself," her mother replied.

"I mean," asked Ella, "how do you know it's a Turkish cigarette?"

"That's what he said," said Vivienne.

"Does he saw a woman in half?" Boppo asked.

"Oh, he saws several women," Vivienne replied. "He saws several women in several pieces as a matter of fact, and he gets them all mixed up. He can't put the right bodies back on the right legs. He saws his wife in half with all the rest, I think. I spoke to her. She's very nice. It never occurred to me, Boppo, that she was your old Ella with her hair falling over her face, but now that you mention it she might be. He shoots flames in the air. They burn in the middle of the ceiling attached to nothing."

"Burn without fuel?" Lance asked, intending to be polite, appreciative, to express a greater interest in the evening's event, especially in view of the size of the dinner bill. The meal was two hundred dollars. For a party of four the magician was two hundred more, in a good cause. Lance admired this Boppo, envying him. The thought crossed Lance's mind that with so much money he would be likely to spend it in other ways. He'd give some to charity, yes, of course, to the League Opposing Violence Everywhere, and to other causes just as worthy. He could see, however, how he might be tempted to divert portions of large sums to the advancement of his own social life. For example, one might fare better with young women if one had more money to spend. One could take women to nicer places. Lance was always taking Ella to freebie things, to the park, to open-air things, bicycle riding. He felt compelled to avoid expensive entertainment, show tickets, dance, recitals, very big night-club stars on tour, and certainly they never dined like this. This Mr. Boppo, Lance supposed, possessed women for the asking, although whether, at his age, he still *cared* for women, Lance questioned. Lance promised himself that some day he, too, would be rich.

Boppo, too, had drifted for a moment into reverie. He had from time to time asked himself the question Lance had asked: had he ever met Konstantinople? For years Boppo's imagination saw Konstantinople, husband of Ella One, as a bridegroom in a tailcoat, as if he wore forever the suit he was married in. Boppo had known nothing of the wedding, or if he had known he had dismissed it from his mind. It was a painful occasion for him, but somehow, for years, he imagined Konstantinople as bridegroom, as if the wedding were still in progress, as if the officiating clergyman had not yet sent forth his question, asking whether anyone objected to this marriage—if so, speak now or forever hold your peace—whereupon, in dreams, the young Boppo cried out against this marriage. Nevertheless, in the dream as in life, the ceremony was carried out, and in time the dream fell from Boppo's repertoire of dreams, and he dreamed others.

But whether he had actually met the person called Konstantinople, who came not from Turkey but from Yonkers, Boppo never knew. Surely he would have remembered the name, but Konstantinople in private life was known by some ordinary everyday name, and he might have been one man whom Boppo had met, whom Boppo never viewed as a rival, and whom he therefore dismissed from his mind. It was long ago, memory twisted events, fabricating, distorting, shuffling people and places about, things were as confusing and terrifying and as irretrievable as time in its savagery could make them, and Boppo could remember only one possible man, old enough to be her father.

Beneath the table Ella's hand groped for his. She was passing him a note. Sometimes she was a child! She gazed innocently forward into her mother's eyes. This little mischievousness in Ella was something of which Boppo was not fond, but he was tolerant of everything she did, everything she craved, she was an angel beyond comparing, but a bit childish, too. He understood that she took a certain pleasure in this, passing a secret note to deceive Lance, deceive Vivienne, it was a kind of thrill of excitement or danger.

Her note would say some empty thing, leaving Boppo with no new knowledge, and an incriminating slip of paper in his hand. It would say, "Telephone me," which in any case he would have done as soon as he arrived home (unless she phoned him first), and talked for an hour with the telephone tucked beneath his jawbone while he pushed paper at his night-desk. Ella would have been furious to see him so inattentive, but he had heard it all, if not from her from some other marvelous women. She was not his first lover. Her mind was filled with myriad topics which she covered with precision.

Her little furtive notes were often written in an ascending scale of capital letters and underlined passages, "You are *the* MOST *FANTASTIC* man," to which he was inclined to reply, in the interest of her ongoing education, that she had not yet polled a fair sample. She was thirty years younger than he, and she would know other men after him. No little note passed in this way had ever been urgent. Even so, he was always impatient to read her message, even when it was nonsense. He took her note between his thumb and forefinger. They rose from the table. In the darkness he could not read it. Lance with his powerful penetrating young new tennis eyes could have read it in this dark, but not Boppo. Near the door of the restaurant, by the light of the cashier's lamp, he read the little note, which said, "You are *more* MAGIC than any *MAGICIAN*."

Maybe so, granted that the word might be used in more than one way, still this man Konstantinople was magic; he did fabulous things; he threw balls of fire into the air where they burned until, with a snap of his fingers, he ordered them to extinguish themselves. He ordered his dog Palooka to become a cat, and the cat to become a white mouse. The dog jumped into a box, the cat jumped out, the dog was gone.

The magic show took place in a small theater, once the ballroom of a once-grand mansion in Muskrat Hill. The mansions of this neighborhood were occupied now not by powerful families, of whom few remained in the city, but by philanthropic institutions such as Vivienne's League. The cat jumped into the box, the mouse ran out, Konstantinople captured the mouse, closed the box, opened the box, and the mouse had become the dog. Konstantinople baked a cake in a hat. He baked as many cakes as gentlemen offered hats, promising in his Turkish accent (made in Yonkers) that after his performance everyone would eat cake washed down with spirituous punch. "Do I care to eat cake tasting of sweatbands?" Boppo asked Ella, seated beside him in the long row of folding chairs.

But it wasn't Ella beside him. It was Lance, who had interposed himself, who had schemed to sit beside her, so that he might talk to her. Then let the boy enjoy this hour, Boppo thought. Let the evening be the boy's. The night would be Boppo's. (So had the afternoon been.) Intermittently Lance spoke to Ella in the fierce whisper he had employed at dinner. Whether she was listening Boppo could not tell. Lance's tone was distinctly angry, pleading, an expression of confusion, of dilemma, of his wanting to know what in the world was going on, what was going to happen to them, were they or were they not engaged. He needed to know. He did not much care any longer what they were, just so long as the suspense ended. He was at the end of his rope. Boppo, too, wondered with less urgency than Lance how things would ever end. Perhaps Ella would succeed without hurting Lance in telling him as much of the truth as he needed to know. "He'll die," she sometimes said. "What worries me," said Boppo, "not that he'll die but that he'll kill me. He's such a strong fellow. I don't care to be shot." "He *is* terribly strong," said Ella, "but he'd never use a weapon." "I don't care to be strangled by bare hands, either," said Boppo.

Lance was hot, steaming. It was Boppo's impression that the boy beside him boiled in a state of massive irritation. Nothing Konstantinople said or did amused Lance. True, the magician's little political patter was unoriginal—Boppo was certain he had made the same jokes about each President before. Konstantinople had practiced magic through several presidencies. He was seventy-five years old. When he revealed his age the sympathetic crowd applauded. He wore a tailcoat and a cone-shaped fez. A tassel bobbed from the crown of the fez. All this left Lance, hot as he was, cold. Balls of fire suspended in the air meant nothing to him, nor cakes baked in hats, nor vanishing animals reappearing, nor the women sawed in half. Lance's fury was his sole distraction.

Konstantinople sawed in half a woman all in green, then a woman all in red, then a woman in blue. He had now six carts, each bearing half a woman, but he complained that he had lost track of things. "I don't think I can remember," he said, "how to put them back together again. I am color-blind." Boppo looked for Ella in all this—for Ella One, sawed in half by her husband. Vivienne had thought she might be in one of those roles tonight, but she was not. "I can't remember whose legs belong to whose head," Konstantinople said. "This is the part of the trick I always goof. Oh well, I will put them back together as well as I can." Willy-nilly he reassembled his women. None matched. The green woman ended half blue, the blue woman ended half red, the red woman ended half green. Now at last even Lance was impressed, scowling thoughtfully while the audience applauded with the most genuine enthusiasm.

A magical trick, to be sure, Boppo thought. He wished he knew how it was done. All rather simple, he supposed, like any trick. Easy enough once you knew how. He applauded this man who was once upon a time, so many years ago, the object of his hatred, who had stolen from him, taken from him, spirited away the one woman for whom, more than any other in his life, Boppo had felt the connections of romantic love. He had never afterward allowed himself to feel so deeply, for fear of being plundered again.

Konstantinople announced his departure. He intended to lock himself up, he said, in a strong container and ship himself home. He hoped everyone had enjoyed the evening. This was a fine old house, he said, and a good cause, and he had enjoyed coming here and doing his magical tricks for everyone. Two young women still wearing their mismatched costumes, smiling their painted smiles, long-legged, prancing on high spiked heels, wheeled a foot-locker to the center of the stage. Boppo recognized it as an army foot-locker, but taller. Upended, its lid swung open like the door of a wardrobe closet.

Konstantinople stepped inside. The door was shut. The young women snapped into place several formidable locks, and one of the women invited members of the audience to step to the stage to examine the locker, the locks, to encircle it testing for trickery, and to speak to Konstantinople, whose voice called muffled from within to complain of the bad air. In his Turkish accent he said, "I was sure I asked for a window seat."

Somewhere, at some time of his life, this had happened to Boppo. He was certain of it. Years and years ago he had come with Ella to see Konstantinople do his magic, to see the man in the tailcoat, seen also repeatedly in Boppo's dreams. Or if he had not come with Ella One to Konstantinople's magic show he had gone with her somewhere to say goodby to Konstantinople, to see him off somewhere, to a railroad station, a bus station, and

Boppo had stood with Ella One in a state of tension, confusion, fear, and heat, like Lance beside him now.

"Goodby, Mr. Konstantinople," cried one of his young women. "Goodbye, maestro," and to the audience she said, "He is gone."

Yet the upended foot-locker remained onstage. It had not been wheeled away. How then was its occupant gone?

The shining, silver locks, snapped shut with such finality only a minute earlier, sprang open now, and the door of the foot-locker opened. A woman smartly dressed in a slack suit stepped forward. The shock of deception was stupendous. Boppo applauded. Everyone applauded. Even Lance applauded.

The woman was Ella—Ella One—Boppo's friend last seen thirty years ago when she christened him "Boppo" and disappeared from his sight almost forever. He knew her instantly. Her hair fell over her face. Her body he remembered, too, vivid and familiar, never so much known to him as imagined. They had skated together, swum together, danced together in the bright nights of their youth. He was a penniless young man. The applause ended. The magician would not reappear. His wife appeared instead, to thank her husband's audience for coming tonight in support of a cause in which she and her husband had always believed. Not violence, but love, she said. "To the cake," she said, with a graceful sweep of her arm. The lights altered, transforming the theater to the scene of a party, a reception, cakes baked in gentlemen's hats, and punch flowing.

Ella One descended from the stage. She approached Boppo. Apparently she had known he was here, and precisely where, and came toward him with her hands before her, palms upturned, and said his name in a voice as recent to his ear as if he had heard it yesterday. "Boppo. We're so glad you came."

"Tell me how he does them," Boppo said. "How did you get in that locker?" He embraced her. She smelled slightly of perspiration, as one might who had been enclosed even for the shortest time beneath hot lights in a sealed foot-locker. When he kissed her she abruptly turned her head, and his kiss concluded awkwardly somewhere below her ear. She glanced about, as if to see who had seen them. "Beware the jealous Turk," she said.

"Oh, come," said Boppo, holding her hands still. "I love his fez," he said.

"His what?"

"His fez. That hat he wears."

"Oh," said she, "is that what you call it? We always just called it a wraparound."

"And once I saw him in that tailcoat," Boppo said. "We saw him off somewhere. On a train?"

"Wear a tailcoat on a train?" She laughed at Boppo.

"At his wedding?"

"You weren't at our wedding," she said.

"Of course not," he said. "But somewhere I saw him in his tailcoat and his fez."

"Only in the show," she said. "It's his working clothes. He takes it off his income tax."

"Did we ever go to his show together?" Boppo asked. "You and I? I swear that I can remember."

"Remember what?" she asked. She released his hands. She appeared faintly anxious or guilty, and clearly she declined to discuss the past with Boppo.

"Everything," he said, although it was not precisely *remembering* he meant, not the past remembered but freshly seen, formed as if new in his mind, as if fresh evidence had been produced—the boy, the girl, the magician the boy had ignored. Everything came clear now. She had been lover to Konstantinople. She skated with Boppo by day in the park. That was how it had been, he knew now, drifting with Ella One to the punchbowl, where they were joined by Ella Two, who introduced herself as "Boppo's friend."

"Oh yes," said Ella One. "I liked your mother so much. She's awfully fine. I hope I'll see her."

"She'll be along," said Ella Two.

"Where is Lance?" Boppo asked.

"Gone," the younger Ella said. "He took off," she added. Swallowed by the night, not remaining even for the cold flowing punch, disappeared, gone from this house, this mansion, into the night, forever.

Hi, Bob!

Dear Bob,

Hi, Bob! When I say Hi, Bob, like that it makes me hear Carol, the girl that answers the phone in your office. She sits there in front of the elevator and the doors open and there you come. Hi, Bob!

Well, Hi, Bob, I want to tell you about a matter arising from the time you went on with Johnny. I'm going to be telling you man to man, Bob, how wrong you were. I'm not gloating, I'm not "rubbing it in," I'm not sneering "I told you so," I'm only saying you were dead wrong. I watched Johnny that night because you were scheduled, and there you were as real as you could be. If only I had my video recorder at that time I'd have recorded it, but we didn't have it until the money started rolling in. So I'm speaking from memory.

Bob, you and Johnny exchanged words and jokes awhile, and when that was over you started telling him about your checkbook situation. It was this. Every week or ten days or so you came down to the end of your check pad, right? All your checks were gone. There was nothing left but the deposit slips because you write more checks than you ever make deposits. Everybody does. So what you've got is deposit slips left over. It varies from bank to bank, but I understood perfectly what you were saying in principle.

After you wrote your last check you took and tore up the deposit slips and threw them away. For years and years you went on doing that. But all the time you were doing this you were thinking about yourself and saying, "Why am I tearing up these deposit slips before I throw them away? If anybody saw me I'd look like a fool. What use is anybody going to make of my old unused deposit slips, right?" You and Johnny were laughing. "Is somebody going to come along and fish in the wastebasket and take them out and put money in my account?"

You knew damn well they wouldn't. Everybody laughed when you mentioned it that way, and Johnny got his usual grin of appreciation on his face, and the studio audience broke up although they are never shown on the air. I wonder why.

So this was a lesson to you. Why should you waste your energy tearing up old deposit slips, right? Nobody is going to deposit money in your name, right? If anybody saw you they'd think you were a fool, right? Nobody but a fool would think some perfect stranger is going fishing for their deposit slips and deposit money in their account, right?

Well, wrong. I have to tell you what happened to me. It's not that I'm simply anxious to show you that you're wrong. I don't get some big charge out of saying to you, "I told you so." Quite the contrary, I like you and all the gang on your floor, Carol and Jerry the dentist and Dr. Bernard A. Tupperman and Howard your neighbor (the navigator), and I am particularly fond of Emily if you don't mind me saying so. My wife's name is Denise. It's only that on the subject of those deposit slips you were dead wrong, Bob, much as I am fond of you.

Not your fault. You couldn't have known. Chicago is miles from Phoenix. The first I noticed anything I said to Denise, "There's an error in our balance." At that time we just had one bank account, an interest-bearing checking account keeping an average daily balance of one hundred dollars if we were lucky at the Seven Cactus branch at 24th and McDowell. We opened it when we were married with money from wedding loot and still have it after more than five years.

"How much of an error?" she said. She really knew it might happen, but I didn't know she knew. I found out a long time later.

"One hundred and sixty dollars," I answered.

She sat straight up. "Oh my God," she said, "call them up right away." She lays on her back watching the tube unless something happens. When anything happens she sits straight up.

It was ten o'clock. How could I call them up right away? "Banks don't stay up all night," I said.

"We're going to be in a pack of trouble when the checks start bouncing," she said.

"The checks are not going to start bouncing," I said. I was playing it cool.

"They are going to start bouncing and mighty fast, too," she said, "and you better remember they charge nine dollars per check when they do." She always thinks we're in more trouble than we are. I let her squirm. I'm not the kind of a person that says "I told you so" at every opportunity, but once in awhile I'll let her go on hanging herself until at the last minute I'll spring the fact.

"There'll be no bouncing," I said.

"There's a hundred-and-sixty-dollar error," she said.

"But the error is in our favor," I said.

Right away her tune totally changed. "Don't tell them anything until they find out," she said, and she laid back down. "It's not like them to make an error in our favor of all people," she said.

"I'm certainly not calling them in the middle of the night," I said.

Hi, Bob!

"They'll find out soon enough," she said, "with all those computers and everything you better believe."

It was like a gift. It *was* a gift, one hundred and sixty dollars deposited in our account and no mistake. The statement showed five deposits. Ordinarily we made only two deposits twice a month, the first and the fifteenth, Denise's payday, my payday. That was the extent of it all, but here it was as plain as your nose. It had to be a mistake.

Well, Bob, suppose the bank made an error in your favor of one hundred and sixty dollars. How far would you exert yourself to call it to their attention? Tell the truth. Talk it over with the gang, Carol and Emily and Howard and the little doctor. I'll bet there's not one of them that wouldn't say to you exactly what I'm saying to you now, "I'd do like he did. I'd let the bank find the mistake for themselves. That's what they're paid for. I'm not going to let them make a sucker of me. A bank is a big institution and Seven Cactus bigger than all the rest, seventy-seven billion dollars in assets, three thousand offices in seven states, that's what they claim on TV. They weren't going to go under on account of the one hundred and sixty dollars they put in my account, were they? If they don't actually have those billions in assets they shouldn't be saying so."

I agree. I didn't mention it to anybody and Denise didn't, either. We went about our business and the bank went about theirs. You notice they didn't kill themselves. When you went in the bank you saw that nobody was suffering. With the extra hundred and sixty in our account we got to the end of the month better than usual. It was a rare sight seeing anything left over. There we were when all the bills were paid with eighty dollars left over.

"We don't have eighty dollars left over," Denise said. "We only have eighty dollars left over if you're looking at that hundred and sixty as ours to begin with. The true situation is we're not eighty over but eighty under."

"It's only an honest mistake," I said.

"Honest!" she said. "It's not honest at all. You know very well there's a hundred and sixty dollars in your account that doesn't belong to you because somebody else put them there. The *bank* put them there."

"How do you mean *my* account?" I said. "You're talking about *our* account. This hundred and sixty dollars doesn't belong to you, too. You're as guilty as I am."

"Under the law we're probably both guilty," she said.

"A wife cannot testify against her husband," I said.

"She can if she cares to," Denise said.

"Why would you care to?"

"I didn't say I would," she said. "Don't tell me anything more about it."

There was nothing to tell until after the middle of the month again, and when it came it was something. I came flying up the stairs with the mail and rushed into the apartment. "You'll never believe the latest," I said. She saw it was the statement in my hand.

"They found out," she said.

"Like hell they found out," I said. "Quite the opposite. We're overbalanced again."

"Are you sure it's again?" she said. "Are you sure it's not the same overbalance from before?"

"No, we are overbalanced six hundred dollars more now," I answered.

She sat up straight. "Let me see," she said, holding out her hand. I took her hand and kissed it before I put the statement in it. "I can't believe it," she said, although there it was, a deposit for six hundred dollars we never put in. She was forced to believe it. She was looking right at it. Denise is the most beautiful girl in the world.

What does six hundred dollars mean to you, Bob? The bank never got in touch with us about it and we never got in touch with it. I wonder if you blame us. We didn't blame ourselves. Let it ride, we thought, let's see what happens. What could happen? As far as I could see all that could happen was the bank would get in touch with us and inform us we were overbalanced and take it away. If it wasn't ours to begin with we wouldn't be any worse off if they took it away. Could they sue us? SEVEN CACTUS SUES LITTLE FELLOW AND THROWS HIM IN JAIL. How would that sound for the bank that advertises "the friendliest heart in the West" on TV? THROWS HIS WIFE IN JAIL WITH HIM, TOO. She was an accomplice and she knew it. She knew we were overbalanced. We both knew we were overbalanced.

We bought several items with the overbalance. We bought an extra telephone for one thing. We always wanted an extra phone and now we had one thanks to the overbalance. We set our sights on a video recorder and paid a chunk down and put it on layaway. All month we nibbled away on that six hundred dollars and when it was gone it was gone.

Suddenly we fell into the biggest overbalance we ever had before or since—the record, the all-time top, thirteen hundred dollars and ten cents, one thousand three hundred dollars and ten cents ($1,300.10) on the sixteenth of May. Beat it if you can, Bob. Do you believe me? You better believe because it is true.

This was not one single deposit like the others. It was three different deposits of seven hundred and fifty dollars, five hundred and fourteen dollars and ninety cents, and thirty-five dollars and twenty cents. Where did this come from? Denise cried for joy and danced around the room, but she was afraid, too. She stopped dancing suddenly and said, "Some way or another this is going to catch up with you."

"Denise," I answered, "come to your senses. If this catches up with me it's going to catch up with you, too, since this is a joint account, you know. Meanwhile let's do something with it that's not too careless and not too careful." We paid off the video recorder and we gave a big party for the car pool and for some people from Imago Industry and two neighbors from the building.

It was one of the greatest nights of my life. We moved the TV into the bedroom and hooked the recorder into it and it played all through the party. After the party we laid in bed all night watching the shows we would have missed. Denise and I talked all night about those thirteen hundred dollars and ten cents. Off and on she dozed off and dreamed about the Arizona lottery. "Everybody dreams they won the lottery," I said. In the car pool we're always telling our dreams.

"I don't dream I win it," Denise answered. "I just dream *about* it."

"Nobody we know ever won in the lottery," I said.

"It's better to just let the bank overbalance you than try for the lottery," she said. "It's a lot less work and nothing to buy. We have certainly earned more money through overbalancing these last three months than we'll ever earn in the lottery."

I wasn't so sure we *earned* it. She said *earned*. "You know what I mean," she said.

I thought we might have come to the end of it but we hadn't come to the end of it. In the statement in June we again overbalanced. It was two deposits but it didn't add up to much. They were small. One was for one hundred and fifteen dollars and fifteen cents and the other was for eighty-six dollars. It was something. You can't be ungrateful. I knew we were spoiled by the thirteen hundred dollars and ten cents in May. We would never see anything like May again. "Whatever amount it is," Denise said, "it's helping us make ends meet and that's what matters."

"You can say that again," I answered.

"We'll take what comes. Don't go wild."

"Easy does it," I said. "Don't press too hard. God knows where it's coming from."

"Somebody is rewarding us," she said.

"For what?"

She couldn't answer that. She didn't know and neither did I. I don't deserve to be rewarded much more than the next man, and she's in the same class as well. She's a good person and I'm not bad. We don't do bad things although we don't do many good things either, and there are a lot of people like us in the building and every place else. We're as normal as we can be. I go to work and return. Denise goes to work and returns.

At least that's what she always said and I had no reason to think she was lying and she had no reason to think I was. I never cheated on her. Sometimes the car pool agreed to stop for a beer, usually on Friday. Two or three times a year we had a shop party and everybody went. It was in the back room of a tavern not far from the shop attended by about twenty men and four women so there wasn't much opportunity for cheating even if you wanted to. I didn't want to. Things were fine with me.

They all kidded me, "Oh, you want to get home to the most beautiful girl in the world" because I once mentioned in the car pool Denise was the most beautiful girl in the world and they never forgot it. I didn't mind the car pool. I kind of enjoyed it. If I was tired I slept, if I cared to read the newspaper I read it, if I cared to join in the conversation I joined. The rule was take it or leave it. I could smoke or not smoke depending on the vote in the car. If we voted smoking I lit up and if we voted against smoking I didn't. So what?

One week out of every five I drove the pool in my big Merc. It's all very loose and rattles a lot but it gets you there, seating five people with ease depending on who. A lot of people laughed at it but when their cars broke down there was the Merc chugging along. It never failed the car pool once.

Denise hated the idea of the car pool. "You might as well be in jail as be in a car pool," she said. Imago Industry had several car pools riding out of our neighborhood but she never joined them. Four weeks in five she drove the Merc and the fifth week I needed it for the car pool she got a lift from a fellow at Imago driving a red Datsun 240z. If it was in good shape I'd have given a million for it.

After the money began to pile up she bought a little frosted lemon Mazda coupe and buzzed all over the valley. It made a sound like a bumblebee. She could weave in and out traffic without turning her head and park in places you'd drive right past in the Merc. She loved her Mazda.

I never told a soul about the extra deposits coming in from the bank. Sometimes I was sorry I even told Denise. She worried about them. "The bank is going to catch up with us," she said. "They can't miss with all those computers."

"You better believe," I said. "We've got computers that can pinpoint bomb a target four thousand miles away; you know we've got computers that can catch errors in a bank."

"Nevertheless," she said, "so far they haven't mentioned anything."

"We'll sit tight until they do," I answered.

"I'm sitting tight," she said.

July beat June and August beat July and September was the bonanza, the record, the all-time top in the number of deposits (four), although it did not beat May for total sum. Nothing ever beat May. We *averaged* four hundred and sixty-six dollars and eighty-five cents per month the first seven months, not a bad windfall at all when you consider it, is it, Bob? It was always deposited in the middle of the month, the 15th, the 16th, maybe the 17th. We wondered why but we didn't know and we didn't care. We were just spending it.

In September we got out of town, loading up the Merc, visiting Denise's folks in Flagstaff for several days, and another week we kept cool camping. One night Denise's father said, "Well, kids, how are things going in the money department?"

"*Very good,*" I answered in an enthusiastic voice, thinking to myself of all those extra deposits in September.

Denise didn't like what I said. "No better than ever," she said.

"Which is it?" her father said. "One of you says very good and the other says no better than ever. For a minute there I thought you might be making some progress in the money department."

"We're making ends meet," Denise said.

Hi, Bob!

"You can't ask a lot more than that," her father said. "And you kids have got just piles of friends so what is there to complain about? Never let the money department get you down. Never try and beat the system because it always beats you instead. Nobody asks any more than making ends meet."

However, the hard facts were we wouldn't have been making ends meet if we didn't have those deposits coming in, and the more we depended on the deposits the farther we stretched the ends.

My opinion was that we were going to be sorry for all this afterward. I'd rather let the system beat me and people laugh at me and call me a sucker than wind up behind bars. There were times when I felt the bank was going to find out any day they were overbalancing our account. We were going to be forced to come to terms with that situation any day sooner or later, and when you consider the computers I was afraid it was going to be sooner. I could see myself in deep trouble. I could see myself in jail. Incarcerated. No car. No Denise. I could see Denise in jail as an accomplice after the fact. We didn't even have a lawyer.

In October we were back in town. "Denise," I said one night, "don't you think it might be a good idea if we had a lawyer?"

She sat up. "What for?"

"Just in case," I answered.

"In case what?" she said, but she knew.

"In case we're apprehended with money in our account we know never belonged to us."

"Who does it belong to?" she asked. "If it doesn't belong to us can you give me the name of somebody it belongs to? Give me their name and I'll give it back."

"Some way it belongs to the bank," I said.

"Oh, poor little Seven Cactus National," she said. "If we give it to the bank who will they give it to? They'll say thank you and put it in their pocket if they even say thank you. *Have a nice day*, that's what they say. I have a lot nicer day whenever I see us overbalanced. What do you think the boys in your shop are going to say when you tell them the bank overbalanced you and you gave it all back? *Sucker, sucker*, that's what they'll say and laugh until they drop."

"It's making me nervous," I said.

"If we were in debt you'd be even more nervous," she said.

"I wouldn't be worried about going to jail," I said. "If you think a car pool is jail just wait until you see *jail*, Denise."

"Nobody's going to jail," she said.

But how could she be so sure?

When the December statement came in we could see our year-end income from deposits we never made.

Month	*Amount*	*Comments*
March–September	$3,267.92	Best single deposit, $1,300.10 Most deposits in any one month (4)
October	299.95	
November	177.74	
December	251.48	
Total	$3,997.09	Average monthly over-balance, $363.37

Hi, Bob! One day unbeknownst to Denise I decided I'd consult a lawyer. I didn't know any lawyers and I didn't know if I even knew anybody that knew a lawyer, but it turned out that Corwin in the car pool knew a lawyer and said he would get me his name and address and so forth. "What makes you think you want a lawyer?" Corwin said.

"To be on the safe side," I answered.

"Did you commit some sort of a crime?" he said.

"I don't know if I did or not," I answered.

"Tell us what you did and we'll tell you if you did," everybody in the car pool said, but I wouldn't tell them. I kept it to myself. The lawyer's name was Mr. Michelin, same name as the tires. "Come with your cash in your hand," he said.

Denise hit the ceiling. "Why are you so anxious to spoil a good thing?" she said. "You live in dread of going to jail for your crimes. Maybe you committed crimes but this isn't one of them. Who is this lawyer to your pal Corwin? Five minutes after you're out of the lawyer's office he'll be calling Corwin on the phone and they'll be having a great laugh together at your expense. *That sucker had a good thing going until he went and spilled it to the lawyer*. It'll be all over your shop, what a *fool* and a *sucker* you are. How are you going to like that?"

"Nevertheless I'm going," I said.

"How much is he going to charge you?" she said. I was surprised she didn't ask it first.

"One-ten," I answered.

"What can that mean?" she said. "One-ten what? I know you don't mean one dollar and ten cents."

"No," I answered, "by one-ten I mean one hundred and ten dollars."

"Did he give you any idea what one hundred and ten dollars covers? Does it cover the whole case from beginning to end?"

"It's one hundred and ten dollars an hour," I answered.

"I'm not going along," she said.

"I wasn't expecting you to go along," I said. "I'm going by myself."

"I mean I'm not going along *moneywise*," she said. "That money is half mine. I'm not pouring fifty-five dollars an hour down some lawyer's throat that might end up advising you to go and spill it to the bank. I love those overbalances. I'll miss them if they stop. Are you taking off from work to go see the lawyer? You're losing pay on top of the one hundred and ten dollars an hour. Where is this all going to end?"

"I'd rather be docked a couple of hours pay than end up in jail," I said. "It seems worth it to me."

"You can spend *your* money but not mine," she said. She was screaming at me.

"Even if you scream, Denise, I'm going to the lawyer. I've been thinking about it since before Christmas and I've made up my mind."

She suddenly stopped screaming and talked in a normal voice now. She knew what she wanted to do, and she knew all along. "I'm pulling out of the account," she said. She had been sizzling, steaming mad, but she was cool now. She wrote a check for half the balance of our old interest-bearing checking account and started up her own. "No hard feelings," she said, "but I'm just appalled at the idea of wasting a lot of money on a lawyer finding out something I don't really care to find out in the first place. You can go by yourself."

I paid the lawyer's secretary one hundred and ten dollars by check before I ever set eyes on the lawyer. She paperclipped my name to a folder and she asked me how I heard of him. I told her Corwin referred me, and the next thing I knew I was in the office with Mr. Michelin himself. He drives a Caddie. I asked him why he didn't use Michelin tires on his Caddie. This was after I knew him. He didn't smile. "I'm tired of hearing the connection between Michelin tires and Michelin me," he said.

I told him about the unusual deposits overbalancing our account. He breathed hard. He wore a white shirt wrinkling and unwrinkling as he breathed and his chest heaved in and out. I thought he was a big man but when he stood up I saw that he was only broad and short. He drank tons of water. He carried water in a thermos in his Caddie. He breathed in and out thinking over my problem. "Here's what we'll do," he finally said. "We'll write a perfectly legal letter explaining to the bank what has befallen you. This mystery money has drifted over in your account. You recognize the money is not your own. You feel guilty, remorseful, ashamed, and chagrined and recognize your obligation to return the sum to its rightful and proper owner."

"We don't have it to return any more," I said.

"I'm not saying we're returning the money," he said. "I'm not even saying we're sending the letter."

"Then what are you saying?" I said.

"I'm saying we're writing this letter and notarizing it and sealing it up and proving your good intentions pending legal advice. As soon as I've written it you and Denise come back and we'll sign it and notarize it."

"She won't come back," I said.

"From the sound of things your wife is not a cooperative girl," said Mr. Michelin. "You should advise her to protect herself with this letter, but of course if she doesn't want to do that we can't make her. Do you suppose she already knows the secret of how that money is getting there?"

"How could that be?"

"I don't know," he answered. "That's what I'm asking you. I don't know Denise or her habits or anything about her. All I know is she's the most beautiful girl in the world, and if that's true that's what could account for it. Somebody is being friendly to her."

"A lover?" I said.

"Anything you want," he said. "It could be anything from lover to a bank error. These computers are not by any means totally foolproof but then women aren't either."

I was in and out of his office in twenty minutes or less at five and a half dollars a minute if you can believe it, his fee being one hundred and ten dollars an hour *or fraction thereof*. They never tell you about the *fraction thereof* on the way in. Later it cost me another one hundred and ten dollers for the time it took Mr. Michelin to write the letter. We took it to the Notary and sealed it up and mailed it back to the law offices and he put it in his safe. He showed me the safe. It was a lot of money but I felt safer doing it. Being free and clear of jail relieved my mind.

After the first of the year the overbalances stopped and never started up again and I sorely missed them. That nice little sum of two-fifty-one-forty-eight in the middle of December was the last I ever saw. "Things are working better this way," Denise said.

They were working better for her but not for me. She bought that little frosted yellow Mazda. She drove twenty-eight miles round trip every day to and from Imago Industry and kept her Mazda in perfect condition and the tank full. Half a week after payday I was flat. One day when the utility bill came in I couldn't pay my half out of my checking. "Denise," I said, "I'm going to have to pass on the utility bill to you because I'm just plain flat broke."

Her answer came as a huge surprise to me. She was the sweetest thing in the world. When I told Mr. Michelin how sweet she was these days he said she was either receiving further overbalances or a lover. "OK, no sweat," she answered, "I'll take care of the utility bill. Hand it here."

"How do you account for the way you're in such fine spirits?" I said.

"Oh, I've got my ups and downs like anybody else," she answered. "Maybe right now I'm on an up."

"Maybe right now you've got a lover," I said.

She sat up. I could see that either I took her by surprise or indignation. I couldn't tell. "You've really got a farfetched imagination," she said. "It sounds to me like this might be some idea your one-hundred-and-ten-dollar lawyer put in your head. Is that where you heard it? From your lawyer? Who do you suggest my lover might be?"

"I don't know," I answered. "I don't know all your friends. I don't see you from morning to night. How do I know where you scoot around in your little frosted lemon Mazda all day?"

"I'm just a working stiff like you," she said. "I work at Imago. I go there every day. Call them and check. I don't lose pay for time off running to lawyers. Maybe that's why my balance is better than yours and I end up paying the utility bill."

"Let me see your statement," I said.

"Madness," she said.

"Why not?"

"Because I'm so overwhelmed with joy I could cry, hearing you think I have a lover. You have made me happier saying that than anything you could have said," kissing me and loving me. We made love beside the television. Did you ever think about that, Bob?—how many people might be making love and watching you on the TV at the same time? It's amazing.

Why was she flattered? Didn't she believe she was the most beautiful girl in the world? It wasn't like I said she was the most honest girl in the world because I didn't say that. If she was the most honest girl in the world she would have showed me her statement but she wouldn't. I didn't know what to think.

Hi, Bob! I'm getting there. What would you have thought if she refused to show you her statement? You'd have thought she must have something to hide and so did I. I started looking high and low all over the apartment for it. I looked every possible place. I didn't want to see anything I didn't want to see. All I wanted to see was her statement. I put everything back the way it was. I looked on top of everything and under everything and in between everything but I never found it.

Well, you know how things happen when you're least expecting them. I came back from playing racket ball with a fellow on the following Saturday morning and looked in the mailbox. It was mostly two envelopes from Seven Cactus National and I knew what they were. They were her statement in one and mine in the other. I was sweating from the racket ball but I didn't even go upstairs. I ran out of the building the way I came in and around the corner to the Circle K and phoned Mr. Michelin at his house and said, "A lucky break. Our statements came in the mail just this morning."

"Are they in window envelopes?" Mr. Michelin said. They were. "Tear hers open," he said. "Don't tear yours open. Hurry up, I can't wait, I'm dying of suspense."

I tore hers open. It showed five deposits for the current month. Two of them were her regular deposits from work and the other three looked like the old-fashioned overbalance deposits to me. "That's what they look like to me, too," said Mr. Michelin on the phone. They were dated the fifteenth and sixteenth again. "Oh, yes," he said, "those are the old overbalance dates. I'm glad we got our hands on this information. Now, take and open yours very carefully with a razor blade, and take your statement out and put hers in so the name shows through the window and glue it very neatly with some glue and when it dries zip it back in your mailbox. Houdini himself wouldn't know it was opened."

About ten minutes before seven in the morning on the fifteenth of the month I kissed Denise goodbye and went down and out of the building with my bag lunch in my hand. You would have thought it was any ordinary car-pool morning. Right on the dot of seven o'clock Mr. Michelin came by in his Caddie and I jumped in his Caddie and closed the door behind me as fast as I could. "Where is her car parked?" he said.

She was parked in the underground under our building. "Where does the underground come out?" he said. I pointed where it came out. "How long before she'll come out?" he said. In about five minutes she'd come out. She was a prompt person. He double-parked down the street. "Slump down low in the seat," he said.

Soon she came driving up out of the underground. She came buzzing past us in her little frosted lemon Mazda. "Well, there she was," I said.

Mr. Michelin didn't make any remark. "So that's the most beautiful girl in the world," he said. Once she turned the corner he hung a U-turn and followed her. "Now what will her approximate destination be?" he said.

"I don't know if she went to the bank yesterday," I answered.

"I asked you to ask her," he said.

"She wouldn't answer," I said. "She might be stopping at the branch at 24th and McDowell on the way to work. If not she might go on her lunch hour, or she might not go until after work."

For a minute she seemed to be slowing down for the branch at 24th and McDowell, but she seemed to change her mind. Maybe she thought it over. There was a line at the Nite 'n Day Machine and she must have thought she didn't have time. She sped up again and headed for the Freeway. "She really moves," Mr. Michelin said.

She really did. She wove in and out of the lanes, although she didn't seem to be gaining especially. Mr. Michelin drove one steady pace in the fast lane, when suddenly she decided she was getting off at Thomas. I couldn't understand why she'd be getting off once she got on. Mr. Michelin swerved across and barely made it off behind her. "She's trying to make up her mind about something," he said.

Soon we saw what she had in mind. It was the Seven Cactus National branch at Thomas and 19th with the friendliest heart in the West flying on the flagpole. It was hard to know what she was doing. "Keep down low," Mr. Michelin said. Denise parked in the lot and jumped out of her car in a hurry and walked at a fast pace to the Nite 'n Day Machine, but when she got there she didn't work the machine. She took a deposit slip and went back to the Mazda and drove off, and we drove out of the lot from the other direction and doubled back and continued following her.

Denise headed north on 19th now, past Indian School and on to Camelback to the 19th and Camelback branch of Seven Cactus with the heart-shaped flag flying in the air, where she jumped out of her car again and ran up to the Nite 'n Day Machine but did not bank. It was Thomas and 19th all over again. "Keep an eye on her closely," Mr. Michelin said, "and whatever you do keep down low." He was looking very puzzled and so was I. He poured himself cold water from his thermos bottle and he began to perspire through his white shirt as early in the morning as it was. "Why is she doing this?" he said. "Keep a closer eye on her than ever and figure out what she's up to."

"It doesn't make any more sense here than it made at 19th

and Thomas," I said. "It'll make sense, though, because Denise wouldn't be doing anything that didn't make sense."

"Then we've got to be keener than ever," Mr. Michelin said, following her down Camelback now and onto the Freeway and off again. She was driving to work now. No more branches. In the Imago Industry lot she hopped out of her car and walked very fast to the door of the plant. The last few steps she broke into a little run. She might have been a little late.

When the door closed behind Denise it suddenly occurred to me that we might now be waiting there all day until she quit work and came out again, and even then we didn't know if we'd find out anything more than we knew. "We will," said Mr. Michelin. "This is the day those overbalances show up on her statement. Either something will happen or it won't."

"Yes, and you're having it both ways," I said, "at a cost to me of one hundred and ten dollars an hour. At noon I'll owe you five hundred and fifty dollars. At three o'clock I'll owe you eight hundred and eighty dollars."

"Won't it be worth finding out at last what it's all about?" he said. "It's your decision." We were circling the Imago lot in his Caddie. "Which is it?"

"We'll wait," I said.

It was going to be a long day sitting doing nothing at one hundred and ten dollars an hour out of my pocket into the pocket of Mr. Michelin, Esquire. We played the radio. We read the newspaper. He showed me some card tricks. "Don't both of us read the newspaper at the same time," said Mr. Michelin. "One of us keep their eye on her Mazda at all times."

About half-past nine the city sweeper came by and the driver leaned out of the cab and said we better move the car or get swept. You couldn't understand what he said. He spoke Spanish. But we knew what he meant, and Mr. Michelin drove around the block and I guarded the space and he came back. About ten o'clock Mr. Michelin said, "I'm going to find a can in that station over there or I'm about to bust, so if she comes out whatever you do blow on this whistle as loud as you ever blew on a whistle." I took the whistle and polished it up with my handkerchief. Mr. Michelin became annoyed by this. "I don't have any sickness," he said, "so you don't have to polish the whistle up so hard." Maybe we were going to blow the whistle on Denise—*blow the whistle on her*—get it, Bob? Suppose she came out of the plant and I blew the whistle. She'd hear the whistle and look over and see me standing by a Caddie. Mr. Michelin knew it didn't make any sense but he wouldn't admit it. We were getting on each other's nerves. He took his thermos with him and strolled away looking for a can at the rate of one hundred and ten dollars an hour.

What in the world was I doing forking out that kind of money even if I had it? I'd be paying him off forever. For what? I had no guarantee we were going to find out anything more today than we knew since the overbalancing began. Soon he came back with his thermos all filled with cold water. "Well, yes we are," he said. "We already found out she went to two branches and grappled around in the paper supply in the Day 'n Nite Machines and drove away like the wind. Think about this with every ounce of your energy."

I gave him his whistle back and I went to the can myself in the Mobil station. When I returned to the car he was playing solitaire with himself in the back seat and looking over at the Mazda every few seconds. For awhile we took turns sitting on the curb in the shade of the car. It was the only shade there was and by eleven o'clock it was gone.

I had my lunch in a bag with me and I thought I'd eat it, but he had no lunch with him. "Go ahead," he said, "don't wait on ceremony." He started the motor and turned on the air conditioning. "Consider yourself in an air-conditioned restaurant," he said. The solitaire game was still laid out on the seat beside me. There I was, eating my lunch that Denise packed for me and spying on her at the same time. "Where will she go for lunch?" Mr. Michelin said.

"I don't know," I answered. "If she brought her own bag of lunch with her she'll eat in the plant. Or else she'll drive away for lunch."

But Mr. Michelin could not remember if she brought a brown bag lunch with her and neither could I. "Two of us didn't notice," he said. "You and I have just got to start noticing things better. We didn't notice closely enough what she did at those Nite 'n Day Machines."

Right then she came out.

"There she is," I said.

"Stay right there ducked down," he said. I was still in the back seat. "Uh-oh," said Mr. Michelin, "here come problems." A tall, athletic, well-dressed man came out of the plant right behind Denise. It was the fellow who used to drive her to work in the red Datsun 240z. I'd have given a million for that little car if it was in good shape. "That's her lover," I said. "I knew it." Yet I continued eating my lunch.

"Remember how I was the first one to tell you Denise had a lover," said Mr. Michelin. "Now maybe we're coming to the end of the mystery."

The tall, athletic fellow walked off and climbed in his Datsun. Denise started up her little Mazda and buzzed out of the lot with her lover right behind her, and Mr. Michelin followed, too, and I was still in the back seat eating my lunch. The solitaire cards flew all over the place. It all happened so fast.

"All right now," said Mr. Michelin, "don't let it happen so fast. Notice exactly what she does."

"Keep on her tail if you can," I said.

"Nobody ever got away from me," Mr. Michelin said. "Remain down low and notice everything."

I did. She was on 19th again heading north until she hung a left on Glendale. We thought she was heading for the Freeway again but she wasn't. Her lover never hung the left on Glendale. He continued north and may be going yet for all I know. She drove right over the Freeway into Glendale, looking for another branch of Seven Cactus. We passed two branches but she didn't want them. "Why one branch and not another?" Mr. Michelin said.

"I don't know," I answered. "But Denise has got some system going. She always does."

There was nobody between us now, and Mr. Michelin let himself fall back a distance. On the straight road clear of traffic the Caddie was too powerful for the little Mazda. "Let's notice everything," Mr. Michelin said.

At the corner of 51st and Glendale in Glendale she drove in to the Seven Cactus branch. That was the one she decided she wanted. "Why this branch and none of the others?" Mr. Michelin said.

We watched her as carefully as we could. Now that the bank was open Denise preferred the Bank-Thru line. She got on the line and turned her motor off. Every time she moved up a space she turned her motor off again and on again, but when she reached the Customer-Serv table she did not reach in and grapple around and take deposit slips out.

No, she put her hand in with papers in it and pulled her hand out *empty*, and when she reached the Bank Thru she drove right through. She did not come to make a deposit but for some other reason. "What other reason?" Mr. Michelin said.

"Just follow her and we'll see," I said. She drove from Glendale to Peoria and hung a left on Peoria into Peoria. Up ahead was another big flag flying "the friendliest heart in the West." "Get right in line behind her," I said. I crouched down a little and hid behind his head. She got on the line, turning her motor on and off each time she moved up. "She thinks she's saving gas," I said.

"She'd have saved more gas staying back there eating her lunch out of a bag in the plant," said Mr. Michelin.

She reached the Customer-Serv table. "See!" I said. I knew what she was doing. It came to me. "She's not taking anything out but putting papers in," I said, "so when you get to the Customer-Serv yourself reach in and grapple around and take out several deposit slips like you were about to make a deposit and I'll tell you what they are."

I was right. They were Denise's deposit slips with her name and address and phone number.

Well, now. Hi, Bob! Does it all begin to come back to you! I bet you know what she was doing, too, or can't you guess? You should be able to guess because she got the idea from you, Bob, that night when you went on with Johnny. When you came to the end of your check pad some deposit slips were left over, right? You tore them up and threw them away. You felt like a fool tearing them up. Was somebody going to come along and fish for your deposit slips and deposit money into your account? You and Johnny were laughing.

Well, Bob, Denise knew a thing or two herself. Nobody was going to fish for her deposit slips in the wastebasket but they might just fill out her deposit slips if they were right there in the Customer-Serv and if they were in a hurry on their lunch hour. It depends on where you put them, Bob, that's all. Denise knew where to put them. You didn't know because you didn't think about it, that's all. She's every bit as smart as she is beautiful.

"She's a crackerjack," said Mr. Michelin.

"We won't say anything to the outside world," I said.

"Of course not," said Mr. Michelin.

"Let's go and I'll buy you a beer," I said, "and you can drop me at the shop. I can still get in an afternoon's work." I folded over one of Denise's deposit slips and stuck it in my pocket. I surprised her with it that very night. She was amazed that I remembered that show with you and Johnny, Bob. She thought she was the only person alive that did. How will it all come out? The overbalances keep coming in month after month, but I guess if I write you the next letter from jail, Bob, you'll be able to guess how it came out. I hope not. I don't know. We'll wait and see, I guess. So long, Bob.

Titwillow

Think of the power of a word. Think of the little word "tit." Think of the inconvenience I caused my beloved counselor Uncle Arnie because I could not sing that little word as part of my role as the Lord High Executioner, in *The Mikado*, on a Saturday night at Camp Secor, on the lake of the same name, fifty years ago.

Uncle Arnie was my ideal, my hero, a tall, muscular, learned, athletic fellow who appeared to me to be the complete adult, but who must have been, when I was ten, not more than twenty; and who, one night, when I was fourteen, disappeared forever from my view into some region unknown to me and to everyone else connected with that heavenly camp. The night of his leaving was a mystery to me worthy of one of those frightening, irrational stories he read to us boys in our bungalows by the light of a flashlight. The bugling of *Taps* ended our day, its haunting notes drifting into the dark, echoing woods.

> Day is done,
> Gone the sun,

From the lake,
From the hills,
From the sky.
All is well,
Safely rest,
God is nigh.

That at least was Camp Secor's version of the words. But day was never done for Uncle Arnie. Almost before *Taps* died away he leaped from the doorway of our bungalow (our "bunk" as it was called), into the night for work or play. Where did he go? We boys in the dark speculated. He went to the Social Hall to build sets for Saturday night's play. He went to the Nature Hut to study Nature, for he was Nature Counselor as well as Drama Counselor.

Yet even greater excitement was possible, for Uncle Arnie often had "a girl," as we put it, some camper's visiting sister, some camper's visiting cousin, aunt, possibly even some camper's visiting mother. Could such things happen? Once, early in the evening, he came to our bungalow with a young woman, and here an amazing event occurred. Uncle Arnie intended to change from his camp clothes (a pair of shorts, a button-down shirt) to more formal clothes of the kind the counselors wore to town for the evening. *With the young woman right there in the bungalow Uncle Arnie changed his clothes.* True, her back was turned, she looked away. For a moment he was naked. Suppose she had turned and seen him so. How brave he was! How casually he flirted with disaster! I was breathless through the crisis.

At Camp Secor, through all the summers of the decade of the 1930s, Saturday night was Drama Night, the formal end to the most formal day of our week, which began with morning Services and was followed by Super Inspection. For Super Inspection we scoured our bunks and cleaned and improved our surroundings in preparation for the weekend visits of our parents. Our parents must see how clean we lived, how free our camp was of contamination, how healthy and pleasant everything was, and how abundant our diet, too.

Above all, our parents must see how safe we were. How about swimming? Were the lifeguards always on duty? Was the water too deep? How about in boats? Could the boats tip over? Was a counselor always in a boat with the boys? Where were the life-preservers? Could a boy become entangled by undergrowth under water? What about undertow? What about water moccasins? Was the doctor always on duty? Could everyone identify poison ivy?

For boys who liked to present plays there was plenty of work. I cared little enough for work—I was never good with tools—but I did love the tension of acting and the praise which often followed: "You were so wonderful in the part I completely forgot it was you." When I was in a play I learned my lines immediately and remembered them for months. I never needed to be cued or prompted. However, although I delivered my lines with perfect fidelity I really had no sense of the whole play. In this I was innocently deficient. I thought the trick of acting lay in memorizing lines. I had no knowledge of what was occurring when I was off-stage, no sense of connection between the actions I was performing and the motives of the other characters. I followed the director's instructions loyally, especially since the director was usually Uncle Arnie, but I never suspected that my actions were intended to reveal some sort of meaning, some idea, some viewpoint.

I played in many plays for Uncle Arnie. When, however, he cast me as the Lord High Executioner in *The Mikado*, an unprecedented problem arose. You will recall the lovely song sung by the Lord High Executioner. It begins—

> On a tree by a river a little tom-tit
>   Sang "Willow, titwillow, titwillow!"
> And I said to him, "Dicky-bird, why do you sit
>   Singing 'Willow, titwillow, titwillow'?
> "Is it weakness of intellect, birdie?" I cried,

"Or a rather tough worm in your little inside?"
With a shake of his poor little head he replied,
"Oh willow, titwillow, titwillow!"

I readily learned the words to the song, and I soon sang it passably with Uncle Arnie's coaching.

From the beginning, however, my body rebelled against my role as Lord High Executioner, singing the tit-willow song in my palace in the town of Titipu. The word "tit" was the problem for me. As a boy at camp I uttered every obscenity I knew, and yearned to know others. Obscenity may even have become a specialty for me. I went overboard. More than once, for excessive obscenity, some counselor only doing his duty forced me to wash out my mouth with soap. But that was only fair and proper—what was the fun of the foulest obscenities except that they were daring, dangerous, against the adult law?

However, obscenities uttered on the run, in the daring hours of the night, or in the midst of a heated game were somehow different from the word "tit" sung from a stage to a passive, waiting audience not only of campers and counselors, not only of fathers, but, above all, of mothers and sisters and cousins and aunts of my fellow-campers.

From the moment rehearsals began I knew I would never go through with the performance. It was never real to me. I could not permit it to happen. And yet, as the days went by I was unable to withdraw. Day by day I became more deeply committed to a role I would never play, and the greater Uncle Arnie's pleasure in my mastery of details the deeper my dejection. At last, several days before the scheduled day of our performance I begged Uncle Arnie to prepare himself for shattering news. "I can't play the part," I said. "I can't do it."

He saw that nothing he could say would change my mind. His own mind turned instantly to his problem. "You've stuck me with some decision," he said, but hardly had he said it than he had solved it.

Uncle Arnie played the role himself, while I sat guiltless with admiration watching his performance. The Lord High Executioner was a foot taller than everyone else, quite as if Gilbert and Sullivan demanded it that way. It was a superb, jolly time, the latest of a series of Saturday night triumphs for Uncle Arnie, to whom I confessed my regret at having abandoned the role. I saw how sterling I might have been. I saw why he had chosen me: Uncle Arnie six feet tall was funny, but I at five or less would have been doubly so. I would have brought down the roof of the Social Hall. And I saw at last how very little the word "tit" had mattered; it came and went like a vapor.

Uncle Arnie had been under pressure to learn in a few days the role he had never intended to play. Afterward he rested from his exertion, lying on his bed staring at the beams of our bunk. My admiration for him soared anew, and in that mood I confessed to him the fact he had never sought. "If you want to know why I pulled out of the part—" I began, but he stopped me. "I know why you did it," he said. "You quit because you couldn't sing the word 'tit'." He saw by my astonishment that he was right. How could he have known? "A little tit-willow told me," he said, and now he spoke to me unkindly, as he had never spoken to me, and never would again. "You were a damn stupid little shrimp," he said. "You could have been the star. The part was written for you."

In spite of my having failed him our relationship was unchanged, and I was never to fail him again, for I adored him, although I was yet to be the instrument of another crisis of his life and mine, from which I at least would never absolutely recover.

Everything I am I owe to camp. Maybe I exaggerate. But we exaggerated a lot in camp, told "tall tales" in the Western tradition. We had never been west of the Hudson.

We came to camp every July first on a ship of the fleet of the Hudson River Day Line. They were graceful, elegant, dignified, lordly white steamboats named for famous men of New York. *The Robert Fulton. The Henry Hudson. The DeWitt Clinton. The Peter Stuyvesant. The Alexander Hamilton. The Chauncey M. DePew.* Why were these men famous? I had no idea. Whoever they were they were of some distant tradition of Yankees, old settlers, Hudson River Valley men, founding families, of whom mine was not one. I was a second-and-a-half-generation American born in Mount Vernon, New York. My maternal grandparents were born in America. My paternal grandparents were born in Europe. So much for genealogy.

I boarded the steamboat in Yonkers, to the cheers of my fellow-campers, who had boarded in Manhattan. They were city boys. I was the rare suburban camper. It was no distinction of mine they were cheering. We cheered at every opportunity. We would spend much of our summer cheering one thing or another. Almost from the beginning we were hoarse. We cheered a boy for his birthday. We cheered him for returning from two days at the infirmary. We cheered every game or match. We cheered parents who bought us ice cream. At the end of August we cheered the future and vowed to return to camp next year.

Of all the campers, however, only I returned every year, all summer, every summer, through the decade of the 1930s. This record was equalled by only one other boy, although his circumstances were so special they must disqualify him: his name was Daniel Vronsky and his parents owned the camp. He was continually exposed to the sarcasm of the campers, whose lore it was that the Vronskys were stingy, frugal, "cheap tightwads." They watered the milk. They underpaid the counselors. The Vronskys were sensitive to these charges. One night—one Thursday night, for Thursday night was movie night—a boy named Zeke Rosenberg punctuated the film we were watching with loud, hyperbolic remarks free-associating events of the movie with the supposed miserliness of the Vronskys. Mrs. Vronsky, who was present, arrived at last at the end of her patience. She was a stout, nimble woman with a powerful but quavering voice, and she came sailing down the aisle between the rows of campers in the Social Hall, to deliver a clever phrase I was now hearing for the first time and heard ever afterward in her voice. "Zeke Rosenberg," she cried, "keep a civil tongue in your head." How marvelous, a civil tongue! And the idea that one's tongue was in one's head, not mouth! I grasped the figurative meaning of it all. It was the cleverest thing I had ever heard.

Years afterward, when camp was over forever and all the boys gone off to work or war, I met Danny Vronsky in an elevator in an office building in New York. Here was my opportunity to ask the question so long on my mind. "Do you know whatever became of Arnie?"

Danny appeared not to want to talk about camp, as if the memory evoked chagrin. He winced at the sour taste. One of the great experiences of my life had been the bane of his. "Everybody scattered to the wind," he said. "Nobody missed them."

"I'm thinking of Arnie specifically," I said. "I thought you might know. He left camp in a terrible hurry."

"Why?"

"That's what I don't know. I never understood it. I thought you'd be much more likely to know than I. He was fired."

"What for?"

"Don't you remember?"

"All I remember is Candy Sale," he said, smiling sheepishly. He stepped from the elevator.

Candy Sale. Poor Danny Vronsky was the unhappy guardian of Candy Sale, which occurred every second evening. Each camper was permitted six cents' worth. Danny strictly rationed us, passing to each of us one five-cent bar, one penny stick, while with the other hand he marked against our names our enlarging debt. It was the custom to revile him. "People as rich as the Vronskys," we boys argued, "could *give* candy away." This was as far as Uncle Arnie's lessons in socialist theory had taken us.

* * *

Boarding the great white ship named for a famous New York man, I sought first of all the face of Uncle Arnie. Year after year he, too, returned. Other boys besides me came because of his being there. He could, if he had wished, have lured twenty Secor boys to a rival camp, but once when I mentioned this to him he frowned in confusion. Opportunism was never his game. "Why would I do that?" he asked.

"For the money."

"Grow rich as a camp counselor," he said, amused, mulling it over. It was a new idea to him.

With Uncle Arnie we boys discussed the meaning of Hitler and the Nazis. Since Uncle Arnie tended to dramatize things he was accused by some parents and fellow-counselors of vivifying the danger of the Nazis. But through the decade of the 1930s the Nazis extended their lands and their power, confirming Uncle Arnie's most fearful accounts. While we boys were playing baseball at Camp Secor, swimming in the lake, cheering, acting in plays, studying Nature, feasting by campfires on salami and watermelon, reading Little Big Books, and hiking dusty country roads, Hitler on the other side of the ocean was planning to kill us. That we were often bad boys we knew, but not *that* bad.

My father paid one hundred and seventy-five dollars each summer to send me to camp. It was a fierce sum. I have heard that he committed himself to my camping when, one summer day in my sixth or seventh year, I had almost been struck by an automobile on the street near our house. But he may not have intended to commit himself for a whole decade. His income was about four thousand dollars a year, and I was not his only child.

No doubt my own enthusiasm was persuasive to him. I pitied the children of my neighborhood who, having missed camp, missed everything. Life without camp was unthinkable to me and I refused to think it. The year was summer, and all the rest was winter. Winter was parents, grandparents, school. Summer was the uninterrupted intensity of the intimate life of bungalow, dining hall, and the benign authority of Uncle Arnie. We who on the first day of every July were innocent boys, by the thirty-first day of August knew everything. Winter was school, but summer was *education*. Why does a prick go hard, eh? Did you ever ask yourself that? How would you know if you didn't hear it at camp from the Health Counselor? One summer when I came home from camp I said to my mother, "You never have to tell me anything again." Surprisingly, she knew what I meant. "Don't give me that book any more *Growing Up*," I said. We had a book on our shelves called *Growing Up*. When I asked a sexual question my mother often said, "It will tell you in *Growing Up*." Why girls had breasts. The idea behind pubic hair. The book had photographs, too, perhaps not very daring by modern standards. My *ultimata* I delivered to my mother as I debarked down the gangplank of the Hudson River Day Lines steamboat at Yonkers. "I know everything now, you don't have to tell me anything."

The Fourth of July came right away, featuring fireworks blown into the sky by counselors on a raft in the lake. As it was with many things at camp (as in prisons, too, I understand), good things came only as our reward for enduring bad things. Every clear pleasure must be preceded by a portion of education. The price of fireworks was Judge Dolph, Uncle Arnie's enemy. Judge Dolph's relationship to our camp was never explained to me, but as I piece it all together now, fifty years after the event, I see that he was the Vronskys' intellectual trouble-shooter, consultant, warning system. He may have been Mrs. Vronsky's cousin. He wore white shoes, white knickers, and a crisp white shirt with a black bow tie. His only other costume was his bathing trunks. He was about forty years old, by training a lawyer who afterward apparently mingled legal activities with illegal activities and was sent to the penitentiary, where he was photographed for the newspapers playing golf and smiling. We were at first expected to call him "Uncle Dolph," but that name never took, and in any case we hadn't much opportunity to address him. He came to camp on the Fourth of July to deliver his oration, once or twice in the weeks that followed, and again at the end of August for the Awards Banquet, where he said "a few words" and laughed, because he knew he could never limit himself to a few words.

His wife was Helen. Once we heard a rumor that she died, but I heard afterward that she had not—that she and Judge Dolph had become separated or divorced, a reality his family could not accommodate and so declared her dead. Death was Nature. Divorce implied failure. My mother, sitting with Helen once on the guesthouse porch, came away with the opinion that she was "forward . . . odd," viewing her, I think, as a woman who had abandoned her duty, or was prepared to. Helen wore daring bathing attire (a "two-piecer") and painted her toenails. When she talked, cigarette smoke poured from her mouth, as if her intention were not to make words but smoke. I forget anything she may ever have said except one sentence, which shocked me. When someone asked her how she was feeling today she replied, "I'm better, only farting up a storm." This was one of my first living hints (although we had discussed this often with Uncle Arnie) that women shared biology with men.

For a short time their son, Jerry, was a camper. He received special privileges, such as chocolate milk upon demand. I recall with a particular exactitude the two sentences he ever spoke to me. When I asked him for a small favor he replied, "Who was your nigger servant last year?" Once he walked from the dining hall with a piece of dessert in his hand, which he flung into the bushes exclaiming, "This tastes like pus from a dead nigger's ear." I sensed in him a sullenness which might at any moment turn to violence. I never saw him smile.

Judge Dolph's July Fourth oration was delivered to us boys at dusk beside our lake. Behind him, against the setting sun, the fireworks raft floated in readiness. Since his remarks from year to year varied very little he was easy prey for a boy-satirist named Billy Dubrow, who anticipated the Judge's figures of speech as they flowed forth. Billy evoked a good deal of stifled laughter. Our counselors called for silence and respect, but they, too, were amused, and found the Judge tiresome.

Judge Dolph's topic was the meaning of America and our duty toward the flag. He was specific in his affirmations, but for change of pace he bombarded us with rhetorical questions. "Is there a boy here who does not know his duty to our flag? Not here." Our duty to our flag was to keep it from touching the ground, to take it down from the flagpole in the event of a rainstorm and fold it neatly and stow it in a box provided for that purpose on the porch of Bunk Six. "Yes. But doesn't every boy here know that our duty to the flag is much more? For what does our flag represent?" Our flag represented freedom and opportunity. "And what boy here is not thrilled to read the Preamble to the American Constitution? Not now, but look into it the first chance you have." The flag meant that by working hard and saving our money we could become prosperous, build houses, own automobiles, and win the respect of the best people in America.

This I too believed, but more and more with greater refinement. Uncle Arnie, often skeptical, also believed in American opportunity, if not in Judge Dolph's terms then in his own. He did not object to Billy Dubrow's satirizing Judge Dolph's style or language, but he warned us against the mistake of rejecting good ideas on the grounds of their being presented by a bad speaker. Judge Dolph ended his speech as dusk turned to darkness. We cheered. At last came the fireworks.

Judge Dolph was that sort of person we boys called a privileged character and about whom we harbored mixed feelings. He parked his car on the guest-house lawn. He demanded meals at his convenience—the only man in camp more powerful than the chef.

He could not swim and was therefore restricted to the "crib," that enclosed space where the smaller campers swam until, as triumph succeeded triumph, they passed their "deep water" tests. Judge Dolph could, of course, have defied the Swimming Counselor and swum where he pleased, but his safety was a factor, and he understood at that level, if not at the level of principle, that men were safest who renounced privilege.

On several occasions, when Judge Dolph chose to cavort in the "crib," we campers were detained upon the hillside. He declined to share the waterfront with us. What an awkward sight he was! He thrashed and flailed, raising a geyser of water so high about him he might have been some sort of water-smashing machine of doubtful purpose. Yet he was unembarrassed by his ineptitude. When at last he emerged from the "crib" he was bold and defiant, snatching his towel from the hook and rubbing himself energetically, as if to say, "On dry land I move with confidence. Any great man might also be a bad swimmer. Real men are land animals. Anyone can swim. A fish can swim." Had he proved his greatness by exhibiting his power to keep seventy campers roasting in the sun? For certain summers of my life I saw Judge Dolph's defiant water-thrashing as the secret of his character. He flaunted his deficiency. He rubbed our noses in it. Afterward in life, when I saw in myself actions reminding me of Judge Dolph I paused to reconsider myself.

Sunday night was Campfire Night, equal in importance to Friday night (Services) or to Saturday night (Drama), for, although many of our parents had begun their journeys back to the city, others remained for the jollity and serenity of the campfire, for little roasted meats and sweets, and for slices of cold, dripping water-melon utterly satisfying. It was an occasion for the unity of voices, as at a moment of devotion, vespers. We sang solemnly, following the flight of sparks drifting aloft but almost instantly flickering out, as the stars themselves, we were given to understand, would someday flicker out—in a billion or a trillion years, but don't worry, not before the Awards Banquet. The firelogs crackled, and at their hearts a red intensity. Long before the evening ended the smallest of the campers—the group called Midgets—had so far advanced toward sleep that they were led away to bed, often followed down the trail by their mothers for one last farewell kiss. The counselor to the Midgets was for several years a man twice extraordinary—first because it seemed to me sensational that the tallest man in camp should be counselor to the smallest children; and second because he was a Gentile (Peter Kelly was his name) and thereby represented to me the buried ideal of the unity of Christian and Jew. My ideal assumed greater urgency for me, summer by summer, as events in the news magnified the terror of Nazi Germany.

Some campfires featured Indian rituals, dances and war cries. We wore feathers and head-dress, painted our skins, carried wooden hatchets, and danced around the fire. From my career as a campfire Indian I learned the word *emanate*: with a wooden stick bound at the end with a rag immersed in lighter-fluid I drew torch-fire from the campfire while announcing the following idea—"From you, O Great Spirit, all blessings *emanate,* like fire for my torch *emanates* from the great fire which is our campfire."

We were made aware, of course, that the Indian gods of Sunday were never to be confused with the true God we addressed on Friday night and Saturday morning. Our little toasted meats were kosher. Once again, especially with our parents present, the theme was safety. Nothing was left ambiguous. Indian gods were irregular gods. As soon as we stopped dancing we put our sweaters on. We were vigilantly supervised to prevent our poking out one another's eyes with flaming marshmallows.

For me, however, one Sunday night was disastrous. Apparently on this memorable night the plan was to review the events of the week. Our parents would hear in the campers' own voices about things we had been doing and learning, about little side trips we may have taken in the company of our counselors, discoveries we may have made, feats and achievements, skills acquired, records posted, and landmarks sighted. Representatives of each of the groups rose to report, beginning of course with the Midgets, before they tired. The Midgets amused us all with their inaudible innocence. Sophistication increased with volume. The Sophomores spoke, the Juniors spoke.

I, an Intermediate, had been chosen to speak for my group, which I eagerly did. Speaking, for me, at that time of my life was pleasant and easy. I was without self-consciousness as a speaker, feeling myself in control: nobody would try to force me to say "tit." Often, as I rattled along with some general plan in mind, I produced words or phrases which had been no part of my plan but which produced laughter or some other delighted response, and this in turn was extremely satisfying to me.

I rose. On similar occasions I spoke two, three, four minutes, and by the feel of things knew I had gone on long enough, and stopped. On this occasion, however, I was able to speak only one sentence. I never got farther. "Well," I began, "this week we caught a poisonous snake."

This uttered, I was halted by a voice out of the darkness, beyond the light of the campfire. I did not know whose voice it was. The voice was distorted by the speaker's rage. And out of the darkness the speaker hurled an accusation at me. "Don't be a little fibber," the speaker called. "You did not catch a poisonous snake." The speaker was Judge Dolph.

"Yes we did," I replied. "You can ask anybody." But I had in fact been caught in a small lie. I had not caught a poisonous snake. I had been witness to Harold Zinavoy's having caught a poisonous snake.

"He did not catch a poisonous snake," said Judge Dolph, shifting the direction of his address from me to the assembly as a whole, and especially to the parents of the campers. The Judge came forward toward the fire. He was dressed in white, a sweater draped across his shoulders, the arms of the sweater knotted across his chest. He had been about to leave camp for the city when my remark arrested him.

"Yes we did," I said.

"You did not catch a poisonous snake," said Judge Dolph.

"Harold Zinavoy caught it," I said. "We caught it and skinned it and dissected it."

"You did not," he cried. "You did not catch or skin or dissect or anything else a poisonous snake for the following reason." His voice now assumed the rhetorical posture of his Fourth of July oration. "I'm asking myself," said Judge Dolph, "do we have poisonous snakes in the vicinity of Camp Secor and my answer is no, we do not have and we have never had poisonous snakes. This is vouched for."

The snake was poison because we dissected it in the Nature Hut and compared its parts with the diagrams in Uncle Arnie's *Giant Book of Snakes*. We very clearly saw that the snake we had caught was identical to the snake in the book, and it was—or had been, until we killed it—poisonous. Of the facts of the case no doubt could exist.

"Therefore," Judge Dolph continued, "please explain to one and all present that the snake you caught was not poison, that we have no poison snakes in the woods."

"We did not catch it in the woods," I replied. "We caught it under Bunk Four." I could not have made a graver error. From the point of view of safety, Judge Dolph's theme of reassurance to the parents, a snake under Bunk Four was much more damaging to his argument than a snake in the woods. Around the campfire some parents seemed to be smiling at me. They seemed to be amused, and their amusement encouraged me to maintain my version of things. I knew that I was telling the truth, but I would easily have lied had I known the danger I was in. The faces of other parents were grimmer, suffering either for the tension of the moment or for the idea that there might be, after all, poisonous snakes under Bunk Four.

"No matter where it was caught it could not be poison," said Judge Dolph.

"It was poison in Uncle Arnie's book," I said.

"All very well," said Judge Dolph. "You may sit down now and where is Uncle Arnie. Uncle Arnie, please rise. Where are you?"

"Right here," said Uncle Arnie, but he did not rise upon command. He wore a white sailor cap he sometimes wore to train his hair. He was handsome, our all-around man, my own personal all time favorite counselor, our scholar, our actor, our athlete. At length he rose, as if his rising were independent of Judge Dolph's command.

"Uncle Arnie," said Judge Dolph, "we want you to tell everyone here the truth about this snake, where it was caught and who caught it and where did they take it and what did you find out about it."

Uncle Arnie spoke promptly and courteously. "The snake was poisonous," he said.

"I am sure you are mistaken," said Judge Dolph, as courteously as Uncle Arnie.

"I can show you in the book," Uncle Arnie said.

"Even the book might be mistaken," said the Judge.

"I'll get it," said Uncle Arnie.

"We don't need it," said Judge Dolph. "We don't need Uncle Arnie, either, who is never mistaken. Always right, so Uncle Arnie believes, Uncle Arnie the show-hogger playing the parts in all the shows the boys should have, stealing the juicy parts from the campers. Our Uncle Arnie." The Judge's case against Uncle Arnie had been building. "Uncle Arnie that sees German Nazis around every corner. Uncle Arnie with his theories of spreading the wealth all around is mistaken in this matter and has been mistaken in many other matters and done many things we disapprove."

"I have the book in the Nature Hut," said Uncle Arnie.

"Get it," said the Judge. Another charge against Uncle Arnie presented itself to the Judge's mind. "Uncle Arnie spends so much time in the Nature Hut we were wondering what kept his interest up so much there. We found out not long ago that Uncle

Arnie takes girls to the Nature Hut. If you want to know the truth about Uncle Arnie the truth is this. Uncle Arnie will not be with us any longer. Uncle Arnie has forfeited the right to our company." Judge Dolph deliberated whether to say more. Instead of speaking he seized the dangling sleeves of his sweater and yanked them hard, propelling himself from our company, striding in his whiteness into the night to his car parked on the guest-house lawn.

Uncle Arnie, too, disappeared. I thought he had gone to the Nature Hut for his *Giant Book of Snakes*. Although Judge Dolph had declared that Uncle Arnie would no longer be with us I had not understood this as a sentence to be carried out but as some sort of symbolic speech appropriate to Campfire Night, like an imprecation to the Indian gods. How could Judge Dolph banish Uncle Arnie from camp? Uncle Arnie *was* camp. Uncle Arnie was my reason for coming to camp. It was Uncle Arnie's face I sought as I walked up the gangplank of the steamboat at Yonkers—never Judge Dolph's: I did not think of Judge Dolph for a moment from one year's end to the next. How could Uncle Arnie have forfeited the right to our company? I knew he had not forfeited the right to *mine*.

But as the evening ended and the fire died and we sang our solemn anthem of devotion to these woods, these trees, this lake, our fellows, I knew that the worst was true. We had all heard of people being fired. This was real, impossible to believe and yet true, even as it was impossible to believe that Jews were being persecuted in Germany. Terrible things happened whether I believed them or not. Things ended. People died. Uncle Arnie would be gone from our bungalow when I returned there, and he would never return, neither tonight nor tomorrow nor next year.

In fact he was. He had disappeared. His shelf was bare. His locker was empty. His suitcase was gone. I ran in the dark up the hillside and through the meadow to the Nature Hut, but it was dark, and the door was locked. I ran to the Social Hall. It, too, was dark. On the road beside the guest house the parents were starting up their cars, calling goodbyes from car to car. Somebody's father smiled at me and clasped my shoulder affectionately and said, "You're the boy that caught the snake."

"Where's Uncle Arnie?" I asked.

He had just gone off in somebody's car. Gone where? To the city. "Where else?" somebody said. To the city. To oblivion. To eternity.

Flattery

One day very recently as we were settling down for class—we had not quite shut the door—a man walked in whose appearance was most unusual. The strangeness of his figure somewhat amused my students, although they were, of course, courteous and non-committal. Perhaps they thought this was some sort of university stunt, one of those experiments the people from Psychology carry out, creating a bizarre or unusual situation to test the responses of unsuspecting subjects.

The man wore coveralls of one piece, criss-crossed front and back with detachable straps fastened by bright, golden buttons. For shirt he wore the top of his winter underwear, clean, white, and worn. He was a tall, sun-browned farmer. He came forward to my lectern with his hand outstretched, and I took it, of course. He said, "You don't remember me, do you?" His teeth were bad.

"No," I said, "I'm sorry to say I don't remember you. I'd remember you if I could." His face was not at all familiar. Nothing about him was familiar to me. Nothing leaped at me out of the past. His speech was an ordinary accent, undoubtedly of the upper Midwest (I am no linguist), neither learned nor distinctly unlettered, except that now and again his grammar lapsed. But his vocabulary was full, as if he was one who read mainly old-fashioned eloquent books in solitude.

He was disappointed in me. He had known how unlikely it was that I would recognize him, and yet he had hoped I might. He had not yet sat. I had not yet asked him to. In his disappointment at my not recognizing him he turned for support to my class, as if they at least would share with him this clear sense of my deficiency. He set the record straight for them. "Your professor was my professor years and years ago in Wisconsin," he said, "before you were born," and he added—flattery perhaps—"and a damn good professor he was, too. He was the best. He changed our life. He tore up the place." His little speech must have struck him as likely to affect my memory in the way he desired, as if I would be delighted to interpret his flattery as proof. "Now do you remember me?" he asked.

"Not quite," I said. My class laughed. I had not meant it to.

His name was Robert Hehlme. He spelled it—not the "Robert," of course, but the "Hehlme"—observing me now with a slight smile. The spelling of his name would certainly supply the proof of our acquaintance; if not the spelling then the pronunciation: his name was to be pronounced "hem" as in sewing. "She sewed a new hem on her dress," he said, clarifying the sound of his name as he had no doubt clarified it ten thousand times. "How about now?"

"Still not quite," I said.

"Not even a little?" he asked. His smile was gone, and he turned again to the class for support. Certainly the class would share his sense of my unreason. They would know my fallibility. But in fact they failed him. They were slow to take sides. They were waiting to see.

"I wish I did," I said. "I would if I could."

"I was in your freshman class," he said.

I was evasive. "Yes, it would have had to be a freshman class because that was all I taught when I was there," I said. "Freshmen."

"I suppose you don't teach freshmen any more," said Robert Hehlme. "These don't look like freshmen to me."

My students were gratified not to look like freshmen, perhaps flattered a little to be seen as so indisputably mature, as I had been a bit flattered, I suspect, to be seen as a damn good professor. The best. It wasn't the kind of professor I now was—I no longer tore up the place—but it offered my students the enlarging vision of someone I had once been, gave them a broadened reality for me, eye-witness proof of my past.

A student asked Robert Hehlme, "What grade did you get?"

Robert was taken a little by surprise. He had not expected to become engaged in a dialogue with the class, and he looked at me for permission to reply. "I got an A," he said to the class. "I was nothing but a straight-A student in everything."

Why then was he in coveralls and underwear top? Scuffed work shoes? (No socks.) Why were his teeth so bad?

He smelled of straw. He was a hayseed. "Robert," I said, "if you'd like to have a seat we'd be happy to have you." He would be pleased to sit, he said. He sat among the students, his long legs stretched before him. "What are we talking about today?" he asked.

"I don't know," I said, "we'll soon find out."

My remark made him gleeful. Once more he addressed the class, turning in his seat to face the students, slapping his hands together, applauding me, in fact, for my clever little speech. "That's just the way he always did," he exclaimed. "He'll never say right out what we're talking about. 'We'll soon find out'—that's a good one, that's our professor all right."

I'm not sure I was happy to think I was doing things today exactly as I had done them thirty years before. What was it I did anyway? I started some place with the intention of ending some place, but where we'd go between the beginning and the end remained to be seen. I tried to keep it open. We'd go where the talk led.

We were talking today about *Paul's Case*. We had talked about it thirty years before, too. Robert said he remembered it. "But I can't say I remember much about it," he added. "I do remember something. Isn't there a part in there where the boy was expelled from school?" Yes, for a thirty-year memory that was close enough. Robert Hehlme had been impressed by Paul's having been expelled from school. Had Robert himself been expelled from school? Was that it? What made me think so? Or if not from school from something else? This now seemed probable to me—that Robert was an outcast, that he had been expelled from school, from society, from the common life, that he had become a lone traveler, a man in coveralls who could have comfortably belonged if only he had been comfortable belonging. He was ill at ease, nervous, out of place generally, as he was out of place here in my classroom. He was a large, awkward man in coveralls, among students half his age.

"You have a fabulous memory," I said. "Paul was expelled, yes. What else do you remember from the story?"

"He stole some money," Robert replied. "And I remember another thing, too—a woman wrote that story. . . ."

"Willa Cather."

"I couldn't remember her name," Robert said. "I should have read it before class, but I forgot the assignment." He laughed at his own wit. A student passed the text to him, which Robert held at arm's length. He was extremely far-sighted. He had neglected his eyes, as he had neglected his teeth.

"I'm afraid I lost my specs," he said, returning the text to the student. "That's what I came to talk to you about."

"To talk to me?" I asked. "About what?"

"I lost everything," he said. "I was robbed down to the last penny. Totally cleaned out."

Of course, a class loves this sort of thing, an interruption, a diversion, a digression, and so do I, although I like to give the appearance of resisting. Often in class, at this hour, in the waning afternoon, my vision of bliss is the inside of my automobile—I am driving home, I see ahead my destination, my liquor cabinet, my refrigerator, cubes of ice.

My students were keen to hear about Robert's being robbed. They, too, had stories to tell. Their quarters were always being broken into; valuable hardware was always being stolen—speaker systems, computers, television sets—and so we turned for the moment from Paul's interesting, immortal case to occasions of our own having been robbed, theories of robbery. I had myself never been robbed.

"The way it happened," said Robert, "was like this. Do you mind if I tell them how it happened? I don't want to interrupt."

"No," I said, "tell," as if we had not already interrupted ourselves beyond recall.

"I'll give you the basic circumstance," he said. "How'll that be? I might give you some background first." He began, then, with background. He was a bachelor farmer in North Dakota, from a town called Bjork, which could be found on most maps. Bjork lay between Bismarck and Minot on the Missouri River. There he had lived all his life except, he said, during a period of military service in Korea. He raised wheat and cattle. He told us the number of acres of his wheat, the number of head of his cattle, and the number of buildings on his farm, and their uses.

For me it all had a prosperous sound. Every winter he traveled. "I'll go one year to Florida," he told us, "and the next to California."

"Glorious," I said, "to be able to travel in the winter. But I thought there was always work to do on a farm in the winter. Don't you mend fences and build things and tend to ailing cattle in the winter?"

He was a little disdainful of my ignorance. Flatly he said, "No, there's nothing to do on my farm in the winter." But he thought then that he might as well tell me the whole truth, immodest as it was. "I've got squadrons of help to work my farm in the winter," he said. "Lots of people lay off their help in the winter, but I never did that once I could afford not to. I don't think it's right, do you, to lay people off in the winter that gave you their labor in the summer?"

Some students applauded. Good for him. He was not only prosperous but humane, kind, a benefactor. "So I go south," he continued. "This year I came here. I don't know why. I just thought I'd stop over on the way to California, and I'm sorry now, although it's giving me," he said, addressing the class, "a chance to see my old professor again. He was a great influence on my life." To me he said directly, to make it official, "You were a great influence on my life."

How could that have been? I made light of it. "I know nothing of farming," I said. "I don't know a cow from a haystack."

"You taught me better things than that. Anybody can learn to run a farm. What you taught me was mellowness of mind. I always meant to thank you for it. Many's the time I was on the verge of sitting down and writing you a letter. I apologize for never doing it."

"How were you robbed?" a student asked.

"Of how much?" another asked.

"How was I robbed? I'll tell you." Robert rose from his chair to face the class. Old-fashioned students sometimes rise for their summing-up, often for speeches or reports they have prepared before class. "I don't know the name of it," he told us, "but it's a little bit of a crummy cafeteria downtown. I'll confess I don't mind eating in crummy cafeterias. I'm used to them. It saves me the price of a sitting-down lunch with a waitress in a business man's place, so sometimes there's something cheap or too frugal about me. This wasn't a fancy place at all, a tray, a napkin, some pieces of silver, a glass of lukewarm water in a dirty glass, just move along and select your food. It's good enough to hold you till you get to a real restaurant. I loaded my food on my tray and I pushed it along to the cash register. When I got toward the cash register I took out my wallet and put it down on the tray with my food. Maybe for a second or two I looked away. When I got to the cash register it was gone."

Of course we could see exactly how it had happened. It was perfectly clear. "I'm always trying to remind myself to keep my hand on my wallet." I said. "Sometimes I forget. But my wallet has never been stolen."

"You've been lucky," he said.

"What did you do?" a student asked.

"Do how?"

"Did you report it?"

"Report it to who?"

"To the police?"

"What do the police know?" Robert accepted his loss. Nothing could be done. Loss was in the nature of things. (Was this the lovely mellowness of mind I had taught him?) His money was gone. His wallet was gone. His cards of identity were gone. His task was not to report it, to wait upon the police, who, in any case, could do nothing, but somehow to put himself together again and get on his way. "I hope at least you reported your credit cards," a student said.

"I've never had credit cards. I travel cash only."

"If you travel with cash," the student said, "you're done for. You must have had a big wad of cash in your pocket and somebody laid low for it."

"That was the case," said Robert.

"How much do you suppose you had in your wallet?" a student asked.

"I don't suppose," Robert said. "I know."

"How much?"

He looked at me. Should he tell them? Was it proper? Why not? He could tell them or not, as he wished. "Something over thirty-five hundred dollars," he said. Several of us whistled between our teeth.

* * *

After class Robert returned with me to my office. I was eager for my automobile, my house, my drink. I was thirsty. In my office I sat. I had been on my feet for six hours. I did not invite Robert to sit, but he appeared, in any case, absorbed by the books on my shelf, whose titles he read far-sighted at a distance, backward leaning, turning at length from the books without comment, as if he could approve—nothing wonderful, merely sufficient. "Professor," he said, "I want you to know I'm just as embarrassed about this as you."

"Embarrassed about what?" I asked, but I knew. He would want to borrow money.

"About losing my money," he said.

"Well, it wasn't your fault. These things can happen to anybody."

"I should have known better. It was dumb, putting my wallet down like that. How stupid can a person be? Now what I'm wondering is this," he said, "can you lend me a sum?"

A sum. What sum? I took a figure into my head. He might require a day or two to get money from home. I thought a man could easily live for a day or two on fifty dollars. I took fifty dollars into my head.

"I think five hundred will be enough," he said.

"I couldn't lend you five hundred dollars," I replied. "I don't have it." Since I do not readily or glibly lie the swiftness of my reply amazed me.

Robert, too, was amazed. "You don't have five hundred dollars," he said. He could not believe it. And why should he have believed it? He knew enough of the world to know the probabilities. "I thought I'd take an airplane," he said. "Fly," he added, as if I didn't know what an airplane was. "Fly home. I've blew my winter. I guess it serves me right."

"Someone could send you money from home," I said.

"There's nobody I'd want to confide in," he answered.

"Your bank?"

"I'd rather not."

I did not ask him why. He had presented Bjork, North Dakota, to us as a small city in which everyone was more or less known to everyone else, and I was moved by the simplicity of his "I'd rather not," the delicacy of it, his assertion of something a man of my learned sophistication ought to be able to share—that in a moment of stupid miserliness he had lost thirty-five hundred dollars in a cheap cafeteria to which he had gone to save the price of a better lunch. He did not really care to publicize those facts to the folks back home. He sighed and sat. I wanted to go home. I foresaw a long delay in our getting out of my office. This felt like the beginning of one of my tormented problem-solving student conferences. The hour was wrong.

And I was chagrined by my callousness. Why shouldn't I lend him five hundred dollars to extricate himself from a scrape? Think how many people had loaned me money to help me along over the years. It was my tone I didn't like, my poormouth lie, as if his demand upon me were less honorable than my demands on other people, as if I were superior to him.

"Fifty can't help," he said. It was clear to me that if I handed him fifty dollars he would not take it. He expressed his disappointment. "I had the idea you'd do it for me," he said.

"I'll do fifty," I said, rising to leave, imagining my telling this tale to my wife in an hour or less, my drink, my body's unwinding.

He was dismayed. His memory of me was of a man of compassion, but the man of compassion had failed him, and he viewed me with pity, sympathy: he, not I, was the man of compassion now. The loss was mine. Remorse was his. His eyes glistened with grief or regret at this bad news of the death of my soul.

I wrote him a check for five hundred dollars. It was not a large sum for me. Nor was it small. My wife would wince. Even as I wrote the check I winced.

Robert read my check at arm's length, swiftly. His arms were almost too short for his far-sightedness. Where were his eyeglasses? They, too, had been stolen. "I thought only your wallet was stolen," I said.

"The specs were in the wallet," he replied.

"Eyeglasses in a wallet?"

"They're just little fold-up specs for reading," he said. "I don't need them walking around. I'm the most far-sighted man you'll ever meet."

Robert mentioned a small problem. In a strange city, without identification, he would have a great deal of difficulty cashing my check. The problem was easily solved. I telephoned the university cashier, who had been about to close his office, but who agreed to remain open for me. He urged me to come promptly. Robert and I walked briskly across the campus. My friend the cashier had, in fact, gone home by the time we arrived, but he had left behind an assistant waiting specifically for me, in his hand a little package already prepared, of fifties and twenties, which he counted out for us in the nimble-fingered way of a young man whose business is cash.

Rather more carelessly than I'd have done, Robert slipped his new money into his coveralls pocket. That seemed to me an unsafe way to carry it, but I said nothing, out of the sense that if I have performed a favor for someone I ought not then to instruct him in anything. His debt has already humbled him.

In my office Robert had promised to repay the money in a week, but, having done some calculation, he now asked me whether ten days would be all right. "I know I said a week," he said.

"Ten days would be perfect," I said.

It was dusk. We walked from the cashier's office to a street-corner, where students waited. "I'll grab a bus," Robert said. I had no idea which bus one grabbed. I had not ridden a city bus in years. One thing I knew, however—the driver was not likely to change a twenty-dollar bill for fare. "Nor even a fifty," I said.

Robert smiled at his old professor's humorous way of saying these things. "It's all right," he said, "I'll negotiate it ," and when his bus arrived he climbed aboard, scooping dollar bills from the lateral pocket of his coveralls. But he had led us to believe he had been robbed "down to the last penny," that he had been, as he said, "totally cleaned out."

To my car, to my house, to my refreshment. I reviewed for my wife in some detail (about as I have told it here) the afternoon's event, the appearance after so many years of my one-time student Robert Hehlme, and the things that passed between us. I asked her if she remembered the name. She considered the name for awhile. "All names are vaguely familiar," she said. "I don't have a face to go with it, either."

"If you come up with a face," I said, "give it ruined teeth. Truly neglected teeth."

"You'd think a prosperous farmer would have gone to the dentist," she said.

"Some people let their teeth rot," I said.

"Somebody so neglectful of his teeth isn't likely to remember to send you your five hundred dollars," said my wife.

So you see it somewhat mattered to her. Notice how she said it—*your* five hundred dollars; *mine*—by which she meant to emphasize not that the money was mine but that the foolishness was mine, the absurdity, and above all my susceptibility to flattery. "Into your class walks this bum," said my wife, "this itinerant tramp, having located this dear old professor from years ago, thinking to himself, 'Boy, can I con this old guy, give him the old dependable line what a fabulous teacher he was back East, what an inspiration he was to all us young people just starting out in life, filling us with all those inspiring feelings about life.' And what did it inspire him to do? It inspired him to hit the road like Jack Kerouac. That was the literature he learned from you, if he learned anything from you. . . ."

"He may not even have been my student at all," I said. "How do I really know?"

"He sounded like it," she said. "He knew that story—the Cather story. He knew your classroom style. Big successful deals these protégés of yours. 'It's not that I'm a bum, it's only that I look like a bum robbed of my fortune in a downtown cafeteria whose name I can't remember.' Sweetheart," said my wife, "that's what you call a North Dakota snow job."

Perhaps she was right. "In a week or ten days we'll know," I said. I mixed another drink. It was one more drink than I usually drink.

"What will we know?"

"We'll know whether we'll get our money back."

"I look at it two ways," my wife said, cooled by her vehemence. "I wouldn't be surprised if he pays you back and I wouldn't be surprised if he doesn't. How about dinner?"

"Why should I wait?" I said, carrying my drink to the telephone. I placed a call to the chief of police of Bjork, North Dakota. He had gone home to dinner. I reached him at home, where he, too, was drinking a drink before dinner. I toasted him. "Sir," I said, "I'll take as little of your time as possible."

"That's all right," he said. "Don't hurry."

"I'm calling to inquire about a resident of Bjork named Robert Hehlme." The chief did not reply. I spelled the name. I pronounced it perfectly: "hem" as in "She sewed a new hem on her dress."

"I can't say the name's familiar," said the police chief of Bjork. "Or the dress."

"I understand he's a big farmer up there," I said.

"I'm questioning that," said the chief. "I'd know him if he was."

"You know everyone in Bjork," I said.

"Just about."

"This is Bjork," I asked, "on the Missouri River between Bismarck and Minot? The farmers raise wheat."

"The farmers mostly raise hell," he said.

"Could he be a farmer," I asked, "but just not as prosperous as he says?"

"Not in Bjork," said the chief, "because I've been chief eighteen years and never heard of your man."

"This is Bjork," I asked. "Am I right?"

"Bjork, North Dakota," said the chief.

"Could there be a Bjork, South Dakota?" I asked.

"Not between Minot and Bismarck on the Missouri River." The chief quickly guessed that I had come to the end of my inquiry. "It's nice of you to call," he said. "Call again if you think of anything more. Enjoy your dinner."

"I will," I said. "You too."

He heard the ice in my glass. "Cheers," he said.

From the Desk of the Troublesome Editor

FROM THE DESK OF
MATT FINKELSTEIN
EDITOR, SPECIAL PROJECTS
Apthorp House

Re: Chronicum's manuscript

Dear Chron,

I'm really awfully sorry not to have been back to you sooner with reactions and responses to your manuscript, but I have been under a lot of pressure here. My secretary called in sick most of last week. I don't know if she was sick or just disgusted. And we have been having more tense, stressful meetings in the house than ever before. Last evening, as everybody was on the verge of going home, Frank came roaring through the corridors crying out, "We're going to come up with a title if we have to be here all night," which we very nearly were. We who were dressed to leave at six o'clock ended up sitting around in our hats and coats until midnight, starving and nodding.

You may be interested to know the title we came up with: *Testament*. It was a kind of compromise, not very inspired, but it's a lot better than some of the awful stuff a lot of people kept coming up with, and Frank and Francine like it because it has that Michener single-word-blockbuster-title sound to it—*Centennial . . . Chesapeake . . . Hawaii . . . Poland . . . Texas . . . Iberia . . . Sayonara . . . Space.*

But I must bravely get on here with the essentially disappointing news I have for you. I proceed, as you will appreciate, with all my humblest assertions of deference to your talent, and to some extent my astonishment at my arrogance in criticizing your work at all. Still, that's what I'm paid for and you always take it so well—you write, I scream, you rewrite, I stand amazed, and everybody ends up happy.

Some of the writers have been coming in with some challenging work, but you may take whatever comfort you can from the fact that none of them, any more than you, has done the job on the first try.

I think the problem with your book at this point is both *structural* and *substantive*. I mean to say that it lacks, on one hand, narrative, thrust, drive; and that it lacks, on the other hand, a satisfying moral, lesson, philosophy. In the subtlest sense, it doesn't speak very well either for the Jews or for mankind. It seems only to say to me, "He who lives by the sword dies by the sword," which I know is not the message you intend, for you are an optimist about man's chances, as I am.

Let's begin with *structure*. Tomorrow.

My secretary says I unfairly satirized the Apthorps yesterday; that what they have in mind is a lasting work; that this Volume is the major project of their lives. A couple of years ago in Francine's prospectus this was not to be a Volume but a series of books. Later it was thought of as a single volume which would be "the biggest and most distinguished of its year." Now they are thinking of it as the biggest book of the decade. Frank sees people curling up with it in hotels with *People* and *The National Enquirer*. A year ago or more when they announced at a meeting that it was to be a Volume instead of a series I said, "It'll have to be on damn thin paper." This made everybody laugh except Frank and Francine. I saw how serious they were and I don't joke about it any more.

Structure. I am sure I'm the last person in the world who ought to be so rash as to tell *you* about structure, or what makes a book work, but as I read along in your manuscript I found myself asking myself, "Why am I reading this?" I had better be able to give myself a good answer or we are in trouble.

Your manuscript should be drawing me forward. But nothing seems to be at stake. I see great high points of narrative, landmarks, peaks you want to reach (and will), but for the moment things are mapped out rather than written, sketched rather than painted. You have a reputation to uphold. We who know your reputation know that your strategy always leads us to satisfying heights. In the present book, however (that is to say, in the present *draft*), some of your digressions lead to dead ends; or the opposite is true—some of your endings have no beginnings. Now and then your climaxes, instead of augmenting the ecstacy of suspense, trail away, as if you have forgotten your plan.

You sometimes interrupt yourself. But for interruption to be effective the writer must have engaged the reader in a plan of action the reader is powerless to abandon; alas, you have not always done this. You interrupt your own interruptions. Bill Gibson once offered me a witty small sentence so durable I have used it for years: "You can't interrupt nothing." Sometimes you intrigue me with the promise of a story, but you distract me by not continuing with it. Please dispose of your abortions. For example, what about the story of Sheshan and Jarha in Chap 2? "Sheshan had no sons, only daughters. He had an Egyptian slave Jarha, to whom Sheshan gave his daughter in marriage." So embryonic is this suggestion you don't even name Sheshan's daughter. In Chap 5 Reuben was deprived of his birthright because he "violated his father's couch." We hear no more. (I'm just mentioning these passages as suggestions.) Perhaps more tantalizing than any other is that moment right at the end of Chap 16 when we encounter Saul's daughter Michal, at the very moment of David's triumph, standing at the window. "Now as the ark of the covenant of Yahweh entered the Citadel of David, Michal the daughter of Saul was watching from the window and saw King David dancing and exultant; and she despised him in her heart." What does Michal know about David that we don't know? We never see her again.

Let's go on. From Word One of the manuscript my flag goes up. "Adam." You're beginning your tale with Adam, which might be suitable as a brief refresher reference to events which have gone before, a little like Alistair Cooke's opening remarks on Masterpiece Theater, but instead of your getting in and out of that moment with brevity you give us *nine chapters of genealogy*. I just honestly and truly can't believe, Chron, that any writer, however fine, however confident he may be of his/her waiting public, can risk the loyalty of his reader with *nine chapters of genealogy* while he is warming up to his story.

At this point, however, I also have a crucial *substantive* question. This goes to the heart of things, to the whole mortal question of mankind, the Jews, and living by the sword, which I mentioned yesterday in this now somewhat lengthening letter. I mean *principle*. I mean, I speculate that this long indulgence of yours into the many generations of your genealogy is intended to show the reader the purity of the Jews. And yet, in my opinion, racial purity can scarcely be a goal we ought to care about. To the extent that we celebrate such a thing as racial purity we celebrate the very lore which has always been the battle-cry of those who would kill us—they are pure and we are not. In our own century the Nazi example is the obvious one, but not the only one, and our object ought to be to rise above ignorance, to see the races of the world as one race, as they fundamentally are. In Chap 17 you have David asking God rhetorically, "Is there another people on earth like your people Israel. . . ." Yes, David, there are other people on earth like Israel, more people like Israel than unlike Israel, various colors, various tongues, but basically one. Our safety—the safety of the world—depends upon our raising nationalism and jingoism to universal appreciation. We are required to celebrate not purity but principle. I remember when Jackie Robinson died somebody in the press asked Roger Kahn what Robinson had done for his race. Roger replied, "His race was humanity, and he did a great deal for us."

Well, I understand very well this genealogical compulsion of yours. It's an old familiar habit and I don't worry about it—you're supporting your story while you're organizing your tools, you're stalling, you're whistling while you're thinking. It's your scaffolding. Then when you get your story up you take your scaffolding down. But there's work, work, work. Don't groan, old friend. You know that we who live the lowly lives of editors possess a certain talent (commonly called hindsight) for perceiving even in the best of authors—and you are certainly one of those—qualities which, in the complicated process of composition, authors can't readily see for themselves.

Your book in its present form tells me that what you're aiming at is this: the death of Saul, the reign of David, the succession of Solomon. I see you struggling to get your rough draft more or less under control before you can begin to swing dramatically free. You want to establish your periphery, your limits. Here are your major structural blocks as you've worked them out so far:

> *Chaps 1–9*: Genealogy from Adam to Saul. (Needs to be reduced to a few lines; a chapter at most.)
>
> *Chap 10*: The death of Saul. (Requires expansion. You have despatched Saul in a hell of a hurry, just as you have virtually eradicated his daughter Michal—see above. Your well-known pro-Davidism was never more conspicuous than in your treat-

ment of Saul. I think we have got to think about this.)

Chaps 11–into 23: David's anointment, his military exploits, especially, of course, his capture of Jerusalem, his recovery of the ark, his taking of the census, God's wrath, God's forgiveness, David's building of the altar, his plans for building the Temple, his secret or private meetings with God, and his aging. (Much of this material raises substantive questions. Clearly the obvious numerical imbalance underscores *structural* questions: David receives 13 times the attention Saul receives; on the other hand, David receives only four chapters more than the genealogy. We have got to think about this.)

Chaps 23–27: An interruption for chapters of names and lists of dubious importance or relevance, the orders and functions of the Levites, the classification of priests, cantors, keepers of the gate, and military and civil organization. (Do we need these?)

Chaps 28–29: Here at last, after an interruption of five chapters, you regain contact with the line of the plot. David retires as king, succeeded by his son, Solomon. Your book ends. (I suspect you will want to expand these two chapters to bring them into line with the earlier material as you redesign the proportions of the manuscript. By the time you arrive again at this late stage of your book you will have appreciated for yourself the demands of proportion.)

I can't resist mentioning at this point my powerful personal emotional identification with your opening of Chap 28. "David held a meeting in Jerusalem of all the officials of Israel, the commissioners for the tribes, and the officials of the orders in the royal service, the commanders of thousands, the commanders of hundreds. . . ." and on and on. Believe me, everybody was there, which is how it's getting to be here at Apthorp House. Frank and Francine have called nothing but meetings as we bear down on later stages of preparation for the Volume, the title of which I no longer know. I thought we had settled it the other night—*Testament*. But Frank came rushing in today with some exciting, inspiring reports on Test Marketing which seem to indicate that the minute the world has gobbled up this Volume it will cry out for another. That will be *Testament Two*. This then is *Testament One*, unless we devise another parallelism such as *Earlier Testament/Later Testament* or *First Testament/ Second Testament*. Cheer up, Chron, you are going to share in some mighty hefty royalties.

In Two/Later/Second *Testament* or whatever we call it, all the contributors will be Gentiles, and I hope, apart from whatever Test Marketing may say, that Two will be a lot shorter than One. We don't really even know how many books we're going to have in the present Volume. It depends, of course, on how many of the writers come through. Maybe 22. Maybe 39. I couldn't help laughing. I asked at the meeting this morning what the justification is for 22. Frank was uncertain. He looked at Francine. "There are 22 letters in the Hebrew alphabet," she said. Are there? Francine always speaks with such authority I keep thinking she's telling the truth. Months later I find out she made it up on the spot, to keep the meeting moving.

"Then why 39?" I stupidly asked. Frank, for some reason or other, became really angry at me for that and began to spin around the ceiling shouting down sarcasm. "Thirty-nine because," he said. "Why three strikes and four balls? Why seven wonders of the world? Why 52 weeks in a year? Why 30 days hath September? Why 12 in a dozen? Why 52 in a deck?"

Why me? He really doesn't like to hear questions at meetings, especially from me. I am exhausted by meetings. I am going home right now.

Since David, of course, is the major character in your story I am hoping you will make him as convincing as possible by sharpening your critical perception of him throughout your revisions. Your reputation as a partisan pro-Davidist is well enough known to place upon you a special burden of perspective. You have got to help me see David in the round.

And so I come to *credibility*. You intend to show us the triumphant David offering inspired leadership to the Jews at an historic moment of relative stability through the years of his long reign. Here is a David you want me to admire, to respect, to love, and to follow—to my death, if necessary.

I know that before you are through you are going to give me the required balance. Reading your manuscript in its present stage, however, I have a certain difficulty in dealing with David's overview, his philosophy, his politics, and the moral idea (if any) which he attaches to his role as king and leader.

If I am to overflow with pride in our Jewish legacy, and if our Gentile readers are to feel themselves strengthened by their association with this era of our common beginnings, we must have a David we revere. Just as *structure* is a device for seizing us and retaining us, so is the characterization of our hero.

I guess what I'm talking about here is that quality we in the trade call "rooting interest." I must root for David and everything he represents if I am to commit to him my posterity and my sacred soul. But I have trouble rooting for David at this point. I don't really like him very much. I might put it more strongly. I dislike him. I begin to loathe him. He begins to strike me as a wanton warmaker. I begin to hear within myself mumblings and mutterings and grumblings familiar to me as inward signals from the early Vietnam days, when I felt myself isolated in my private thoughts and began to look anxiously around me for signs of sympathetic viewpoint in the public. I feel myself left out. I keep wanting to call out, "But you are omitting me, and if you don't start including me I'll start retaliating with graffiti on the walls." I am the brooding dissenter, of whom there must have been proportionately as many in David's time and place as in our own. I'm sure you remember Anatole France's story, "The Procurator of Judaea." In that story Pontius Pilate observes: "The Jews alone hate and withstand us. They withhold their tribute until it is wrested from them, and obstinately rebel against military service. . . . They are secretly nourishing preposterous hopes, and madly premeditating our ruin." When he is asked by his old friend Lamia if he remembers a particular Jew—Lamia names the man and his town—he cannot remember: there were so many young radical troublemakers. He tries to think. "Pontius Pilate contracted his brows, and his hand rose to his forehead in the attitude of one who probes the deeps of memory. Then after a silence of some seconds—'Jesus?' he murmured, 'Jesus—of Nazareth? I cannot call him to mind.' "

So you see, it is not my imagination that I was at least sufficiently numerous to be individually anonymous. In my silent, fearful, minority heart I resist this David. He makes me feel disvalued. Why then should I follow him, revere him, praise him, or root for him? The men who "rallied to David" in Chap 13 are those "who could handle the bow with right hand or with left, who could use stones or arrows." I don't fit into that bunch. Even as a kid I didn't. My God, look at the crowd that came to Hebron in Chap 12 to join David "in accordance with the order of Yahweh": Judah sent 6,800 "warriors equipped for battle." Simeon sent 7,100 men "valiant in war." Levi sent 4,600. Benjamin sent 3,000 "kinsmen of Saul." Ephraim sent 20,800 "valiant champions." Zebulun sent 50,000 men "fit for service, marshalled for battle, with warlike weapons of every kind." Naphtali sent 37,000 men under 1,000 commanders "armed with shield and spear." From Transjordania came 120,000 men "with warlike weapons of every kind." And that's only part of it. I count in that chapter a total of 326,000 men, all armed, all "fit for battle." But are they fit for civilization?

In Chap 11 the *minute* David is anointed king you have him marching on Jerusalem and capturing the fortress of Zion—which he immediately renamed after himself. Right away he offers a prize to the first man to kill a Jebusite. Oh, these damn prizes, these Pulitzers, prize-winning this, prize-winning that, and now David comes up with prize-winning killers. Couldn't he have given prizes for something else? I do so much wish that the first act of David's reign might have been some break with ancient barbarism. I should love to read of a David who takes down walls instead of putting them up. I saw a bumper sticker this morning: *Visualize World Peace.*

Of course, facts are facts. David built the wall. He did not take it down. But history might also be the record of men and women who sought to take down the walls. History need not be the conventional account recording the dates of battles and the numbers of people killed. What news of the arts in the year of David's anointment? What news of peacemakers, negotiators, mediators, and ecologists, of whom there were some, for my imagination tells me so, and Anatole France's Pontius Pilate felt besieged by them. Writers can change the world by helping the world to imagine the unseen. You may show the undernourished public good things it didn't know it wanted until it saw them. Once Saul Bellow was asked why he hadn't written about war. He replied that he chose to write about the *causes* of war.

A few lines before the end of Chap 18 you give me a little bit of a hopeful lift: "David ruled over all Israel administering law and justice to all his people." I hope I'll hear more about law and justice and how it was administered to "all." When you say "all" I keep thinking maybe I'm to be included even though I'm not an ambidextrous switch-hitting bowman. I don't mean to be picky. I have started and stopped this letter several times today. I need the weekend to recover from Apthorp House. I'm sure I'll love David better on Monday.

* * *

Viewpoint. Attribution. I think we've just got to try throughout the text to cut down the number of occasions of *hearsay,* which make me so skeptical of David's motives and virtue. Lose David and we lose everything, don't we? There goes my rooting interest. So we've got to get to the heart of the problem, which at this point seems to me to be this: I just really can't tell the difference, Chron, between David and God. They sound alike and think alike and have the same value system. Whose fault is this? I cringe at my own audaciousness, but in trying to size up our problem as honestly as I can the thought keeps coming back to me that the responsibility is the writer's—yours—that if God and David are indistinguishable the reason is that you have made both of them spokespersons or (shall I say it?) mouthpieces for your own point of view.

When you want something to happen, you arbitrarily make it happen. You put orders in God's mouth. But what motivates God? What makes God think David's so wonderful or Israel's so terrific that he should produce miracles for them. You can't just make God do the things you'd do if you were God. A character has got to have a motive—that's basic to all storytelling. I'm awfully bothered by your bad practice of introducing disembodied speeches reported by unidentified sources. Readers demand credibility. Voices out of nowhere turn people off. For example, I was mentioning to you on Friday that business in Chap 12 whereby the tribes send all those warriors to David at Hebron. My eye catches the passage asserting that this was done "in accordance with the order of Yahweh." I haven't begun to count the number of times you cause things to be done by the order of Yahweh, but as a critical citizen I find myself bursting to ask, after a great deal of anguish and hesitation, "Where is the evidence for this order from Yahweh? Who heard Yahweh give it?"

Yahweh and David seem to be masters of the self-fulfilling prophecy. When they want something, public opinion backs them up. You underestimate the prevalence of human variety.

Thus you are not credible when you give the multitude a single voice, as if it were a consenting person. "All the tribes of Israel then rallied to David at Hebron. 'Look,' they said. . . ." How can tribes say "Look"? As I mentioned on Friday, there were 326,000 people there, counting warriors only, not even counting women, children, and servants, "all of one mind in making David king. For three days they stayed there, eating and drinking with David." I just can't see this crowd of 326,000 people plus women and children and servants, many of whom are by now as drunk as you might expect, crying out at any moment all in one voice the clear syllable "Look."

In this matter you cross-pressure the reader. My reason or pride might make me want to dissent, but I think I'd remain terribly damn silent about it, knowing David's tendency to strike down his supposed enemies, or his single-mindedness in pursuing his ends. (Several of the other writers in the Volume have brought in some awful stuff about David. The worst is a terrible rumor of his having gone about windowpeeping, seen a voluptuous woman at her bath, seduced her, and shipped her husband to battle to die a cuckold's certain death. I fear that people these days are much more likely to give credence to that sort of realistic rumor than they are likely to believe reports based on secret channels to God.)

Or even assuming that David (or you) has access to Yahweh, I find myself troubled to think that you might not be interpreting him correctly. You make him so very earthly, so helplessly in the grip of mere human desire, as if you are projecting your wishes or character on him. You make him a *quid pro quo* God, a God very often given in a most unbecoming way to personal spite and violent vengeance, bitterly disappointed by his mere terrestrial failures, as if he were mortal and short-lived like us. Why, for example, does God save David after David has sinned in Chap 21? He saves him because David has built him an altar. This is bribery; it is the demand for fealty made by any everyday pirate. Frankly, it sounds more like Man than Yahweh. God should be different from us, and he should act like God, not like David—not like you or me or Frank Apthorp.

In all this you've really avoided the important political question, "Who is really running things?" Israel is really a democracy, if only the people knew it, and David's great fame (how he loves fame!) could rest upon his showing the people how powerful they really are. Whatever David does, he claims that he has been ordered by Yahweh to do it. And the people in turn claim that they are obeying their king. In this, David perpetuates the public ignorance, for he knows that what the people are doing is what they really want to do. They know no better. If he seriously proposed to introduce into Israel a more contemplative, peaceful life, the people in their ignorance would rebel against him. Therefore he permits them—God orders them, he says—to ravage, reduce, dismantle their "enemies," to carry off spoils and bring him home ornaments. He releases his people to their furies and their savagery, and he and they and God all together sustain the illusion that David obeys God, and the people obey David. The public requires a leader. David plays the role of leader, though in fact he is a tool, a puppet. The more willingly he serves, the more willingly his people love him and honor him and celebrate his greatness.

But a truly great leader, in my opinion, a truly great king, by educating people and refining popular assumptions could carry his countrymen further than he found them toward a fully realized humanity, decency, and restraint. If David were that kind of king I would love him better than I do.

Another thing I notice with dismay is your opening to Chap 20: "At the turn of the year, the time when kings go campaigning, Joab led out the troops and ravaged the land of the Ammonites. . . ." Do kings "go campaigning" by the calendar? Do you mean there's a war season like a hunting season? If so, wouldn't it be wonderful if you created David the Educator (as opposed to David the Warrior) struggling to end such a thing as ritual war, war by the calendar, substituting for it some more constructive activity, in which masses of people (not only men "fit for battle") could participate with pleasure. But no, not your David; he sanctioned this Ammonite expedition as he sanctioned every other. Joab brought home to him the crown of the king of the Ammonites—"it weighed a talent of gold; in it was set a precious stone which made an ornament for David's head."

It amazes me that God puts up with all this warfare and then, on the other hand, becomes angry with David for conducting a census. What's so terrible about a census? It seems to me better to count people than to slaughter people. David appears to miss the point of this issue, at least as you present it. Satan incited David; God punished Israel. How? Get this: God sent a pestilence and slaughtered 70,000 Israelites. Holy Christ. Where is justice? God in his crazy wrath sounds more like David, who killed seven thousand Aramaean charioteers and forty thousand Aramaean foot soldiers (not to mention General Shophach) in retaliation for the Aramaeans having *mildly* abused *three* of David's servants—"shaved them, cut their clothes half way up to the buttocks, and sent them away." Whatever happened to that earlier resolution to administer "law and justice to all"? Gone with the wind.

I think you might make this scene stronger if you got at the issue of the *substance* of the situation: Satan tempts David; David conducts the census; Joab presents David with the figures: "The whole of Israel numbered one million one hundred thousand men capable of drawing sword, and Judah four hundred thousand capable of drawing sword." Possibly you might have a more sensitive God see things in larger perspective than David, and hint to David, "According to your census nobody matters except men who are capable of drawing sword. Go and do better. Establish a Bureau of the Census. Find out how many people are ill-fed, ill-housed, ill-clothed, and ill-educated. Do something about it." In all this talk of the power and the greatness of the Davidic kingdom I know what we'd see if we walked the streets: we'd see hideous poverty. And you know that, too, Chron, for you and I have walked about together in some of the cities of the world. Sam Johnson has said that we know the virtue of a nation by measuring its solicitude for the poor.

I pray you won't think I'm being hypercritical. I know that you know that all of us here in the house want to make this Volume the best it can possibly be, and the way to do that is to be relentlessly self-critical as we work with our authors on the individual books—none of which, when all are done, are going to have the power and breadth of yours. You bring pleasure to your readers and credit to yourself with every new work.

One more subject and I'll go away. Let's examine that fabulous scene among David, God, and Nathan the prophet for the ultimate word on *viewpoint and attribution*. This scene, potentially so crucial, so climactic, plunges to depths of self-serving rationalization, a four-way farce of deception and egomania. I say "four-way," Chron, because you must be counted a presence: you are the omniscient, all-seeing reporter telling us what happened when God, David, and Nathan conspire to justify David's affluence.

As the scene opens (Chap 17) David is relating his distress to Nathan: "Here am I living in a house of cedar, while the ark of Yahweh's covenant is still beneath the awning of a tent." I think he is reacting to some public criticism, of which he has become aware. Rumblings have begun to drift upward, vibrations of radical young troublemakers, socialistic "madmen" of the left known to Pontius Pilate. But David loves his cedar house. He does not care for tents. What shall he do?

Nathan grasps the problem perfectly and sees the way out. They know what they're up to. He gives a blank check to David, *carte blanche*, cart before horse. "Do all that is in your mind," says he to David, "for God is with you." Nathan will tell God what David wants to do, and God will approve it.

Nathan wastes no time, and God is acquiescent—"that very

night the word of Yahweh came to Nathan." So Nathan says. Or you say. How do we know? God, through Nathan, for the benefit of a momentarily uneasy public, delivers the most satisfying endorsement any man could ask for. Do you remember Eisenhower's endorsement of Nixon—"he's my boy"—after Nixon's speech explaining that he had not taken the money he had taken?

God swiftly disposes of the charge. He tells Nathan (says Nathan) that the ark of the covenant has never reposed in a house but has gone "from tent to tent, from one shelter to another." In half a dozen lines you've done it. God also (Nathan? you?) takes advantage of the occasion to expatiate on David's past, to guarantee him fame, and to promise his protection to Israel.

> I took you from the pasture, from following the sheep, to be leader of my people Israel. I have been with you on all your expeditions: I have cut off all your enemies before you. I will give you fame as great as the fame of the greatest on earth. I will provide a place for my people Israel; I will plant them there and they shall live in that place and never be disturbed again; nor shall the wicked continue to destroy them, as they did in the days when I appointed judges over my people Israel; I will subdue all their enemies. I will make you great; Yahweh will make you a House. And when your days are ended and you must go to your ancestors, I will preserve your offspring after you, a son of your own, and make his sovereignty secure. It is he who shall build a house for me and I will make his throne firm for ever. I will be a father to him and he a son to me. I will not withdraw my favor from him, as I withdrew it from your predecessor. I will preserve him for ever in my house and in my kingdom; and his throne shall be established for ever.

Hearing this "revelation" (broken promises and wishful thinking, I'd call them), David "went in" to Yahweh and addressed him in humble terms, rephrasing God's promises and praise as God presumably announced them to Nathan, but speaking to God in the way of a trader, a deal-maker, *quid pro quo*, swapping flattery: "There is none like you, no God except you alone, that we have ever heard of." He instructs Yahweh to remember his promises: "Now, Yahweh, let the promise you have made to your servant and to his House be always kept, and do as you have said."

No right-minded citizen, hearing through Nathan God's blazing endorsement of David and of Israel, could continue to bicker about David's living in a cedar house. And yet, relieved that the hint of scandal has passed, a good citizen might begin to wonder how he/she truly knows God said these things to Nathan. One has only Nathan's report, really. David put the report to no test, certainly. Nor is there much to give us confidence in David's deal-making language.

I know you'll want to strengthen the dialogue throughout Chap 17—Nathan's *tête à tête* with God; then David's. You've got a big job if you're going to make a closed-circuit revelation credible. Sooner or later people will ask questions. And I wish I could believe, at this point, that David's session with God nourished him with a powerful resolution to lead a different life, to carry the Jews as the world's best model toward a national life of peace and tranquility. I regret to say that nothing in the language or the substance of these sessions—first Nathan and God, then David and God—assists us to imagine a God of sublime vision or a David of noble intention. The scene ends. Immediately David is whacking away again at the Philistines. Chap 18 begins: "After this, David defeated the Philistines and subdued them . . . he took Gath and its outlying villages. He also defeated the Moabites. . . ." He consolidated his power over the Euphrates. You enumerate the loot: one thousand chariots, seven thousand charioteers and twenty thousand foot soldiers. He killed twenty-two thousand Aramaeans. "Wherever David went, God gave him victory."

Will it ever end? I question Chap 17 as relentlessly as I have only because alert readers are going to question it, and certainly Frank and Francine are going to question it.

My secretary reminds me that I have here a little memorandum from Frank regarding some small matters of style, which I enclose herewith:

Matt—

I'm reading Chron's ms and enjoying it. It's great. Here are some small matters of style meanwhile basically having to do with difficult words. Get Chron to eliminate difficult words when possible. In Chap 11 seventh pgh he has a character named Benaiah strike down two champions and one snowy day killed a lion in a cistern. He was a huge man five cubits tall. Nobody knows what cubits are any more. We're not into cubits. We couldn't even get into the metric system. Change the cubits to feet and inches. The same is true of a talent of gold. Gold is enough. Talent is something else.

Have him change Yahweh to God. They're the same, aren't they? Many readers aren't going to have any idea who Yahweh is and they aren't going to be able to pronounce it. I understand it's related to Jehovah. That doesn't help any. There's Jehovah's Witnesses for one thing. Let's stick to God throughout the book and throughout the Volume, changing over from Yahweh to God wherever necessary—all very simple with computers.

Have him change ark to something else such as receptacle. I had to look it up. It's the chest they carried the ten commandments in but many readers hearing the word ark are instantly going to think back to the first book of the

Volume where one of the characters set out in an ark. Did you read Joe Heller's novel *God Knows*? David himself wasn't even sure what the ark was. "To tell you the honest truth, I had no clear idea what the ark of the covenant even was when I decided to move it up into the city from the house of Obededom the Gittite etc. etc."

Frank

Well, dear Chron, we're on the way now. I've discovered a lot of things writing this ever-lengthening letter, and I'm sure you have too. With you, as with so many writers, the first couple of drafts are a process of self-illumination. I know that you are going to take this the rest of the way, and this will be one of the very good books of the Volume. You are going to create a balanced and sympathetic David, showing the elevation of his consciousness toward the ideal of justice. If the Jews have anything to give to mankind it is that sense of law and justice arising from the experience of having suffered life under tyranny. The experience of oppression must make us principled, not merely turn us into oppressors. We want justice and freedom not only for ourselves but for everybody—even for the Philistines.

I love David's choosing Solomon as his successor. The very name *Solomon* means peace, does it not? David, seeking support and help from Solomon among the leaders of Israel, praises Yahweh for having "given you peace on all sides." I don't see evidence of God's having done so, so your job, as I see it, is to reinforce the foundations of your tale to make the achievement of peace coincide with David's enlarged understanding. He will articulate a vision of the end which shall be more beautiful than profits and weaponry.

Take your time. Don't rush it. A lot of this is our fault. Maybe we've emphasized too much the pressure of the deadline. But you've got things in place now. The Volume will wait for you.

You know your beginning and your end. With new confidence you'll not need to engage in those long digressions, the endless genealogies and the household inventories.

I'm sending my marked copy of the manuscript back to you Express Mail—Federal Express, my secretary says. If Frank and Francine have things to add to my letter I'll send their comments along to you, too, of course. We've all been awfully tied up in meetings. We still aren't even sure how many books there are going to be. Some of the writers are coming through better than others. Some aren't coming through at all. Not everybody is an Old Dependable like you, Chron. If you have any questions, as I suspect you will, call collect. It's always a pleasure to hear your voice, even if you're angry.

I send my best wishes and warm regards to you and Emily and the children.

Yours very affectionately,
Matt

FROM THE DESK OF
MATT FINKELSTEIN
EDITOR, SPECIAL PROJECTS
Apthorp House

Re: Chronicum's manuscript

Dear Chron,

By now you have no doubt received the manuscript. Ordinarily I'd be waiting in some trepidation for those howls of protest from your direction which always precede your rolling up your sleeves and getting to work, your reshaping your manuscript, and your whipping it back to me with lots of praise and thanks for my having made you do what you should have done in the first place.

Well, my dear friend, if you love me, find me a job. Recommend me to a respectable book publisher of your acquaintance, which is only to say, by way of backing in, that this will be my last letter to you on Apthorp stationery, and Friday will be my last day of work at Apthorp House. Frank and Francine have fired me.

Frankly, I've been wanting for some time to resign, but if I resigned I couldn't collect unemployment insurance. Now I can collect unemployment insurance. I'll also get a vast sum in severance pay from Apthorp House.

Yesterday Frank just simply stormed into my office. Usually he phones ahead. The last time he stormed in without phoning was a couple of years ago to tell me he was firing Aaron Goldstein and to appoint me to succeed Aaron. I said no, Special Projects was the place for me, I was more of a literary person myself, I didn't think there was much room for a literary person at the top of a publishing house. Frank has been going about boasting to people of my "integrity" ever since.

Now, however, the uses of my integrity have expired. He had in his hand a copy of my long letter to you. A lot of it bothered him, though I don't think that at the moment he walked into my office he intended to fire me. He felt that I had taken too long with your manuscript. "You dawdle and delay," he said. (I denied that. "I work as fast and as thoughtfully as I can," I said.) "You think too much," he said. "You took a week to write this letter you used to write in half a day. We want to keep this project moving. It doesn't have to be all that good. It's been Test Marketed. It's going to go big on the strength of the popular elements, sex and violence etcetera etcetera. Who needs all this?" he asked.

By "this" he meant my letter to you. "We don't need all this soul-searching and hair-splitting. There's nothing wrong with David. I like him. He's my own kind of man. I love him. He doesn't put up with this Philistine shit. He goes out and kicks ass. I understand him. I like God and Nathan, too. I have no objection to their secret meetings. It's a committee. People do it all the time. You know who I don't like?"

"No. Who?"

I'm absolutely positive that when Frank came into my office he had no intention of firing me. But suddenly he was seized with a fabulous idea and propelled into action by the force of his anger. For a fraction of a moment he restrained himself. His eyes darkened with a sudden thought, and I know what that thought was, and you can guess, too: my severance pay. If he fired me, he'd have to pay me severance pay. But his eyes had a second thought. It would be worth it. A few thousand dollars and it would all be over. "You're fired," he said, "because I've become so damn impatient of the way you'll take a lot of simple reading material and make it dense. Who needs density? People read on the run. They read while they're dressing for parties. They read while the commercials are on. The only people who read the dense parts of books are poverty-level students standing up in used bookstores. We asked Chron in on this project because we knew he could do it and he's done it, and you are rewarding his beautiful effort with a long letter that sounds more like a sermon than a letter. I love the way he outlines things so the reader knows where they are. I love that genealogy with millions of names. I love the credibility he's got into it. He doesn't need all your advice about structure and substance. I don't want him wasting his time with Sheshan and Jarha and Reuben and Michal and all these minor characters you're driving him crazy with"—referring, of course, to my arduous letter to you. "Let old Chron go back to Adam if he wants to. I love Adam. Adam is a big name. Bring in all the big names he wants, the more the better. Millions of small names in the genealogy and a few big names in the action is ideal. I see television specials left and right. I see Richard Chamberlain as David. I've got plenty of rooting interest for David, and I believe every word David speaks and every word he and God exchange because Chron draws me into their characters as far as I care to be drawn in. It's wonderful. It's marvelous. I don't for one single minute question viewpoint and attribution and hearsay and all those other bundles of shit you've wrapped up in here." By "in here" he meant my letter to you. "I don't want a single word changed in Chron's stuff. I want it just the way it is from Word One [Adam] to the end except as noted regarding the words 'cubits,' 'Yahweh,' 'talent,' and 'ark,' and if Chron objects to changing those I'll respect his objection. Matt," he said, "when I saw this letter you wrote to Chron I was going to write you a letter in reply, but I said to myself, 'When I find myself writing letters in reply to a letter from one of my own editors, one of us have got to go.' "

Since it can't be Frank, it's got to be me. For your sake, Chron, I hope the Volume sells a million and your royalties roll in forever. I can see that it's going to be an uneven Volume. Some of the books make more sense to me than others; and if Frank says the Volume is going to be a big seller it's going to be. He's usually right. I'm usually wrong. Do you remember Lee Youngdahl's book *When Your Bicycle Tires*? I took the manuscript to Frank and Francine. I said, "Is this supposed to be humor? I didn't crack a smile." Francine replied, "We laughed, so it must be funny." It sold 1.25-million copies.

And now they have provided me with unexpected freedom, unplanned vacation. At least I won't have to work on *Testament Two*. If you know anybody who wants a good, steady, sober, literary-minded editor please have him/her give me a call (at home). Leave a message on my machine if I'm not there.

Yours very affectionately,
Matt

The Bonding

I

The telephone rings. I know who it is. It is a chunky, powerful boy with a thick, bushy red-haired mustache and a name, Christy Ratherbiglongname, I can seldom remember, and when I remember it I can't pronounce it. He wants me to come out and play. He is nineteen years old and I am sixty-nine.

One of the things that made me a baseball fan is its democracy. Lines of snobbish distinction go down. (On the other hand, I was fifty-five years old before I ever played with a black teammate.) On the telephone Christy calls me Professor. On the ball field he calls me by my first name. Only on the phone or at the ball field do our lives intersect. Baseball is our *lingua franca*.

"Where?" I ask.

"Lafcadio Park," he says. "It's a trophy game."

"When?" I ask.

"Saturday," he says.

"What time?" I ask.

"Get there maybe half-past seven, seven-thirty," he says, "give us time to warm up a little. Do you see what I'm saying?"

He needs me and I need him. He knows what I can do. I'd

been recruited by Christy Ratherbiglongname at a senior citizens' game at Chaparral Park, in Scottsdale. He'd been driving by and he just happened to stop and watch. So he said. My impression is that he'd stopped deliberately to see what he could see, and I was the man he saw. He'd be able to count on me. Nobody wanted me but him. I'd be grateful to be his eleventh man. I'd show up for every game. I could punch singles through the infield. I could play right field, first base, pitch, coach.

He was a supremely energetic young man. He slept four hours a night whether he needed it or not. My wife once said she was pleased he was not a military person—he'd attack other countries out of restlessness. "If you come and and play with us," he said when he recruited me, "the church gives you a free T-shirt."

"I don't like playing at night," I said.

"We don't play at night," he said. This was absolutely false. The league I joined him in played half its winter games at night and *all* its summer games at night. But he knew that once I'd been bonded to the team I wouldn't mind his having lied. He had seen by my way of playing that I was longing to be bonded.

This sport I am talking about is an extremely popular variation of baseball called slow-pitch. The pitcher pitches an underhand arc. Strikes are determined by whether the ball in its arc lands on the plate. If the pitch does not land on the plate the umpire calls it a ball. A third-strike foul is out.

The ball is larger than a Florida grapefruit, smaller than an Arizona grapefruit. It is not a hard ball but it is not a soft ball either. The most endangered player is the pitcher, who is often struck by line drives. The distance to the plate is fifty feet. Infielders are often struck by bad-bouncing ground balls, frequently in the crotch, which is painful for the victim and inspires other players to offer bad jokes as consolation. It is a hitting game. A player seldom strikes out.

The bases are sixty-five feet apart, much less, of course, than a hardball diamond. The distance down the foul lines is usually well under three hundred feet. Players' batting averages are closer to .400 than .300. Although these are high-scoring games they move quickly. A nine-inning game seldom takes as long as ninety minutes.

Slow-pitch is an ideal game even for teams composed of combinations of skillful and unskillful players, male or female. In hundreds of schools and communities sponsoring "co-rec" slow-pitch leagues, women's participation is governed by local rules. Every team must field a specified number of women. More and more these days, of course, many women players play very well. Christy, in behalf of the Salt River Pentecost Bombers, led us into a male league. Thus we have no women players, although I have heard some of our players speak fondly of women.

2

I too was once the whip—

> So was I once myself a swinger of birches.
> And so I dream of going back to be.

—the Christy Ratherbiglongname of my team, pouring half my energy into the telephone, rounding up the guys, routing them out of bed, out of the house, rounding up our transportation, pleading with my players against their mothers' tying them up with dental appointments, music lessons, visits to their grandparents. Baseball was urgent. Its urgency addicted me. We needed to win every game. The urgency of baseball made me a fan. Every game was crucial. One might be casual about many other things in life, such as love, learning, literature, morals, ethics, politics, religion, and college entrance examinations, but baseball mattered. I hated those mothers.

My father took me to the first big-league baseball game of my life. I know that the place was the Polo Grounds, in New York, and the time must have been the summer of my sixth year. The immense expanse of the grass was awesome. The feats of the players were marvelous. For example, batters hit balls which seemed to fly so high and far they would never descend. Yet soon enough they descended into the hands of players waiting far out on the grass. Such a relationship in distance astonished me. I was breathless to observe that a ball should be struck by a man with a stick at one point of the vast universe, and be caught in a glove by a man far away at another.

I was entranced by one of the Giants outfielders. What a peculiar name he had! Ott. I see it yet in my memory of that day's scorecard, and often on the Hall of Fame fence at Candlestick Park in San Francisco. Such a name began to suggest to me the diversity of the world: nobody on our block in Mount Vernon, New York, was named Ott. Rosenbaum and Schwartzman, yes. Ott, no.

Thus baseball expanded my provincial world. Ott's teammate Carl Hubbell was called the Meal Ticket. I had no idea what a meal ticket was. My mother put our meals on the table. The sportswriters offered thousands of figures of speech to amuse a boy who loved the way words could be slung all over the place in a billion combinations. Hubbell "hailed from" Carthage, Missouri. Ott was called Master Melvin. Bill Terry was Memphis Bill

Carthage? Missouri? Baseball introduced me to geography. The cities of the east were New York, Brooklyn, Boston, Philadelphia, Washington. The cities of the west were Cincinnati, St. Louis, Chicago, Pittsburgh, Detroit, and Cleveland. West of St. Louis lay the Rocky Mountains and China. My active sympathies for people who did not live near big-league cities were mingled with a certain contempt for their having got themselves in such a fix.

Baseball made a reading fan of me. I was introduced to the connection by my father's evening commuting companion, the *New York Sun*. On the front page of the *Sun* one night I saw a boisterous, effervescent player named Pepper Martin sliding home on his chest to score the winning run for the St. Louis

Cardinals in a World Series game against the Philadelphia Athletics. For me, that was the night of the wedding of baseball and reading, two pleasures conjoined.

As my mind embraced the game, the game enlarged my mind. Baseball taught me things even adults approved. *The game is never over until the last man is out.* Teachers and family relations thought this was a good philosophy of life. They liked to hear me say such things.

For me, however, traits of good character, if I had them, had nothing especially in common with life, only with baseball. Certain things adults morally approved I found simply useful.

Consider arithmetic. Adults approved my sitting there doing arithmetic problems, but in fact those were not problems I was doing. They were batting averages. It never occurred to me that this skill I was acquiring for the purpose of following the game would serve me afterward for other purposes. These arts or skills were pleasures in themselves. It was all one unified endeavor, baseball and reading and geography and history and arithmetic and newspaper report. I became a fan of baseball because I had once glimpsed the green expanse of serenity, and because the game called upon me for all those other arts and skills which were play in themselves, no matter what teachers or other adults called them.

As a boy I adored Camp Secor in the summer, especially our baseball games. I remember a game we played on a ragged, stony field against a team of boys from another camp on the other side of the lake. Their field was pocked with cowflop. So was ours.

When the game was over we boys of Camp Secor piled into the truck that had brought us there. Our driver was Uncle Arnie Cohen, who was also our counselor, mentor, and nature teacher. Beside our truck Uncle Arnie was shaking hands good-bye with his counterpart uncle from the other camp. The moment remains in my head half a century later. The other uncle says to Uncle Arnie, "Who's that little brat of yours who . . . ?" That was me he meant. Uncle Arnie replied, "That kid eats and sleeps baseball." I was proud to be noticed in that honorable way.

Once when we returned from a game across the lake I tried to convey to the folks of our camp the impression that I had won the game all by myself. Uncle Arnie challenged my report. "Nobody wins a game all by himself. Nobody loses a game all by himself."

Uncle Arnie taught me the idea of team, celebrated bonding. I understood as time went by that nobody wins a game single-handed. That was the thing that made me a lover of baseball, the bonding with one's fellows, the possession of their confidence.

Somewhere, some years in the past, I am playing my position. I think I am playing shortstop. Two men are out. The batter hits a pop fly. It should be mine. Everybody sees clearly that it is mine. I am under it. I gather it in. But even before I gather it in I feel around me my teammates begin to jog toward the bench. They know that I am going to catch that ball. They have confidence in me. They know what I can do. They know my skills side by side with my limitations, and I know theirs. We are bonded. Baseball was bonding.

Uncle Arnie also said, "In the field. Want that ball. Want that batter to hit the ball to you. Don't pray the batter hits it someplace else to save you disgrace. Pray that he hits it to *you*."

"Two hands for beginners." Of course it wasn't original with Uncle Arnie. I caught fly balls two-handed. I still do. Uncle Arnie and every school coach in the universe commanded boys to clap that bare hand over the ball in the pocket.

It's no longer the style. The modern one-handed style is casual, confident, and cool. No matter how critical the moment may be—the final out of a one-run game, let us say—the outfielder plays the fly ball one-handed. He is too proud for precaution, for safety, his peers would laugh at him if he required two hands to do the work of one. But I haven't been able to change with the style, and I'm not sure I care to. I appreciate the security of that old-fashioned second hand.

Baseball was my model for the good life. "When a poor American boy dreamed of escaping his grim life," David Halberstam has written in Summer of '49, "his fantasy probably involved becoming a professional baseball player."

My life was neither poor nor grim, but I had my necessities. One summer, when I was a boy at Camp Secor, I wrote my fantasy in lying letters to a friend back home whom I meant to wound with accounts of my own great good fortune. I have written about these letters elsewhere, but an account of them is relevant here, too. Fantasy and fandom were bred together. For me, to invent the richest possible dream was to weave it of the stuff of baseball. I could imagine no life more desirable than the life of a baseball player, the luxury of travel, hotels and chambermaids, worshipful girls, players' uniforms, natty umpires, and, perhaps above all, the strictly scheduled reliability of life, for baseball could be relied upon to be present and to be prompt like nothing else I knew: if Cincinnati was to be at the Polo Grounds at 3:10 P.M. on August 12 *they were there*.

> I do not know what name my mind gave to those letters—*letters*, I suppose, although I knew that letters were true and mine were not. Mine were wholly lies, fiction, deceitful inventions created to excite my friend's envy. At their core were descriptions of an elaborate Inter-Camp Baseball League, in which boys in the most elegant uniforms traveled about like professionals.
>
> Each camp (I wrote) was required to maintain a perfectly barbered diamond and sparkling dressing rooms. Oh yes. Each camp was required to supply new, white baseballs—none of your old tattered,

ragged baseballs held together with black electric tape. Umpires were to be formally attired. The grandstands were spacious, girls pressed forward for our autographs—how boring to be giving out my autograph all day!

In spite of that hardship (I wrote) I enjoyed myself. Saying this, I permitted a tone of world-weariness to creep in. Some people might find this sort of thing exciting, but I'd much rather be home with *him* all summer on the good old baking streets and good old rocky choke-dusted sandlots of Mount Vernon. Sometimes in a letter I'd "correct" an "error" of an earlier letter. I provided settings for the act of composition: today I am writing to you on the train between Camp Indian Pines and Camp Lakadaka. Listen to the dumb thing that happened: on this trip our clubhouse man packed our *home* uniforms instead of our *travel* uniforms, ha ha, that's life, I guess. Oh nuts, in this hotel the electric fans work very poorly, the chambermaids are very slow. Rochester looks so much like Buffalo looks so much like Syracuse looks like Troy like Utica it sure is boring I sure look forward to getting home to school in September. (Glad we don't play *through* September like the big leagues.)

These letters were written on my cot at rest hour at Camp Secor. We almost never left camp between the first of July and the end of August, and when we did it was to hike two or three miles with canteens slung across our shoulders in order to justify our mothers' having bought the canteens. My letters were mailed by the most careful calculation, bearing in mind our eight-day swing through Schenectady, complicated by the tedious necessity of coming back through Albany to make up a washed-out game. My dates were painstakingly computed. Thirty-one days hath July. No Sunday baseball at certain church camps. Follow the weather reports and allow for rain. Follow maps for useful details: in Ogdensburg (I wrote) I picked up some Canadian money, in Lockport some of the kids went to see Niagara Falls falling, but I stayed in the hotel resting my pulled muscle. I had never been to Ogdensburg, never been to Lockport, never pulled a muscle. Where I *was* was on my cot at rest hour at Camp Secor on my way to becoming a novelist.

3

My back aches. I want to go lie down somewhere. I want to call Christy and tell him I can't play ball with him any longer. Kid, it's over. Do you see what I'm saying?

Saturday has come at last. It is Saturday dawn and my alarm clock wakes my wife, and my wife wakes me. "Why do you set it if you're not going to get up?" she asks. "That's not fair."

"Of course I'm getting up," and to prove it I cover my head with my pillow.

"You were sure out," she says.

Yes, I had slept deep. I'd had a little bedtime sedative to ease my back. "How's your back?" she asks, and I reply, it's OK, it's OK, but I don't really know how my back is. I won't know until my feet hit the floor. I don't really want to leave this bed, but I cannot disappoint Christy G., boy whip, who's expecting me, counting on me. Right at this moment I truly couldn't tell my wife or myself if I'm going to play ball today or if I'm going back to sleep.

But this is nothing new. This is how it was when I was a boy and my bruises from last week's game were raw and the scabs were still bloody wet and my mother said if I played ball unhealed like that I was inviting infection, infection would course through my body—"gangrene will set in"—the doctors would amputate my legs and that would be the end of baseball.

The day is cold. Even so, I swing myself out of bed. I am terribly stiff, I can hardly move. Even so, I know that I am going to play ball today. I am going to get loose. People advise: "Use it or lose it." I am going to play ball and might even play it well, might even win the game with a sharp ground ball sliced down the right side. That's my specialty. They play me to pull and I fool them.

Tonight I will not be able to believe the misery in which this day begins. But it has always been like that. Indeed, I quite retired from baseball on May 27, 1960: "I played center field for Language Arts, against Social Science. We lost, 7–1, my legs are unendurably stiff, & I have the feeling this may be my last game. . . . Baseball is for boys." So said my diary one day when I was only thirty-seven and a half.

Baseball taught me to know I could rise to the occasion (once I got out of bed). Baseball acquainted me with my own resources, with the outer limits of my body. I rise, I dress. I pull over my head my Salt River Pentecost Church T-shirt blazing blue bearing some sort of design on the back I have never really identified. I think it may be a box kite, though I don't know why it should be.

Some of our T-shirts include the word Bombers. I don't know whether the word is an addition to the shirt or whether it had been there in the first place and was removed as an ethical afterthought. I have never been to the church for which I so faithfully play. I have never seen it. I do not know where it is. I do not know anyone who belongs to it except Christy Ratherbiglongname, who alludes to it often as a checkpoint on his daily rounds. But I have never heard any of our teammates mention it. (In 1941, when I was employed in New York by Paramount Pictures I played on the Paramount baseball team. I slowly discovered in my sweet innocence that I was the only member of the team actually employed by Paramount.)

* * *

Once I told Christy my best religious baseball joke, but it offended him:

Two baseball players were lounging in their hotel room one night. One player was a pitcher and the other was a third baseman. They began to talk about heaven. They wondered if baseball is played in heaven. They agreed that whichever of them died first would notify the survivor whether baseball is played in heaven.

The years passed. The third baseman died. He remembered his promise to communicate from heaven. He spoke through the spiritual ether to his old-time friend and teammate, the pitcher. He said, "You know, I promised to find out if baseball was played in heaven and let you know first thing, and I've done it just like I promised."

"I knew you would," the pitcher said. "What's the scoop?"

"Mixed," the third baseman said from heaven. "There's good news and bad news. Which do you want first?"

"Start with the good news," the pitcher said.

"The good news is," the third baseman said, "that we play baseball all the time on a regular schedule in heaven."

"And the bad news—" the pitcher asked from earth.

"The bad news is you're scheduled to pitch tomorrow."

Christy did not laugh. The funny part eluded him, violated his picture of reality. "Going to heaven can't be bad news," Christy said.

I devour half a grapefruit and a slice of toast and half a cup of coffee. Play first, eat a second breakfast with the Bombers later. Small breakfast digesting, I lower myself to the living-room floor. My wife leads me through a series of stretching exercises to prepare my back for the game.

I pack my equipment bag: glove, extra shoelaces, a small roll of adhesive tape, and my sturdy pair of Sportgoggles.

When I leave the house I hurry. Apparently I am afraid of

missing something. Butterflies flutter in my stomach. It was always true of me that I approached a baseball field, whether as player or as spectator, with a feeling of rising excitement, eager to be there early, fearful of something happening without me. Maybe I'm afraid of being left out, kicked off the team. "Late! You're off the team!" the tyrant manager shouts at me.

Full daylight now, dawn has dissolved, the temperature is forty degrees on a December morning in Tempe, Arizona, on the way to seventy, and the time is seven-twenty. I'll be at Lafcadio Park at seven-thirty, Christy will direct our warmup, and at eight o'clock we'll take on those Ball Crushers.

We'll beat them, too, I think. We have played them twice and they aren't much. These games are just fun, of course, but the fun is greater when we win than when we lose. When we lose we are filled with the necessity to apologize, to confess our errors as a way of emphasizing that they weren't the whole story, that it was the *team* that lost: our undoing was a collective enterprise. When we go for a second breakfast everything tastes better if we have won.

My car radio tells me the temperatures around the country. The wind-chill factor is forty-four degrees below zero in Minneapolis. I arrive at Lafcadio Park. I have hurried to get here. Christy will be there before me, ready to start our practice. He is persuaded that practice is the secret of our success, and I am inclined to agree with him. When we practice we start each of our games with a thirty-minute advantage. Our slothful opponents are never warmed up until the third or fourth inning, and by that time we have sunk them. They have lain in bed too long.

Nobody is here but me. I am standing swearing to myself in the cold at seven-forty in the morning at Lafcadio Park. Not alone the Ball Crushers but the Salt River Pentecost Church Bombers lie home in bed. To hell with this childish game. I am through with it forever. I quit. I will never get out of bed again. I will rest my aching back.

Since I'm here anyhow I'll run my back a little. I set my equipment bag on the player bench and jog across the grass. A humorist has planted a flag on a stick in a small mound of dogshit behind second base. The American national game is cowflop and dogshit, then and now, from Camp Secor in the Hudson Valley to the Arizona desert. This is the first time this morning I have smiled. I move stiffly. I feel awkward. I jog toward the left-field fence. I decide to jog another fifty paces and turn and break into a run. I imagine that just as I make my turn I will hear the roar of Christy's truck and the clamor of our team leaping to play.

I am warming. I am getting ready to play. I turn. Now I am running well and reasonably gracefully. I no longer feel awkward. My back is loose. The home stretching did good. I am grateful to my wife for her exercise leadership. The impossible has happened, as in bed I knew it would: my body has returned to me one more time. I will not hear from my back again until tomorrow.

But neither Christy's truck nor anything nor anyone else has arrived. When I reach the player bench I am breathing hard, and for a moment the mass failure of Christy and my teammates strikes me as an event of no consequence. Indeed, they did me the greatest favor. If I had not got up to meet them here I would not have run, and if I had not run I would not feel as great as I do this minute. I pick up my equipment bag and drive home. By the time I arrive home I am damn mad.

My wife says, "There just must have been some misunderstanding." "There was no misunderstanding. It's the price I pay for playing with kids. They don't think. They don't keep track of things. They don't write their appointments down. They don't remember anything." "They're not all kids," my wife says. "I thought you had one other old guy." "We got one guy about forty," I say. "I call forty a kid."

I telephone Christy. I reach his machine, which blesses me and instructs me to leave my name and number and the time of my call. I say, "Christy, this is Mark, I just want you to know how damn mad I am, I just got back from Lafcadio Park, I was there at half past seven and I waited until eight and nobody came, so to hell with it after this, I'm just going to play with the seniors in Scottsdale, to hell with you and the Bombers."

I return to bed. I sleep for one hour. I rise. I read pages in two manuscripts in progress, one of mine and one of a student.

My wife and I walk in the neighborhood. On the golf course the gray-haired snowbirds from North Dakota, South Dakota, Montana, and Minnesota fire away. Golf must be a great game. You do not need eighteen people to play. "I'm going to take up golf," I say. "I doubt it," says my wife. We return home.

A message is on our machine. "Hi, Professor, this is Christy, got your message. The game is still at eight, we need you, be there at seven-thirty we can warm up. Do you see what I'm saying? It's a funny thing you went there this morning, trophy games are always night."

The night is as cold as this morning was, without even this morning's prospect of warming. I wear a jacket during batting practice. I slash a couple of pitches to the left side. I made good contact. I like the sound. Right away I know that I am hitting well tonight. My hands sting in the cold. A teammate says I should buy myself batting gloves. In my generation batting gloves were unheard of, unthinkable. God did not intend us to wear gloves while batting—nor to bat with aluminum bats. I slash two or three more ground balls to the left side. I feel that they were hard-hit. I do not think the Ball Crushers' third baseman would have had an easy time handling them.

I jog to right field. If I play tonight that's where I'll play. I need to catch one fly ball for confidence. That will do it. However, none of my fellow Bombers hits anything in the air to me. We have only one left-handed batter, and he is a light hitter like me. He and I are the only players who have never hit a home run for the Bombers. (I have not hit a home run for *anybody* for nineteen years—I hit my last home run playing at the California Institute of the Arts in 1972.) He strokes two or three balls to right field but with only the force of singles. Playing them off the grass in no way assists my confidence—almost anybody can pick up a rolling ball.

As our practice ends, my alert boy Christy considerately fungoes a couple of fly balls my way. The first ball Christy hits to me I catch almost without moving a step. For the second ball I backpedal a dozen steps to the fence, and as the ball smacks the pocket of my glove my confidence rises to its comfort level. Christy has done just what I need. He knows my requirement for confidence. He is grateful to any player who shows up. I am one of his faithful. I am ready to play.

Eleven Bombers are here tonight, and I see that I will not start. "You'll get in," Christy says. "Stay warm and coach third." We join him for prayer. Some time ago when I told Christy I did not believe in God he said, "He won't mind." We form a circle around him, we extend our arms and clasp hands, we bow our heads, and Christy prays. His red-haired bushy mustache quivers. "Dear God, we sincerely love You and pray You will help us do the right things when we play this game right now. We know that You will keep us from doing anything we don't want to be sorry for doing, and in Your mercy help us show good sportsmanship to the adversary."

Our adversary is formed from a pool of discount-store employees and United Parcel Service drivers and handlers. We are a much better team than these Ball Crushers, and we are warm and they are cold. They have barely made their way into trophy play. I expect a lot of traffic to be coming my way at third base. I love it. I love waving my teammates home. I am their guide and protector. I also love halting them, keeping them safe. As they charge at me from second base I cry, "Look at me, look at me, look at me," and if they do as I say I will keep them from harm. Some Bombers base runners sometimes defy me, ignore my signals, charge past me, passionate to score, and although I am first and last a devoted team person, I feel at such times a secret satisfaction at their getting their asses thrown out at the plate.

We score abundantly without delay. In the coaching box I am waving home so many of my mates that I heat up as if I were playing. We score ten runs in three innings. We are secure. We will never blow a ten-run lead. The Ball Crushers score once. We lead by 10–1. We lead by 11–4. We lead by 12–6.

After five innings our dependable shortstop must go home—not to home plate but home to his house. Our right fielder comes in to play shortstop, and I go to right field where I am instantly employed. The first Ball Crusher to come to bat hits a line drive to me. He is a right-handed batter. He had looked my way when he came to bat, and I knew he had it in mind to try out the old man. The ball begins to float, catching me unprepared. For a moment I am alarmed that I have misjudged it. I envision its sailing over my head. But I need only to rise on my toes and reach for it, and catch it in the pocket of my glove with a satisfying sound.

For some reason we Bombers cannot sustain the success with which we began, while the Ball Crushers begin to hit safely repeatedly. This is one of baseball's perpetual recurring mysteries: why does one player, one team, inexplicably lose its command, or another inexplicably exceed all expectations? The score is 12–8, then 13–11, and soon thereafter 13–all.

Nothing comes my way in the air. At bat I ground very hard to third base, but the Ball Crusher third baseman throws me out. When I come to bat again a Ball Crusher calls out, "Watch the line." The third baseman moves toward the line, and I think I can hit it past him to his left, but once again I ground to him. They've got my number. They've got me "defensed."

This is not to be believed. We are really a much better team than they are. They go ahead of us, 16–15.

In the top of the ninth inning when my mates are on the bases and everything depends on me, and all the Ball Crushers are playing me to the left, I punch the ball down the first-base side between the wide-playing baseman and the line. Nothing is lovelier to me than the sight of the ball I have hit skipping over the dirt to the outfield grass.

I had done it again. It was my specialty. More than once in a late inning I've whacked the ball just right through that wide-open space between the first baseman and his base. The Ball Crushers were playing me to pull—that is to say, to hit the ball in my natural direction, down the left-field side. They shifted to the left for me. The second baseman played almost on the bag. The first baseman played wide. The famous old logician said, "Hit it where they ain't, " and so I did, and ran exalted to first base.

I am in paradise, I am praised by my mates. They say, "Hey, good job, man." Christy says, "You did a smart thing, I knew you'd do it." They all knew I would do it. They knew that my moment had come. It was the secret we shared together.

In right field, in the bottom half of the ninth inning, beneath the bright lights and the depths of the blackness beyond, in the cool night growing colder, in my exhilaration, my spirit glows with triumph. Through me the voice of Uncle Arnie speaks out of the past: "I want that ball. Hit it to me. Batter, hit that ball to me, I pray you hit it to me." Whereupon, with two Ball Crushers on base and two men out the batter does in fact hit it to me. It is a soft fly ball, spinning in the lights. I am under it. But even before I gather it in I feel around me my teammates unburdened of their tension. They know that I am going to catch that ball. They have confidence in me. They know what I can do.

I think I'll make a one-handed catch of it. I'll join the modern world, stick one hand up and allow that ball to settle in, which it does, and then pops out again and falls to the grass, while our adversary dashes across the plate with the winning run.

Christy, almost as if he were not about to cry, rallied his men to his truck. He would not bring himself to look at me. Eliminated in the first round of trophy play! This was unspeakable.

At last he looked at me and said, "You got your car, you don't need a ride. I'll give you a call." I always had my car. I never rode in his truck.

I was about to fall into depression. My worst moment would occur on the following morning, when I awoke to the dreadful memory of that ball's having popped out of my glove. It was a moment of my baseball life I will always want back. In the end I might deliver one of those oblique deathbed statements for which mildly eccentric men become famous: "I should have caught it two-handed."

But this is no fatal wound. It is a memory, not a traumatic incident. I am sustained by the truths I have learned from baseball. All the game's commonplace wisdom serves me. "You can be a hero one day and a goat the next." I was a hero in the top of the ninth and a goat in the bottom of the same inning.

"That's baseball."

"You can't win 'em all."

"People forget, tomorrow's a new ball game." I don't know about that. I don't think Christy has forgotten. He said he'd call. Where's his call? I'm waiting.

Everybody learns in her/his own way about losing. For me, baseball taught me losing and winning, taught me never to let anything get me too far down or too far up. You not only can't win 'em all—you can't win much more than half, hard as you try, long as you live.

Baseball was my path to self knowledge. Baseball made me a fan by telling me truths about myself. It taught me to know what I can do and what I can't. I will make good plays and bad plays. Every so often the easiest pop fly is going to pop out of your glove. I don't care who you are. It's the iron statistics. It's fate. If baseball taught me—I heard it first from Uncle Arnie—that I don't win games single-handed, then neither do I lose them, either. *It takes a whole team to lose a ball game.* Hey, look, I didn't blow that ten-run lead all by myself, did I?

Acknowledgments

Grateful acknowledgment is made to the editors and copyright holders who granted permission to reprint the essays in this book.

"At Prayerbook Cross" is reprinted from Mark Harris, *Short Work of It: Selected Writing* (Pittsburgh: University of Pittsburgh Press,1979). This work first appeared in the *Cimarron Review* (no. 6 [December 1968]) and is reprinted here with the permission of the Board of Regents for Oklahoma State University, holders of the copyright.

"The Bonding" is reprinted from *Birth of a Fan,* edited by Ron Fimrite (New York: Macmillan, 1993).

"Carmelita's Education for Living" is reprinted from *Esquire* (October 1957).

"Conversation on Southern Honshu" is reprinted from *North Dakota Quarterly* 27 (summer 1959).

"Flattery" is reprinted from *Sequoia* 31 (winter 1988).

Acknowledgments

"From the Desk of the Troublesome Editor" is reprinted from *Virginia Quarterly Review* 65 (summer 1989).

"Hi, Bob!" is reprinted from *Arizona Quarterly* 42.2 (1986), by permission of the Regents of The University of Arizona.

"The Iron Fist of Oligarchy" is reprinted from Mark Harris, Josephine Harris, and Hester Harris, *The Design of Fiction* (New York: Thomas Y. Crowell Company, 1976). It first appeared in *Virginia Quarterly Review* 36 (winter 1960).

"Jackie Robinson and My Sister" is reprinted from Mark Harris, *Short Work of It: Selected Writing* (Pittsburgh: University of Pittsburgh Press, 1979). It first appeared in *Flashes of Negro Life*, 1946.

"La Lumière" is reprinted from *Denver Quarterly* (fall 1983).

"The Self-Made Brain Surgeon" is reprinted from *Noble Savage* 1 (March 1960).

"Titwillow" is reprinted from *Michigan Quarterly Review* 25 (summer 1986).

"Touching Idamae Low" is reprinted from Mark Harris, *Short Work of It: Selected Writing* (Pittsburgh: University of Pittsburgh Press, 1979). It first appeared in *Esquire* (April 1978).